Praise for Jenna Black's
WATCHERS IN THE NIGHT

"Clever plotting and terrific supporting characters elevate this novel into a first-rate romantic thriller."
—*Romantic Times*

"Jenna Black has crafted a fine story with *Watchers in the Night*. She supplies deft handling of plot, characters, and genre, and I enjoyed the novel tremendously. I see many more fascinating novels coming from this author in the future!"
—Heather Graham, *New York Times* bestselling author of *Kiss of Darkness*

"You'll want to bare your throat to Jenna Black's enthralling heroes. This cleverly plotted romantic tale will leave you hungry for more!"
—Sabrina Jeffries, *New York Times* bestselling author of *Only a Duke Will Do*

"Jenna Black's *Watchers in the Night* is a sexy, fast-paced, totally engaging read. She's built an exciting world of vampires and added a 'to die for' hero and a kick-butt heroine! This is a book you can really sink your teeth into!"
—Rhonda Thompson, *New York Times* bestselling author of *The Untamed One*

"Mystery, magic, and vampires! In *Watchers in the Night*, Jenna Black has created a fresh and fascinating vampire universe. What more could any lover of the paranormal ask for?"
—Lori Handeland, RITA Award–winning author of *Midnight Moon*

THE DEVIL INSIDE

JENNA BLACK

A DELL SPECTRA BOOK

THE DEVIL INSIDE
A Dell Spectra Book / December 2007

Published by
Bantam Dell
A Division of Random House, Inc.
New York, New York

This is a work of fiction. Names, characters, places, and incidents
either are the product of the author's imagination or are used
fictitiously. Any resemblance to actual persons, living or dead,
events, or locales is entirely coincidental.

ISBN 978-0-553-59044-9

Printed in the United States of America
Published simultaneously in Canada

www.bantamdell.com

OPM 10 9 8 7 6 5 4

In loving memory of my mother,
Carol Arnold Bellak, who always supported
my dreams of being a writer 100%

Acknowledgments

Thanks first of all to my wonderful editor, Anne Groell, whose input and suggestions without a doubt made this into a better, stronger book. Thanks as always to my agent, Miriam Kriss, who always believes in me even when I have trouble believing in myself! Thanks to Cynthia Cooke and Kelly Gay, who were my critique partners for this book. And lastly, thanks to all the wonderful urban fantasy authors who got me so hooked on this genre I had to write one of my own!

THE DEVIL INSIDE

Chapter 1

Topeka, Kansas. Demon capital of the world. Not!

Demons, the illegal ones at least, tend to like the biggest cities. More anonymity. More prey. But every once in a while, one would pop up in the most unlikely place. Like Topeka.

I flew into Kansas City, Missouri, then had to rent a car for the ninety-minute drive to Topeka. I live in the suburbs, but I'm a city girl at heart. Driving ninety minutes on toll roads out in the middle of nowhere is my idea of Hell. But wait, it gets worse—no one bothered to tell Kansas it was spring, so it was snowing.

I can count on one hand the number of times I've driven in the snow. If I hadn't known they might burn an eleven-year-old girl to death if I didn't show up, I'd have ridden out the storm in Kansas City.

The speed limit was seventy, but I drove about thirty-five, squinting out the windshield, hoping there weren't any cows grazing on the interstate under cover of the blizzard. Okay, so maybe it wasn't a blizzard by Midwest standards, but it's all a matter of perspective.

Kansas is one of ten states—including my home state, Pennsylvania—that allow the execution of humans hosting illegal demons. I called from the airport to let them know I'd be late. I almost choked when I noticed the area code for Topeka was 666. Gotta love the irony. Luckily, they weren't anxious to put a cute little girl to flame, despite the fact that she was allegedly possessed by a demon who'd murdered at least three people, so they agreed to wait for me.

The demon containment center–cum–execution chamber was in the basement of the courthouse and had more guards than most maximum security prisons. Why the idiots used legions of armed guards was beyond me. What were they going to do, shoot the host to death if a demon escaped? Yeah, that might solve the immediate problem and leave the demon without a body to inhabit, but if it found another host, you can bet revenge would be high on its to-do list. The only way to *kill* a demon is to exorcize it or burn its host alive. Lovely, huh?

I'd read little Lisa Walker's case on the plane. She and her parents had been visiting New York. They'd gone to a Broadway show, and when they were leaving, Lisa got knocked down by some thug who was running from the cops. Probably they thought it was exciting, because, hey, things like that just don't happen in Topeka.

It wasn't until they'd gotten home that they'd noticed anything wrong. She didn't do a Linda Blair and spit pea soup, but she definitely wasn't herself. It was the little things that gave it away—a suddenly more sophisticated vocabulary, a hint of attitude, the occasional expression in her eyes that was too old for her age. They'd called in a priest, and he'd immediately declared her possessed.

Me, I'd have been skeptical. Demons usually prefer strong adult bodies to inhabit, not delicate eleven-year-old girls. And no matter what they claim, priests aren't qualified to declare a person possessed. Yes, some of them are sensitives, and can see auras, but it's not a job requirement like it is for an exorcist.

So if I didn't think the kid was possessed, why had I flown all the way out here to bum-fuck Kansas to perform an exorcism? Because the court had ordered it, and the parents had approved it—and if the kid really was possessed, they'd barbecue her if an exorcist couldn't cast the demon out. The parents had demanded the best, and they could afford me, so here I was, freezing my tailfeathers off in Corn City, USA.

I had to clear two checkpoints before I even got close to the containment center. I'm sure I'd have made it through faster if I'd dressed the part, but if I'd wanted to wear suits, I'd have gone to business school. My uniform was a pair of tight low-rise jeans with a clingy sweater and a pair of kick-ass pointy-toed boots.

The director of the Topeka Containment Unit was one Frank Jenkins. He was a short, pudgy guy who looked harmless at first glance. He came out from behind a steel-barred door, smiling until he got a good look at me. Then the smile faded from the outside in until it morphed into a frown of disapproval. The frown didn't look anywhere near as harmless.

I put on my best hail-fellow-well-met smile and held out my hand. "Morgan Kingsley," I said, sounding almost perky. "You must be Mr. Jenkins."

He shook my hand and nodded, but he didn't look happy about it.

"I suppose you came straight to the courthouse

without stopping by your hotel," Jenkins said, the frown still firmly in place.

That was true, though I wouldn't have changed clothes even if I had checked in. "I thought it would be best for everyone involved if we got this over with," I said. Which was also true. I couldn't imagine what the parents must be going through. Not to mention Lisa, trapped inside a body she could no longer control, a helpless passenger while the demon rampaged.

The theory was that the thug in New York had been hosting an illegal demon who was on the run, wanted for three murders. When he bumped into Lisa, the demon thought it had found the perfect escape. Just hitchhike out of New York in an adorable little girl's body and hope to find a more suitable host later. The police had caught the fleeing thug eventually, only to find his brain fried.

"Well, let's get to it," Jenkins said, still frowning at me. At five foot nine, I was about three inches taller than him. I got the feeling he didn't like that much. Actually, I got the feeling he didn't like much of anything about me. Maybe I was a little too big-city for him.

Without another word, he led me through the steel doors into the heart of the containment center.

Why, you might ask, would a small-time burg like Topeka, which hadn't had more than one or two illegal demons in the last five years, need its own containment center? Because Kansas didn't take well to demons, legal or otherwise. Enough of their citizens believed in the Biblical view of demons as minions of Satan to keep execution legal, and they wanted to be prepared in the event they had a chance to rid the world of one more evil.

What did this mean to me? It meant that while the

personnel had all been trained for the job, they had little or no practical experience. And I saw evidence of that every step of the way as we walked to the execution chamber.

"Mr. Jenkins," I said when we stopped outside the chamber for him to key in the passcode, "why are your people not wearing gloves when you have a known illegal demon in custody?" An incorporeal demon needs an invitation to possess a human body, but one that already has a host can transfer from one to another through skin-to-skin contact. No one within a hundred yards of an illegal demon should be showing more skin than absolutely necessary.

Jenkins glared at me, liking me even less. "I can assure you, Ms. Kingsley, the demon is contained."

I bit my tongue to stop myself from reminding him of several incidents of "contained" demons escaping and wreaking havoc. He didn't strike me as being open to constructive criticism.

The door mechanism made a few clicking and ratcheting sounds, then Jenkins swung it open. It gave a sigh when it opened, as if the room behind it had been vacuum sealed.

I'd thought the containment center staff not wearing gloves was unprofessional. Brother, I hadn't known what unprofessional was until I stepped into that room.

Lisa Walker was strapped onto a sliding steel table. At one end of the table were a pair of heavy metal doors that led into the oven. She was positioned so that her feet faced the doors. So that she could stare with her wide little-girl eyes at the oven that would burn her alive if I failed to exorcize the demon.

Tears had matted her eyelashes and the fine yellow hair that framed her face. Her whole body was shaking with terror, and pity stabbed through me so hard I had to fight not to put a hand to my chest. I reminded myself that I could very well be looking at a demon giving an Oscar-worthy performance, but the pity didn't go away.

If the child wasn't possessed, she might never recover from this trauma. If she *was* possessed, then this was a new low for demon-kind.

But Lisa Walker's pitiful little frame wasn't what horrified me the most. No, what horrified me the most was that her parents sat huddled together on a bench at the other end of the room. Mrs. Walker's eyes were swollen with tears, and Mr. Walker's face was pale and tense.

I whirled on Jenkins. "You're letting the parents watch? Are you nuts?"

Exorcisms are never a pretty sight. There's usually a lot of screaming and cursing. From the demon, not from me. And about seventy-five to eighty percent of demon hosts end up dead or catatonic when the demon is cast out. So far, no one has come up with a reliable method of predicting which hosts would survive intact.

"She's their daughter," Jenkins said, drawing himself up to his full, not very impressive height. "If you fail, they'll have to sign the consent form."

I looked at Lisa Walker and a very unpleasant lump formed in my throat. I hate demons with a passion. And I don't like the legal ones much better than the illegal ones. But even *I* wasn't sure I could sign the order to burn an eleven-year-old girl alive to destroy the demon. Especially not if the girl was my daughter!

"You could have had them sign the consent beforehand," I muttered, disliking Jenkins now as much as he disliked me.

"They'd want to say goodbye."

I glanced over at the parents, who hadn't said word one to me. They couldn't even bear to look at me. Can't say I blamed them. I wished I'd worn a conservative business suit after all. I don't think my jeans and sweater gave them great confidence in my competence.

But the worst thing I could do now was make them wait and worry any longer, so I settled my shoulder bag on the floor and slipped out of my full-length leather coat. I glanced around for somewhere to put it, but there wasn't anywhere, and Jenkins didn't offer to take it for me. He was being juvenile, but then I'd insulted his facility more than once. I'd probably have been juvenile in his shoes, too.

I laid my coat carefully on the floor, which was spotless white tile anyway, then unzipped my bag. A muffled sob from Mrs. Walker made my shoulders hunch. There were only three times in my career when I'd faced a demon I couldn't cast out. But none of those three had been in execution states, and none had been inhabiting adorable little girls. If I failed, this was going to suck on so many levels . . .

The execution chamber was so spare and sterile there was nowhere to put my candles except on the floor. I could have asked Jenkins to get me a couple of tables, but it didn't matter where the candles were, and I was betting all of us wanted to get on with it.

Every exorcist has a ritual he or she performs to get into the trance state. Some are really elaborate, with chants and special clothing and incense—the works. Mine is disarmingly simple. I place vanilla-scented candles all around the room, then turn off all the lights. Then I stand over the demon-possessed body with my hands about six inches above it and just close my eyes.

Usually I'm already starting to slip into the trance after my first deep breath. Today I was having a harder time. Jenkins had taken to fidgeting with his ID badge. The noise was slight, but annoying. And I could hear Mrs. Walker's persistent sniffles. I imagined the table sliding into the oven with little Lisa Walker on it. I imagined hearing her screams.

I took another deep, vanilla-scented breath and reminded myself that, in these enlightened times, they'd anesthetize her before sliding her into the oven—there would be no screams. But that didn't make the image any more bearable.

The pressure was like nothing I'd ever felt before, and something akin to panic stirred.

Then Lisa Walker spoke.

"What's happening?" she asked in a quivering little-girl voice. "Mommy?"

It broke what little concentration I had, and my eyes popped open. I met the gaze of a pair of red-rimmed eyes of cornflower blue. So innocent-looking. But her words and her voice were so patently pathetic, so manipulative, that they gave me pause. So I watched closely, and something stirred behind those eyes. Something not so innocent. And I knew that they were right, that there was a demon inside this little girl. A demon who had no qualms about using the body of a child like a disposable plastic cup. When it found a more suitable host, it would slither out of her body, not caring that it might leave her dead or brain-damaged.

I gave the demon a nasty smile. "Fatal error," I told it in a low whisper that I hoped to God the parents didn't hear. "You should have kept your mouth shut."

The Cupid's bow mouth widened. I closed my eyes. And the trance took me immediately, fueled by my anger. Distantly, I was aware of that little-girl voice making pathetic noises, pleading with me and with its mommy, but I was too far gone to hear the words.

In my trance, I see with my otherworldly eyes. Everything looks different. Simpler. I can't see *things*. All I see are the living, and I see them as patches of primary colors. People show up as blue in my otherworldly vision. Jenkins was a dark, solid blue, like a person at rest. If he felt any strong emotions about this whole procedure, I couldn't sense it. The parents, on the other hand, were a mess, their auras roiling with every shade of blue imaginable.

But on the table under my hands, the aura glowed blood red. A demon aura, so overwhelming there was no sign of human blue beneath it. The aura squirmed, and I realized that the body was struggling against the restraints. The demon saw its destruction coming and was making a last-ditch effort to escape. I hoped they hadn't gotten squeamish when they'd secured the restraints. The supernatural strength of some demons is enough to bend steel, but even an inexperienced staff would know that.

I heard the distinctive sound of groaning metal. Alarm trickled down my back. This thing was strong. And desperate. Behind me, someone cried out. The yellow tint of fear blended with the blue of their auras to make the humans look almost green.

Just like everyone has their own ritual to get into the trance, everyone has their own mental image they use as a metaphor for casting out a demon. Mine is wind.

I imagined a gust of hurricane-force wind hitting that red aura. If it had been your average, run-of-the-mill demon, that one blast would have been enough. But this fucker was tough. The aura didn't waver, and I heard an echo of laughter ringing in my ears.

There were more cries of distress from the humans, and again metal groaned as the demon struggled. My heart pounded in my throat, and fear almost stole my concentration.

None of the three demons I'd failed to exorcize had come close to escaping, thankfully. I may be the scourge of demon-kind, but I do *not* want to be trapped in a room with a loose, angry demon in need of a new host.

The fear radiating from Jenkins and the Walkers pounded against my concentration, worse than my own fear, because there were three of them feeding one another's panic. I prayed Jenkins wouldn't do anything really stupid, like open the door to take himself out of harm's way.

As soon as I thought it, though, it happened. My concentration snapped completely, and I was out of the trance in time to see Jenkins shove the Walkers out the open door before he dove out himself.

At least he had the good sense to swing the door shut behind him. I really didn't want to see what would happen if the demon got loose in the containment center halls with all those inexperienced armed guards wandering around.

Of course, I really didn't want to be trapped alone in a room with a powerful, pissed-off demon, either.

I looked at the table, and my heart stuttered at what I saw.

Steel restraints bolted to the table held Lisa's thin arms and legs down, and there was another steel restraint around her waist. She'd pulled so hard on those restraints that the table had buckled beneath them, though so far she hadn't managed to break free. Blood poured from her wrists and ankles—the demon didn't much care what happened to this poor little body. It just wanted out. It pulled Lisa's lips back in a feral snarl. The metal groaned again.

Shit.

I drew in a deep, quavering breath and forced myself to close my eyes. If I gave it enough time, this thing was going to free itself. And I was going to become an unwilling host to an illegal demon myself.

No pressure.

Sweat trickled down the small of my back. I tried to calm myself. My life depended on it.

I slipped back into the trance more easily than I'd expected. Amazing what desperation will do for you. Once again, I hit that demon aura with a blast of wind. It wavered for a moment, then settled firmly back in place.

The metal didn't groan now so much as scream. The temptation to open my eyes and see what progress the thing was making was almost unbearable, but I resisted.

A small, delicate hand clapped onto my arm with a bone-crushing grip. But her hand was over my sweater, no skin-to-skin contact.

I stifled a scream and sent another blast of wind at the aura. Somehow I managed to stay entranced, even with a demon squeezing my arm so brutally I'd wear bruises for days even if it didn't break anything.

My breath burned in and out of my lungs and my heart slammed against my chest. I was so scared I could taste it, but if I let the fear win, I was demon-chow.

I gathered my power into me, concentrating on drawing every ounce of my strength into my center for one last try. There was another scream of tortured metal, and a second small hand grabbed me.

I almost panicked and let my next blast loose at that moment, but I knew I had only one more chance. If I didn't throw enough power against the demon, I was toast. So I fought my instincts and held myself together a few seconds more.

The demon's fingers tore through the fabric of my sweater, and that little demonic hand pressed against the skin of my forearm.

I screamed louder than I'd ever screamed in my life, overwhelmed by terror, horror, revulsion. My worst nightmare come true. A demon forcing itself into my body, taking me over, destroying everything I was without actually killing me . . .

I shoved my gathered power at it, knowing it was already too late—demons can transfer from one host to another instantly. The millisecond it touched me, I was gone.

Except, I wasn't.

That red, red aura crept up my arm from the demon's hand, and then withdrew, half a heartbeat before my power hit it.

I'd thrown everything I had into that blast. The aura shattered into a million tiny pinpricks of color; then it was gone.

I opened my eyes, hardly believing my good fortune, hardly believing I was still myself.

I wobbled on my feet. The floor bucked under me. I felt myself falling in slow motion but couldn't even get my hands under me to cushion the fall. My head hit that cold tile floor, and I was out.

Chapter **2**

I woke up staring at a white panel ceiling. My head ached like a son of a bitch. My arm throbbed where the demon had squeezed it. And I was so weak it tired me out to breathe.

I blinked a couple of times, happy to be alive and myself, but wishing I didn't feel like I'd been run over by a truck. My body groaned in protest when I pushed myself up into a sitting position.

I was still in the containment room, sitting on the white tile floor. But the room was completely empty. My candles were gone, as was my bag, my coat, Lisa Walker, the now-ruined table. Even the bench the parents had been sitting on was gone.

What the hell . . . ?

I pushed to my feet, wobbly and woozy. My stomach turned over, and I almost lost my lunch. I clutched my belly and felt something that shouldn't have been there. When the nausea passed, I lifted my sweater to find myself equipped with a stun belt.

And I suddenly knew what had happened.

I glanced up at the ceiling, and, sure enough, spotted a surveillance camera. Somebody had watched my little performance, had seen Lisa Walker touch me. Which explained my lovely new fashion accessory. Someone thought I was possessed.

About the only thing that has any effect on a rampaging demon is electricity, which messes with their ability to control the body. I supposed trying to take the belt off would be a very bad idea.

This was turning out to be just a joy of a day.

"Hello?" I yelled. "Can anyone hear me?" And does anyone care?

No one answered, so I tried again. "Hello out there! I'm not possessed. I cast the demon out. You can let me out of here now."

Still no answer. Can't say as I was shocked. After what they'd witnessed, the staff here was bound to be paranoid. They were going to treat me with the same caution they might treat Satan himself.

"Can you at least tell me how Lisa's doing?"

A microphone clicked on. "She's alive," a disembodied voice told me. Jenkins, I think, though the voice sounded tinny over the speaker.

"How badly is she hurt?" Human bodies just aren't made for ripping themselves free of steel restraints. If I hadn't felt those little hands digging into my flesh, I'd have thought the arms would give before the steel.

Another click. "She'll recover. Physically, at least."

Well, shit. That meant her mind was gone. Not that I hadn't expected it, but it still sucked. There was a slim chance that someday her mind would come back. Most likely, she'd be a vegetable for the rest of her life.

I wanted to say I was sorry, but I had a feeling

Jenkins would take that as some kind of confession. Like I was harboring a demon with a guilty conscience.

"I'm really not possessed, you know," I said.

"We saw the demon touch you."

"Yeah, and I *felt* it touch me. But it didn't take me. Maybe I didn't taste good." I couldn't imagine why the demon would choose not to transfer to me when I was its only chance of escape, but it hadn't.

"Was that supposed to be a joke, Ms. Kingsley?" The speaker might be tinny, but the disapproval came through just fine.

I glared up at the camera. I had plenty of disapproval to go around. "Was it supposed to be a joke when you locked me in here with a demon that was obviously not as contained as you claimed?" I hadn't had time to get really angry about this yet, but give me a few minutes and I'd be pitching a world-class fit. "You've got a stun belt on *me*. Why didn't you have one on *it*?" I knew the answer to that: they'd believed she couldn't break free of the restraints. Hell, *I* hadn't believed it, either, or I'd have complained the minute I stepped into the room.

"It was an unfortunate oversight," Jenkins said in his best bureaucratese. It didn't improve my attitude.

"And thanks for helping me out when you saw I was in trouble," I snarled.

He lost his good-little-bureaucrat voice and suddenly sounded miserable. "I'm very sorry, Ms. Kingsley. I had to get the civilians out of the room."

Yeah, and you just had to follow them out while you were at it.

I kept my mouth shut. Maybe because in my gut I thought he'd done the right thing. Only a moron would try to take on a demon one-on-one. Jenkins was a bureaucrat, not a foot soldier. He'd probably left the room to gather a small army of guards with their Tasers and rifles.

"We have asked Father Ben to come down and look at your aura," Jenkins continued. "If you truly are not possessed, Ms. Kingsley, then I apologize for the inconvenience."

I sighed. The last thing I wanted was to be a suspected demon host in an execution state and have my fate rest on a priest who might or might not be able to read my aura. Especially when priests universally believed demons were creatures from Hell, sent to plague mankind. I might not be overly fond of demons myself, but I didn't believe they were the embodiment of evil, either.

"Tell Father Ben to stay home," I said. "Please call Valerie March and ask her to come make a diagnosis."

Val has been my best friend since high school. She's a fellow exorcist, though we each came into the field with a very different agenda. Val's noble cause was to root out the bad eggs among demons so the rest of them wouldn't get such a bad rap. Me, I just wanted an excuse to kick some demon ass.

But Val is a damn good exorcist, one of the few I'd trust when my life was hanging in the balance. Unfortunately, she lives in Philadelphia, so it would be tomorrow before she could get here and spring me. But better an extra day in this lovely facility than a date with the oven.

"Father Ben can be here in a little over an hour," Jenkins said. "Is this Valerie March a local?"

I shook my head. "No, but she's a trained exorcist."

"I assure you, Father Ben—"

"Call her, Mr. Jenkins. I'll give you the number."

There was such a long silence, I feared he'd decided to ignore my request. I had visions of some superstitious priest condemning me as a demon, of being Tasered into a quivering mass of Jell-O and then strapped to a brand-spankin'-new table. All I'd need was an apple in my mouth, and I'd be ready to cook. Because if they thought I'd been taken over by Lisa Walker's demon, then they thought I, the most successful exorcist on record, couldn't cast it out. Which would mean there was no point in trying another exorcism. Just get straight to the burning alive part.

I shivered and hugged myself.

"Very well, Ms. Kingsley. Give me the number."

I was so relieved I almost collapsed. But I gave him the number. Now all I had to do was wait.

No one looking at Valerie March would believe she'd be friends with someone like me. We are almost polar opposites. I'm tall, big-boned—*not* fat—with red hair I like to keep cut short. I've been known to dress outlandishly, and my left ear is pierced in five different places. My right ear's only pierced twice. I also have a small, tasteful tattoo of a sword on my lower back. It's got a fancy hilt with a Celtic knot design, and the blade points directly to my butt crack. When I wear low-rise jeans, you can see the hilt.

I got it when I was fifteen. My only reason was that I'd admired a tattoo I'd seen on a woman on TV. I mentioned it to my parents, who naturally told me how uncouth it was for a woman to have a tattoo. They should have known better. I was at the tattoo parlor the next day. I was grounded for a full month, but I climbed out my window at least two or three times a week.

Val is a strictly-by-the-books kind of gal. The woman wouldn't even jaywalk! She disapproves of at least two-thirds of my life decisions, but she loves me anyway. That's true friendship.

By the time she reached the courthouse, I'd been in custody a little over twenty-four hours. They were not the best twenty-four hours of my life.

They kept me in that completely unfurnished room the whole time. I didn't mind having to curl up to sleep on the tile floor. Well, yes, I minded, but I didn't mind it as bad as the bathroom situation. As in, I didn't have one.

I had to ask permission to take a pee. When I did, an army of six or seven guards would show up at the door, fingers on the triggers of their Tasers, as if the stun belt wasn't deterrent enough. They came with me into the bathroom. Worse, I couldn't even go into a stall for privacy. I had to do my business while they surrounded me, pointing their Tasers, just itching to shoot me.

Of course, if I *was* hosting a demon, letting me out of sight would have been a bad, bad idea. Any demon worth its salt can pull a toilet free from the floor. And believe me, if a demon hits you in the head with a toilet, you aren't getting up afterward.

I held it as best I could, but I couldn't hold it for more than twenty-four hours. I planned to harbor a grudge about this for the rest of my life.

When Val came into the containment room, the goon squad came with her, fanning out in a semicircle on both sides. I was sitting on the floor when they came in, my back against the wall. I'd have stood up to greet her, but I was pretty sure the guards would shoot me if I moved.

She was wearing the conservative business suit I'd refused to wear myself, and she radiated an aura of competence. Not a literal aura, mind you. Competence doesn't show up in auras, or life would be a hell of a lot easier. Her blond hair was pulled back into a French braid, and she wore a pair of wire-rimmed glasses. Off duty, she wore contacts, but the glasses made her look more serious and professional.

She smiled at me and shook her head.

"Morgan, you have the most chaotic life of anyone I've ever known," she said.

I grinned at her, but still didn't stand up. The guards had eased down a bit, but not enough that I'd trust them not to shoot.

"Tell me about it!" I replied. "Can you get me out of here, please?"

"I'll do my best."

Another guard entered the room, carrying Val's suitcase. As I said, some exorcists have fancier rituals than others. Val is one of them. Not because she needs all the trappings, but because she thinks it impresses her clients. Who am I to argue?

Right now, though, I wished she'd go for something a little more understated. I wanted out. But she's a by-the-books gal, so she was going to put on the whole show, though I suspected she knew right away that I wasn't possessed. Demons have full access to our memories and can get quite good at pretending to be the person they've possessed, but it normally takes a little time and practice. When someone's first taken, people who know them well can usually see it. Whether they know what they're seeing or not is a whole other question.

I wanted to ask Val to hurry up—I needed to pee again, and I really wanted to do it without an audience—but I knew better. She was determined to give them the whole frickin' show, and I was just going to have to wait. I pressed my thighs together and prayed I wouldn't pee my pants before she got through.

Val's ritual involved music, candles, and even a circle of power made out of salt. I could see the guards were impressed, their attention occasionally drifting away from me to watch her. If I'd really been a demon host, people would have died while they watched the show.

Finally, Val rose from her trance and declared me clean. Her ritual had been convincing enough that the guards immediately lowered their Tasers and I was able to make a dash to the bathroom.

Jenkins was waiting for me when I got out. I think he was going to apologize for the inconvenience, but I was *so* not in the mood to hear it. Val, standing beside him, easily read the look on my face. She reached over to put a hand on my arm—right where the demon had crushed my muscles—and smiled up at Jenkins.

"Let me give you a word of advice, Mr. Jenkins," she said. "I love Morgan like a sister, but if you say anything to her right now, I might end up having to pull her off you."

Her smile was sweet as spun sugar, but her tone was utterly convincing. Jenkins looked unsure of himself and I almost felt sorry for him. If this had all happened to someone else, I might have said he hadn't done anything wrong. But it had happened to *me,* and forgiveness isn't one of my strong suits. Just ask my family.

Jenkins took her at her word and nodded curtly. He unlocked the stun belt without speaking to me. I clamped my jaws shut to keep myself from starting anything, then let Val lead me out of there as fast as my legs could carry me.

Naturally, I'd parked in a two-hour parking spot, so my car had been towed. Val drove me to the impound lot so I could get it back, along with my luggage, before finally checking into the hotel. The good news was the snow had stopped overnight, and the roads were all nice and clear. Val wanted to talk, but I insisted I needed a shower and a change of clothes first.

I met her at the dinky little hotel bar about an hour later. She'd changed out of her business suit and into a pair of gray wool trousers and a midnight blue turtleneck. This was her idea of casual wear. Me, I was feeling pretty ornery, so I changed into a pair of low-rise black leather pants and a low-cut emerald cashmere sweater. The sweater tended to ride up my rib cage and display my tattoo. There were only four other customers in the bar, all men dressed in business suits, and I felt each one of them take a good long look at me.

I'm not one of those women who pretends she doesn't know she's attractive to the opposite sex. My style might be a tad aggressive for a woman, but it goes well with my height and my bone structure, and I'm used to being stared at. I even enjoy it—though my boyfriend, Brian, hates it. He keeps asking me to tone down my wardrobe when we go out in public. We've been dating for a little over a year, and we have enough physical chemistry to set the bed on fire, but he still doesn't know me well enough not to make that kind of request. I always wear my sexiest outfits when we're going out. Funny how we end up staying in for so many of our dates.

Val had already ordered me my favorite drink, a piña colada. Yeah, I know I looked silly with a total of seven earrings in my ears, wearing black leather pants that showed my tattoo while drinking something so froufrou. But I hate the taste of alcohol. Whatever I drink has to mask the alcohol or I just can't force it down.

Val laughed at me when I plopped down in the chair beside her and took a long, grateful swallow of my drink.

"Should I ask why you brought black leather pants on a business trip to Topeka?" she asked, still smiling.

I grinned back at her. "Call it a premonition."

Actually, I'd brought them because they made me feel feminine and attractive. Yeah, I know black leather isn't what most people consider feminine, but judging from the way guys look at me when I wear them, I beg to differ.

Her smile faded into a look of concern, and she cocked her head. "So tell me what happened."

I told her. I didn't enjoy reliving the memory, but after she flew out here to save my ass, I owed her the full monty.

She was frowning when I finished, and her martini glass was empty. She ordered another, and I stirred the melting remains of my drink.

"Why didn't it take you?" Val murmured, biting her lip.

I sighed. "I don't know, Val. I just don't get it." I'd spent most of the last twenty-four hours examining the question from all angles, but I hadn't come up with any answers.

Her second drink arrived and she took a sip. A worry line creased her brow. "Maybe it was just slow for some reason. Maybe it hadn't had time to take over before you hit it."

I wished I could believe that. "It was pulling away before I hit it." I shook my head, fighting an urge to hug myself. I'd never been so unnerved in all my life. Considering what I do for a living, that's saying a lot. I forced a phony smile. "Look at the two of us—all somber and upset because a demon *didn't* take me."

Val laughed, but it was a tight sound. "Yeah. Silly, I guess." She raised her glass and tried to look less worried. "Who cares why it happened? Here's to you still being alive and whole!"

"I'll drink to that!" I clinked glasses with her, and we moved on to lighter topics of conversation. But I was still unnerved.

After our drink, we went for a fabulous Midwest steak dinner. My appetite wasn't up to the task, but I tried my best to enjoy it. We went back to the hotel right after dinner, and I called Brian to let him know I was okay.

I didn't want to rehash everything again, so before he had a chance to ask me for details about my ordeal, I said, "I'm thinking of a number between one and one hundred. Can you guess what it is?"

There was a momentary pause on the other end of the line. Either his mind wasn't as dirty as mine, or he was debating whether to let me distract him. My money was on the latter.

"Um...ten?" he said, but the mingled laughter and lust in his voice told me he knew exactly what number I had in mind.

"Strike one."

A dramatic sigh. "Let's see then...How 'bout thirty-five?"

I swear, I think I giggled. I am *so* not a giggler. "Strike two."

"Hmm. This is a hard one."

"Hey! Isn't that my line?"

He ignored my protest. "Would that number be sixty-nine, by any chance?"

Nice to know we were on the same wavelength. My

mouth suddenly watered at the memory of the taste of him. "Slugger, you just hit a home run."

"Too bad home plate is in Topeka."

"Yeah," I agreed. "Guess we'll just have to improvise." With the phone cradled against my shoulder, I pulled back the comforter on the bed and fluffed up the pillows before climbing in.

"I like the sound of that," Brian said in a low, husky voice. "Are you making yourself comfortable?"

I snuggled into the pillows. "Yup. And you?"

"Oh yeah," he responded.

I heard the distinctive rasp of a zipper being dragged down. I closed my eyes, the better to picture what lay behind. I rubbed my thighs together, loving the mental image and wishing I could be there in person to see the real thing.

"You're whipping it out already?" I asked in mock disapproval while I unzipped my own pants, fingers playing over the strip of lace between my legs. "I thought you had more stamina than that." I pretended my fingers were Brian's tongue, and my breath hitched.

He made a sound halfway between a chuckle and a growl. "Not when I'm imagining your mouth wrapped around my cock. And where, might I ask, is *your* hand at the moment?"

I laughed. Caught red-handed, so to speak. Awkwardly, I maneuvered my way out of my pants and underwear while still holding the phone. "Where I wish your tongue was," I answered breathlessly.

He groaned, and I think I heard him lick his lips, but that might just have been my imagination.

I swear, Brian has the most amazing tongue in the history of mankind. Far and away superior to any other specimen I'd sampled. I squirmed, the touch of my own fingers inadequate in comparison. "What are you doing?" I panted.

"What do you think?" he asked in reply, and another distinctive sound came over the phone line. My mind's eye filled with the vision of his fist wrapped around his cock, and my own arousal reached new heights. Watching him touch himself always drove me wild.

Just as I was really working up a head of steam, however, the sounds and comments stopped, replaced by a harsh breathing. I knew he hadn't come yet—he wasn't one to keep quiet about it when he did. Fighting against frustration, I stilled the hand between my legs.

"What's wrong?" I asked.

"Nothing," he said between panted breaths. "It's just that you're going to be home tomorrow, and I'd rather wait for the real thing." I groaned, and Brian laughed. "You don't have to wait just because I do."

Patience has never been my virtue, but his words sounded almost like a challenge, and I don't like to back down from challenges. "I'll wait," I said between gritted teeth.

"It won't be long," he assured me. "I'll pick you up at the airport."

I shook my head, even though he couldn't see it. "Don't. I'm going to need some time to decompress after all this. I won't be good company." Quick, hot phone sex I could handle, but I doubted I could have in-person sex without having to tell him all about my lovely trip to Topeka. And I needed a little distance before I could manage that.

"I don't need you to be good company," he assured me.

A thread of irritation wove through me. Brian

wasn't much for giving me my space, and right now I badly needed it.

"I'll call you when I get in," I said firmly.

He hesitated like he was going to argue, but then he didn't. "I never pegged you for such a tease," he grumbled.

My shoulders sagged a bit with relief. Usually he didn't make things this easy for me. Maybe he was finally getting to understand me just a little bit. But if I left him unfulfilled, he might change his mind tomorrow night and show up at the airport.

My hand started moving again, and I didn't try to stifle the low moan that rose from my throat. Brian might fully intend to abstain until he had me in person, but I was betting his self-control had limits.

"Changed your mind about waiting?" he asked. His voice had dropped to a low growl that raised goose bumps on my skin.

"Mm-hmm." Listening carefully, I could hear the quickening of his breaths. I closed my eyes and once again imagined the sight of his hand stroking the smooth, silky skin I so loved to touch. The sensation was achingly real, heating my core.

"You're killing me."

My laugh was low and throaty. "What are you going to do about it?"

"Not a damn thing," he replied, but it sure sounded like his teeth were gritted.

"I'm so wet," I murmured in my best fuck-me voice. "Don't you wish you could touch me to see for yourself?"

"You're an evil, evil woman."

"Yeah, but it's fun to be bad." The heat gathered in my center, and I had to slow myself down. I had to push him past the point of no return before I let myself tumble over the cliff. "Are you being bad, Brian?"

"I'm being a perfect angel," he gasped, but that wasn't what it sounded like.

"I don't think that's your nose that's growing, Pinocchio."

His laugh sounded almost desperate. I closed my eyes and visualized the sweat that glowed on his skin, the flush that colored his face, the salty-sweet drop of pre-cum that beaded on his tip. I bit my lip, hard, on the edge of control.

"Can you feel me squeezing you tight with every stroke?" I asked, amazed I could form coherent words.

"Don't," he protested, his breath coming ever faster. His rational mind might have wanted me to stop, but his body sure as hell didn't.

"Can you?" I asked again. Another muffled protest told me all I needed to know. My self-control broke, and I went screaming over the edge.

Brian let out an anguished groan as he stopped fighting against the climax he knew damn well he wanted.

For a few minutes afterward, we were both silent except for our gasps for breath.

"I love you," Brian said when he had the air for it.

I sighed in contentment. "I love you, too."

"Call me the minute you get home."

"I will," I promised, crossing my fingers like a ten-year-old. I'd call him when I was good and ready, and he knew that. But I promised myself that I wouldn't make him—or myself, for that matter—wait long. As sweet as our mutual release had been, it couldn't compare to the feeling of having the man I loved inside me when I came.

When I hung up the phone, I had every intention of

getting the rest of my clothes off and properly preparing for bed. But my limbs felt so languid, my body so limp, that I decided to close my eyes for just a few minutes first.

I awoke the next morning groggy as hell, yawning every five seconds. It was weird, because according to the clock I'd slept a good ten hours. I should be fresh as a daisy. I chewed my lip as I made my way to the bathroom for my morning shower.

Had I been sleepwalking again? It had happened on and off for the last couple of months, and this was how I usually felt in the morning. Of course, those other times I'd known I'd been sleepwalking because I'd awakened in the middle of it. Let me tell you, it's disconcerting to wake up wandering around your living room at oh-dark-thirty.

As far as I knew, I hadn't been up and about last night, but I still felt like shit. Maybe it was just all the stress and trauma of the last couple of days. Yeah, that was it.

But when I was packing my bags for my flight back to Philadelphia, I found a note, scribbled in my own handwriting, sitting on the desk by the phone.

The demon didn't take you because you're already possessed.

Damn. I guess I'd been up and about last night after all. I ripped the note off the pad of hotel stationery, crumpled it into a wad, and tossed it into the trash can. My skin felt cold and clammy.

It was my subconscious at work, I knew that. As an exorcist, I just couldn't leave the puzzle of why the demon didn't take me alone. So clearly my subconscious had leapt to the most alarming conclusion it could manage, then left this little love note for me while I was sleepwalking.

Nothing to worry about. I mean, if I was actually possessed, then the demon would be in full control of my body. You can't be possessed and not know it. Besides, Val had looked at my aura and declared me clean.

But demonic possession is my personal worst nightmare—hence, my career choice. And rational thought is no match for irrational fear, so that stupid note creeped me out no matter how I reasoned with myself.

If the city of Topeka ever needs an exorcist again, you can bet I won't be volunteering for the job.

Chapter 3

Guess who met me at the airport despite my very clear instructions not to? I should have known he wouldn't give up so easily. Brian's about as good at following orders as I am. When I saw him standing there waiting for me at baggage claim, I couldn't decide if I was more pissed off he'd come or happy to see him.

"He's a keeper," Val said out of the corner of her mouth, and I gave her a dirty look. She winked at me, then hurried away, leaving us two "lovebirds" alone.

Val thinks I should have married Brian by now, and she rarely misses a chance to tell me so. He hasn't asked me to marry him yet, but he has hinted—broadly—that we should move in together. Sometimes I think he and Val are tag-teaming the matchmaking game. Lucky for me, I see through their evil plan.

I hugged him when he came to me, but I didn't exactly melt into his arms.

"I thought I told you I *didn't* want you to meet me," I muttered by his ear, then pulled away.

Brian flashed me one of his all-American-boy smiles—the kind of smile that almost always defused me. Sometimes it was just easier to bask in the warmth of that smile than to fight with him.

I sighed, still a little peeved, but that one damn smile had taken the edge off. "You're a pain in the ass, you know that?"

He snorted. "If that isn't the pot calling the kettle black." He bent to pick up my suitcase, and I just shook my head in defeat.

"If I'm such a pain in the ass, why are you here?" I asked as I followed him out to the parking lot. I stayed a couple steps behind him, not because I couldn't keep up but because I was annoyed.

"Because you give such fantastic blow jobs," he called over his shoulder, loud enough for everyone in a ten-yard radius to hear.

My face went red hot, and I kept my eyes locked on the back of his head so I wouldn't see how many people were giving me speculative looks. Brian loves to embarrass me. He thinks it's funny that he can make this tough broad with the multiple earrings and the tattoo blush. When I'm in a good mood, I think it's funny, too. I wasn't in a good mood.

I'd taken the train in from Bryn Mawr, so my car wasn't here. Brian would drive me all the way out there, then drive all the way back to his condo in Center City. If I was a good girlfriend, I'd ask him to spend the night, spare him that extra drive. I doubted I would, though: not tonight.

We didn't say a word to each other when we got in the car. He was still grinning a little, enjoying my lingering embarrassment. I curled my sour mood around me like a security blanket.

After he'd paid the exorbitant parking fee and got

onto I-95, he opened his mouth to say something, but I cut him off immediately.

"If you're planning to make another blow job comment, you won't get another one for at least three years." I can hold a grudge that long, easy.

He laughed and put his hand on my thigh. I was irritated enough to push him away, but like I said, there is a lot of physical chemistry between us. The touch of his hand on my thigh instantly raised my pulse. And when his hand came right back, I let it stay.

"There are only two ways to coax you out of a bad mood," he said, watching the road instead of me. "Teasing and sex. You looked like you were in a bad enough mood to need a little of both."

I wanted to argue with him, but his fingers were moving up my thigh, finding their way to my zipper. When he started sliding the zipper down, I gathered my wits enough to grab his wrist.

"Shouldn't you be concentrating on driving?" I said, but my voice came out a little breathy. There's always a lot of traffic on I-95, and technically he really should have had both hands on the wheel.

"I'm concentrating enough. What are you wearing under these jeans?"

My face heated. I really didn't want to be jollied out of my mood, but it was hard to stay pissy when I was squirming with desire. Still, I tried.

"White cotton granny panties."

A taxi cut us off, and Brian had stomp the brakes to prevent us from rear-ending the cab.

The near-death experience didn't faze him. "You don't own a pair of white cotton granny panties."

Yes, Brian is that well acquainted with my underwear. "I didn't pack enough underwear for an extended stay, so I bought some in Topeka."

"That so?" He gave me a sly look out of the corner of his eye. "Show me."

I grimaced. "Knock it off, Brian. I'm not in the mood."

He grinned at me. "I've noticed. And I'm doing my best to change that."

Why is it I never come out on top when arguing with Brian? Maybe because he's a lawyer? Never stops me from trying, though.

"Is that why you came to pick me up?" I asked. "Because you want to get laid?"

"No," he said slowly, patiently, "I picked you up because you've just been through hell and you don't need to be alone tonight."

I crossed my arms and hunched down in the seat. "You don't get to make that decision."

"You could have told me to shove off. But you didn't."

I groaned and shook my head. The guy was like a little yappy dog that sinks its teeth into your pants leg then refuses to let go. Which is why he wins so many arguments with me—most sensible people would run the other way when I was in this bitchy a mood, but not him.

"So are you going to show me these new white cotton granny panties of yours?" he continued. Yap, yap, yap. Grrr. Grrr.

"Have I mentioned that you're a pain in the ass?"

"Yup," he said cheerfully.

And, damn it, I couldn't help smiling. "Okay, you win. I'm not wearing any panties. There. Happy?" I tried to sound grumpy, but it didn't work.

"Ecstatic!" He reached for my zipper again. I batted his hand away.

"Please can the foreplay until we get off the

Expressway, okay?" Those of us who know and love it refer to the Schuylkill Expressway as the Sure-Kill Expressway, because you take your life in your hands every time you get on it. And I'd rather Brian take my life in *both* his hands instead of just one.

Hot-blooded though he was, Brian didn't have a death wish, so he kept his eyes on the road and his hands on the wheel until we'd gotten all the way past the Main Line and were on our way out to the suburbs. Then the banter and suggestive comments started again. And yes, he coaxed me into showing him my invisible panties. We're lucky he didn't slam into a tree while he inspected them.

By the time we reached my street, my jeans were distinctly damp, his khaki trousers were about ready to explode, and I was seriously considering jumping his bones in the car.

Until we pulled into my driveway, that is, and I saw a very familiar, very unwelcome car parked there.

I muttered about twenty-three curses under my breath. Brian's shoulders slumped, and he groaned in frustration. Nothing could kill the mood better than a visit from my big brother, Andrew.

Andrew got out of his car and leaned against the driver-side door, waiting.

Brian shook his head. "I guess this means I'm not getting laid tonight, huh?"

"Apparently not."

"Bummer."

He startled a laugh out of me and I turned toward him as I undid my seat belt. I reached out and touched his face.

"Thanks for coming to meet me," I said. It was a bad precedent to thank him for doing something I'd specifically asked him not to do, but I couldn't deny I felt better now than when I'd gotten off the plane.

"You're welcome," he murmured, turning his head to plant a kiss on my palm.

His kiss seemed to burn, and I realized I would need a cold, cold shower tonight before going to bed.

I reluctantly lowered my hand from his face and reached for the door. He touched my arm, and I raised my eyebrow.

"Your zipper," he reminded me with an evil grin.

I mumbled a curse and zipped up.

"I love you," Brian said as I slipped out.

"Love you, too," I replied automatically, then dragged my luggage out of the backseat. "Drive safe."

"Your place or mine tomorrow night? We have unfinished business." He leered at me, and I probably leered back.

"Mine," I told him, and he nodded agreement.

I took a slow, steadying breath as he pulled out of my driveway. Then I turned and headed for my front door without sparing a glance for Andrew.

I felt him following me, but I didn't turn around until I'd unlocked my front door and turned the lights on.

"Wait here," I said over my shoulder, then closed the door in his face.

I dropped my bags by the front door, then retrieved my Taser from the coat closet. I don't carry it very often—by the time I'm called in to deal with an illegal demon, it's already in custody and contained. But sometimes it's comforting to own the one weapon that can bring a demon to his knees.

I checked the battery—good to go—and turned off the safety. When I opened the door again, I pointed the Taser smack-dab at Andrew's chest.

Now, you might think this is a strange way to greet

my own brother, but the last time he'd paid a visit, we'd gotten in one hell of a fight, and the bastard had punched me. Knocked me out cold. When I came to, I'd seriously considered filing assault charges against him. In the end, it hadn't been worth the hassle, and I knew nothing would come of it. Yes, technically assault was a violent crime, and the state could throw the book at him. But though he'd knocked me out, he'd hit me with only human strength. If he'd hit me with his full strength, I'd be dead.

Oh, did I forget to mention my brother is a demon host? Ever since he turned twenty-one, the legal age of consent. I've never forgiven him.

We were pretty close as kids. Well, as close as a brother and sister can be when only three years separate them. Up until I was about ten, I practically worshiped him. But when he hit puberty, the Spirit Society's brainwashing started him seriously thinking about becoming a demon host, and he changed.

He'd always been more into the Society than me—no doubt a large reason why he was the family favorite—but when he started thinking about hosting, he became almost a fanatic. My parents were so proud of him, but I knew it meant I'd lose my big brother someday soon, and I hated it.

Andrew looked at the Taser and raised his eyebrows. "Are you planning self-defense, or revenge?" he asked, his voice mild.

I thought about that a moment. I didn't think he was going to hit me again. I'd had to work really hard to get him that angry last time. Now that I knew he had a temper under his usually calm exterior, I wasn't anxious to bring it to the surface.

"Revenge, I guess," I said, then shot him. The probes

latched onto his leather jacket, and fifty thousand volts slammed into him.

He gratifyingly collapsed into himself, landing on the doorstep in fetal position, screaming.

When I got my Taser license, one of the requirements was to take a shot yourself, just so you'd have a real clear understanding of the power you hold in your hands. I'd seen two-hundred-pound macho men scream like little girls. I wish I could say I'd taken it in stoic silence, but I'd screamed as loud as anyone. Never felt anything like it. Never want to again.

"Sorry, Andy," I said softly, talking to my *real* brother, the one who was imprisoned somewhere in that body. I wasn't clear if the host could feel the demon's pain or not, but just in case it could, I felt the need to apologize.

It took the demon more time to recover from the shot than it would have taken a human. The electricity really fucks up their control of the nervous system. He lay in a panting heap for a while, then uncurled and pushed himself to his knees, looking up at me from behind a lock of reddish blond hair that had fallen over his eyes.

"Should I bother getting up," he asked, "or am I in for some more fun?"

He was still so infuriatingly calm it made me want to zap him again. But he'd only hit me once. Fair's fair. That didn't mean I was putting the Taser away, but I ejected the cartridge and let him pluck the probes out of his jacket.

"Remember," I warned him, "I can still use this like a stun gun without reloading."

He laughed and pushed his hair out of his eyes, then stood up slowly, keeping a close watch on the Taser. "I'll keep that in mind."

"So, what, the pain doesn't even bother you? You just laugh at it?"

He shrugged. "It bothers me. But I deal with pain all the time on the job. If I fell to pieces every time something hurt, I'd be useless."

Andrew is a firefighter. Almost all of the legal demons make themselves into ultra-useful members of society, using their powers for good, justice, etc. They know they have to do a lot of good deeds to make up for their occasional bad eggs, like the one I'd encountered in Topeka. Because demons can heal the bodies of their human hosts, they often take on really dangerous jobs. Andrew is always rescuing people from burning buildings. He's a fucking hero.

Okay, so maybe it's not fair to be mad at him for being a hero. But, see, I'm *not* a hero, and I never will be. Sometimes that makes me feel small and selfish in comparison. I'm all for doing good deeds. Just not at the price Andy paid.

"What do you want, Andrew? I've had a really shitty couple of days, and I *so* don't want any family drama right now."

He ran a hand through his hair—a very human gesture, but then if you just met him on the street you'd never know he *wasn't* human. "It's been two months since our, uh, problem. I thought maybe it was time we buried the hatchet."

Oh, yeah. *This* was a conversation I wanted to have right now. Personally, I'd have been just as happy if we never spoke to each other again.

"Andrew—"

"Morgan, we're family, whether you want us to be or not."

This was somewhere along the lines of the conversation we'd had last time. I wondered if slamming the door in his face would be my best option right about now.

"*Andy's* my family! *You're* just a parasite using his body, like a big, lethal tick sucking the life out of him."

He grimaced. "Lovely image. You've always had such a way with words."

I went for the door slam, but he stopped it with the flat of his hand. I was pissed enough that I tried to use my Taser like a stun gun, but he saw it coming and knocked the Taser out of my hand. He could have broken bones in the process, but somehow he hit just the right spot to make my fingers loosen without even hurting me.

I cradled my hand to my body anyway, hating him, wishing it wasn't illegal to exorcize a demon from a willing host. But it's considered murder, and no matter how strongly I felt about Andrew's demon, I wasn't willing to go to prison or face execution.

Andrew pushed past me into my house, shutting the door behind him. Anger glinted in his eyes, and there was a steely set to his jaw that Andy would never have been able to pull off.

"Violence isn't the answer to everything," he said, sounding disgusted. "Stop acting like a two-year-old having a temper tantrum!"

I glared at him. "*I* wasn't the one who threw a punch the last time we argued."

He lost some of his righteous indignation, and his lips pursed like he'd tasted something sour. "I really am sorry about that, Morgan. The last time I walked the Mortal Plain, my host was an inherently violent man, a warrior. We may suppress our hosts' personalities, but some of it does leak through, and a lifetime of it can affect our behavior. I am . . . embarrassed that I allowed that to happen. It won't happen again."

I cocked my head at him. "So you're saying it wasn't really *you* that hit me? That it was some remnant of your last host?"

As an exorcist, I'm technically an expert on demons. And being raised by a Spirit Society family, I have a little bit of extra expertise from up-close-and-personal experience. But even us "experts" don't really know all that much about them. We only know what they tell us, and I would bet my life that they're not telling us everything. That's one of the things that scares the shit out of me. What aren't they telling us? And why?

Andrew took my question as evidence that I was ready to have a lovely little heart-to-heart chat and invited himself into my living room.

My house looks nothing like me. I look like the sort of woman who should live in some kind of ultra-modern condo with spare, sleek lines and uncomfortable furniture. Instead, I live in a little cottage that could have been plucked straight from the English countryside, complete with hedge roses and a cobblestone walk. My living room features an overstuffed floral chintz sofa and a butter-yellow love seat capable of swallowing a medium-sized adult whole.

Andrew is not medium-sized, though he's not huge, either. He's right around six feet tall, two hundred pounds of pure muscle. If he weren't my brother—sort of—I'd think he was pretty nice to look at. He sank into the love seat, but managed not to be smothered by it.

Bowing to the inevitable, I sat on the sofa and clutched a throw pillow to my chest. My nerves were too raw from the nightmare in Topeka. I didn't feel like coping, and I didn't feel like having any deep conversations with this creature I despised.

Andrew clasped his hands between his knees and stared at them intently. "I take the full blame for what I did, Morgan. I'm not a Viking anymore, and I should have had better control over myself. Yes, Einar affected my personality, but I've been with Andrew for ten years. I should have been able to readjust by now." He looked up at me, and his lips twitched with a hint of a grin. "Though you could bring out the devil in anyone."

I laughed, though grudgingly. Then I swallowed back the moment of humor and fixed him with my steeliest gaze. "Like I told you before, I've had a really lousy couple of days. I just want to take a long hot bath and then go to bed. Can you hurry this along a bit?"

His raised eyebrow made me blush, because of course he'd seen me drive up with Brian, and he'd known that meant it wasn't relaxing I'd had in mind. Luckily for both of us, he let it drop without teasing.

"All I want is to make things right between us. Or at least as right as they can be. What can I do to apologize for my horrendous behavior?"

My first instinct was to tell him to shove his apology where the sun didn't shine. But I must be gaining a little maturity in my old age, because I managed to squash that first instinct. Things would never be "right" between us as long as he possessed my brother's body. But since he was offering me something...

"You can tell me your name," I said, almost holding my breath, wondering if he would do it. The demons adopt their hosts' names when they're in the Mortal Plain, but they have names of their own. Names have power for them, though I've never been clear what kind of power. Another one of their damned mysteries.

He gave me a long, searching look. "If I tell you my

name, will you promise not to address me by it in public or tell it to anyone else?"

"Cross my heart and hope to die," I said glibly.

He thought for another moment, then nodded. "My name is Raphael," he said, and I had to fight not to let my jaw drop in amazement.

He'd believed me? *I* sure as hell wouldn't have!

Damn. If he was actually trusting me with the knowledge, I might feel honor bound to keep his secret.

"I'll be your friend, if you let me," he continued.

"Hell will freeze over first." Maybe that was mean-spirited of me after he'd just made such a nice peace offering, but I tend to be honest to a fault. And I wasn't going to pretend we'd be best buds.

The pronouncement made him look very sad, which made me feel like a heel, but I wasn't about to take it back. He sighed and stood up.

"Be that as it may, I'm here if you need me, Morgan." He flashed me a sad smile. "I think your Taser landed under the couch."

"Thanks," I said, and walked him to the door. He took a step out, and I found myself reaching out and grabbing his arm. I let go hastily, surprised at myself.

He turned back to look at me, waiting patiently for whatever I was going to say. I cleared my throat, wishing I'd just let him go.

I'm a lot of things, but I'm not a coward, at least not most of the time. So I held my head high and met his sad brown eyes.

"I just want you to know, it's nothing personal," I said. "You seem like a decent guy, for a demon. But my brother's dead because of you, and that's just not something I can forgive."

"He's not dead," Raphael said, his voice gentle.

"He might as well be." As far as I was concerned,

Andy was *worse* than dead. He was a prisoner, his mind alive in a body he couldn't control. He could never speak to anyone, never touch anyone, never have any human interaction whatsoever. And I would never understand how anyone could willingly submit to such an invasion, no matter how many heroic deeds it allowed him to do. Maybe that makes me shallow and selfish—that's certainly what my family thinks—but I can't change who I am.

Raphael looked like he might say something else, but thought better of it. With a little shake of his head, he turned away and walked to his car.

Chapter 4

I woke up to find myself seated at my desk in my study. I blinked a couple of times, groggy, disoriented.

The room was dark, save for the moonlight that streamed through the open curtains of one window. The digital clock perched on top of the bookcase across from me said it was one-thirty.

I groaned. Not again! This sleepwalking shit was really getting on my nerves. As I started to push back from the desk, I noticed the pen clutched in my hand. Then I saw a sheet of paper lying on the desk. I could tell there was some writing on it, but it was too dark to read.

I didn't feel sleepy anymore. My pulse shot up and my mouth went dry. Maybe I should just tear off that sheet of paper and throw it away without reading it.

Yeah, that's what I should do. I didn't want to face any more of my subconscious fears. But instead of listening to my own advice, I reached for the desk lamp and turned it on, shutting my eyes against the glare.

I took a long, deep breath before I opened my eyes and read what I'd written in my sleep.

Morgan, this isn't your subconscious. You really are possessed, but you're so powerful in your own right that I can't get a foothold except when you lower your guard—like when you sleep. I don't want to hurt you. I'm as unwilling to possess you as you are to host me, but

That was it. All it wrote. No, all *I* wrote, because there was no way I was possessed. None!

I was so freaked I was shaking. I crossed my arms over my chest and hugged myself.

"Calm down, Morgan," I told myself. "You know you're not possessed. Val would have seen it in your aura in Topeka."

I didn't feel reassured.

Once again, I tore my note off the notepad and wadded it into a ball. This time, though, throwing it in the trash wouldn't be enough. I didn't want those words on that paper to exist.

I grabbed the wad of paper and carried it to the living room. Then I stuck it in the fireplace and burned it. And though I went back to bed and cuddled comfortably under the covers, I didn't sleep a wink the rest of the night.

Brian came over at seven the next evening for dinner and sex, not necessarily in that order. I'd been miserable all day from the combo of sleep deprivation and worry. He judged correctly that it was a dinner-first sort of day. And he cooked. Like Val said, he's a keeper.

That thought made my mood sink even lower. Brian might be a keeper, but I couldn't see him keeping *me* indefinitely. Yeah, he talked about moving in together, but let's get real. He's your all-around, mom-and-apple-pie nice guy. What was he doing with me, anyway? He should be with some sweet, girl-next-door type. Not some surly exorcist chick with an attitude problem.

Yeah, that's the kind of mood I was in. And I'll freely admit I was feeling sorry for myself. Another of my not-so-appealing features. Sometimes I'm secretly jealous of Brian and his normal life. No fanatics in his family. Everyone gets along like family is supposed to. Doesn't mean they don't fight sometimes, but it's *healthy* fighting, if you know what I mean. He has a nice, steady, safe job—he's a lawyer, but the boring kind, not the sleazy kind—and he believes that people are good at heart as a general rule. What he sees in me is a total mystery.

I think even your usual unobservant guy would have noticed my mood, so I wasn't surprised when as soon as the table was cleared, Brian pulled me into his arms for a hug and asked, "What's wrong?"

I sighed and snuggled into the warmth of his body. "Nothing. I just didn't sleep well last night."

He pushed me away gently then raised my chin with his finger so I'd have to look at him. His whisky-brown eyes were full of concern. "Sleepwalking again?"

I swallowed hard, fighting down a hint of panic as I thought about waking up with that damning piece of paper in front of me. I nodded, not sure I could trust my voice.

Brian smoothed his hands over my hair. "You should see a doctor."

I wasn't sure if he meant a physician or a shrink, but I didn't care either way. "No doctors," I said, and my voice came out sharper than I meant it to.

I hate doctors. Almost as much as I hate dentists. I never like to be around people who make me feel powerless.

"Morgan," Brian started, and I could hear him slipping into his persuasive lawyer voice.

"No, Brian. Don't push this."

He held up his hands in surrender, and I thought I was home free. He slipped an arm around my shoulders and guided me toward my bedroom. I went with him, but my mind really wasn't on sex right that moment. Which says something about my state of mind, because I'm always thinking about sex when Brian's around.

We kissed as soon as we stepped over the threshold. I melted against his body and opened my mouth for him, stroking his tongue with my own, but my heart wasn't in it. I thought I was faking it pretty well, but when we lay down on the bed together, Brian pulled away a little bit.

He was leaning over me, one leg thrown over mine as his face hovered inches away. His hand cupped my cheek, his thumb stroking idly.

"It's more than just being sleepy," he murmured. "Come on, Morgan. Tell me what's wrong."

I mentally cursed him for being such a sensitive modern male. A drunken Neanderthal would have suited me better at the moment. We could have some spirited sex, I'd fake an orgasm, then he'd go away happy and leave me to my gloomy thoughts.

I speared my hand through his hair and tried to pull his head down to mine for a kiss, but he wasn't about to let me distract him. He pulled back a little farther.

"Talk to me," he urged.

"There's nothing wrong, Brian. I'm just tired is all, so I'm not quite myself."

His eyes narrowed. It wasn't quite a glare, but it

wasn't a happy look, either. "That's bullshit, and we both know it. Why won't you tell me what's wrong?"

I wriggled out from under his leg and sat up. It was my turn to glare, and I'm better at it than he is. "Because there's nothing to tell!" I snapped. Okay, so I was lying, but I had no desire to share my worries with him. He just wouldn't understand.

He sat up, too, and now there was almost a yard separating us on the bed—a nice metaphor for the emotional chasm that was forming.

"I'm not an idiot," he said. He was trying to keep his voice mild, but anger crept in anyway. Brian isn't very comfortable with anger, which is why he's no good at picking fights.

Anger and me are bestest buds, so I'm damn good at it. "You will be if you don't drop this."

"Damn it, Morgan!" Oh yeah, I was making him feel much more at home with his anger right now. "I love you." He made it sound like a curse. "You can talk to me. Share things with me. It's what people in love do."

"I'm not the touchy-feely, crying-on-shoulders type of girl. I've never pretended to be."

"It's not 'touchy-feely' to answer me when I ask you what's wrong! For God's sake, it's a simple question. All I'm asking is for you to share just a tiny bit of yourself with me. Is that too much to ask?"

I ran a hand through my hair and tried to tamp down my anger. He was right. But so was I. If I told him about the notes, about what was bothering me, it would lead to a long, heartfelt discussion. And it wouldn't matter what I said, he wouldn't understand.

He tries his best, he really does. But he's never been the kind of control freak I am. He's never understood why I'm so fanatically anti-demon. And he'd never understand how the thought that I might be possessed—

even when I knew it was just a product of my overactive imagination—could turn me into such a quivering bundle of nerves.

"I'm sorry, Brian," I said. "I know you think I'm being a coldhearted bitch, but I can't help being who I am. And I'm not the kind of woman to open a vein and bleed all over her boyfriend. If it were something I thought you could help me with, I'd talk about it." I wasn't sure that was entirely true, but it might have been. I'd have to wait until I had a problem I thought he could help with to see.

He shook his head and slid off the bed. His anger had faded, and now he just looked hurt. "I'm not asking you to open a vein," he said softly, not looking at me. "I'd be happy with even the tiniest crumb, but you just won't give it to me."

I held my breath, sure this was it, the moment I'd been dreading—the moment he decided I was more trouble than I was worth.

As usual, I'd underestimated him.

"I'm going to go home now, before we have a chance to do permanent damage to each other," he said. "But I'm not giving up on you, Morgan. I love you, and eventually I'm going to figure out some way to make you trust me enough to talk to me. I'll call you tomorrow."

I stayed sitting on the bed as he walked out of the room. He didn't even slam the door when he left. I took a couple of deep breaths and wiped my sweaty palms on my pants legs.

Much as the thought of losing him made my heart ache, I knew the best thing I could do for both of us was to break up with him now, before I had a chance to hurt him any more. Because if he was just staying with me because he believed he'd change me, then our relationship was doomed. If I were a good, nice person, I'd save him a lot of heartache and set him free.

I guess I'm not a good, nice person. That sucks.

The weekend passed uneventfully, which was a nice change. Brian called on Saturday, just like he said he would, but it wasn't a very productive phone call. I suppose the fact that he didn't break up with me over the phone could be considered a good thing.

I awoke Monday morning feeling much better, having slept well for three nights in a row. Maybe the sleepwalking had run its course.

I decided after all the unpleasantness that I had to make the first move to patch things up with Brian, so first thing Monday morning, I went online and ordered a big, honkin' vase of white roses. I had them sent to his office. I wasn't up to a mushy card, so all I said was *I'm sorry I was such a bitch.*

I spent a lot of time smiling as I rode the good ol' Paoli Local into Philadelphia. I could just imagine what the rest of the stuffy lawyers in Brian's firm thought about him receiving flowers from his girlfriend. He wouldn't hear the end of it for weeks. But I knew the ribbing wouldn't bother him, that he'd probably secretly enjoy it.

I got off the train at Suburban Station and walked to my office near Liberty Place. It was a beautiful March day, sunny and warm and full of promise. I was feeling damn good about myself for once.

My office building houses two mid-sized accounting firms, a private investigator, and me. We make for an interesting assortment. I don't keep what you would call regular office hours because I travel so much. But whenever I'm in town, I try to spend a little time there,

catching up with the paperwork. You wouldn't believe
the paperwork that goes with being an exorcist. I have
to document every exorcism and file a report with the
US Exorcism Board, our governing body.

I hadn't even finished booting up my computer
when someone knocked on my office door.

"Come in," I called, not fully paying attention yet. I
was trying to will my computer to hurry up and get
booted. It was past time I upgrade to a new one, but it
was such a hassle I kept procrastinating.

My computer was still chugging away when I finally
gave up and turned to the doorway. I froze in surprise
when I saw Adam White standing there.

Adam is the head of Special Forces, the branch of
the police department that deals with rogue demons.
Coincidentally, he's also a demon himself. There are
lots of people—including me—who think this is a case
of the fox guarding the henhouse. But in some ways,
it's very practical. Adam can take on another demon in
hand-to-hand combat and win. That's not something
you can say about us mere mortals.

When he saw he had my attention, he smiled and took
a seat in front of my desk, stretching his long legs out in
front of him. He's quite a treat to the eyes, and he knows
it. About six-two and a little over two hundred pounds,
all of it sculpted muscle. Short, dark hair that's almost
black, and bedroom eyes that remind me of hot caramel.

Of course, I don't know why he's so proud of his
appearance. It's not *him* that looks so good, it's his
host.

The Spirit Society favors the good-looking to host
the Higher Powers, as they call demons. Higher Powers
my ass! Demons call *themselves* demons. They say they
predate the Bible by a long way, and that their name for
themselves has been corrupted by humans. But the

Society has decided "demon" is some kind of ethnic slur. I can't tell you how many times my mom washed my mouth out with soap for calling them "demons."

Naturally, since Adam is a demon, I dislike him on principle. He knows that, so I was surprised to see him in my office.

"What can I do for you, Adam?" I asked, sounding wary even to my own ears.

One corner of his mouth lifted into a hint of a grin at my tone, but it dropped quickly. I realized belatedly that he wasn't a happy camper at the moment. There was a hint of a frown line between his brows, and I might almost have called the look in his eyes "haunted."

He took a deep breath, as though bracing himself, then held his head up and met my eyes. "I need you to perform an exorcism."

My jaw dropped, and I was at a loss for words. A rarity for me, let me tell you.

He didn't seem to need me to say anything just yet. "Did you hear about the attack by God's Wrath this weekend?"

God's Wrath is one of the many anti-demon hate groups. Some of them try to battle the Minions of Satan—as they call demons—in the courts, trying to have the Spirit Society outlawed once more. God's Wrath is more on the militant side. One of their specialties is arson, burning demons and their hosts alive in the Cleansing Fire of God. Yes, when they talk, everything sounds like it has capital letters.

I'd been too self-involved this weekend to read the paper or watch the news, so I didn't know what God's little helpers had been up to.

"Do you remember about three weeks ago that fire they set in South Philly?"

I remembered. The fire had killed an upstanding legal demon and his pregnant lover. They'd had another child, a little girl, who was trapped in the house. One of the demon firefighters rescued her, grabbing the child and then jumping from the top of the three-story building to the sidewalk below, taking all the impact with his legs to protect the child he held. That had to hurt. The child had lived, and the demon's legs had no doubt healed within a few hours.

"I remember," I said, because Adam was waiting for my answer.

Adam's face was grim and tight. "The firefighter was Dominic Castello. This weekend, God's Wrath decided to punish him for rescuing the Spawn of Satan."

I groaned. I hate demons with the best of them, but even *I* don't think it's a bad thing to rescue a three-year-old girl from a burning building just because her daddy happens to be hosting a demon.

"They wanted to teach him a lesson, not kill him," Adam continued. "So nine of them ambushed him in front of his house, armed with baseball bats and crowbars."

I winced in sympathy even as I began to realize where this story was going.

Adam looked miserable. "He was only trying to defend himself." He met my eyes, a look of earnest entreaty in his own. "We feel pain, you know. We can tolerate it better than humans, but we have our limits."

"What happened?" I asked softly. But I already knew.

Adam hung his head. "They beat him until he lost control. He went berserk and fought back. Only until he was able to break free and run, but the damage was already done. He killed one, and another is in the hospital on life support."

I'm not used to sympathizing with the demons, but I was making an exception this time.

Demons don't have the same rights as humans. According to the law, it doesn't matter what the extenuating circumstances are. If a demon goes rogue—in other words, is involved in a violent crime—it's going to be exorcized. Period. And there would be no long, drawn-out trial. Hell, they didn't even have the right to a lawyer, though some judges let them have one anyway. Certainly there was no jury of their peers.

"So he's the one you want me to exorcize."

Adam nodded. If I hadn't known better, I would have sworn there was a hint of tears in his eyes.

I'm usually hired by family members, and only when the court-appointed exorcist has already failed. I couldn't think of another time when a *demon* had hired me, but it sure looked like that was what was happening here.

"Why are you coming to *me*?" I asked, then winced at my less-than-tactful tone.

Adam didn't take offense. "He and I have what you might call a history together. We've been friends ever since we came to the Mortal Plain, and our hosts were friends even before that. This is going to be difficult for all of us. We need the exorcism to work smoothly and quickly. And you're the best there is."

That made me squirm. "So your host is . . . aware of what's going on?"

Adam's eyes skewered me. "You know he is."

I looked away. Yeah, I knew. And this was one exorcism I wasn't too eager to perform.

"Will you do it?" Adam asked.

I sighed. How could I refuse? Dominic Castello was getting one hell of a raw deal. Better to get it over with quickly than to make him suffer. "Yeah, I'll do it."

He couldn't quite bring himself to thank me, but he managed a little nod of acknowledgment.

Chapter 5

The exorcism of Dominic Castello will haunt me for the rest of my life.

Not for any reasons I might have expected. Unlike Lisa Walker, he didn't fight it. They had him bolted to the table and fitted with a stun belt, just in case, but from the moment I walked into that execution chamber, all I saw was resignation.

Adam came with me, to bear witness and provide moral support. Moral support for Dominic, not me, in case you were wondering.

Dominic was a typical demon host—meaning he was gorgeous. Coarse, wavy hair of Italian black, with large, expressive hazel eyes framed by thick lashes. Not as muscular as some hosts—like, say, Adam—but I'd bet he'd have a wiry strength to him even without his demon's help.

There wasn't a mark on Dominic's body, at least not on what I could see of it. He'd had to do a lot of healing over the last couple of days. He'd turned himself in to Adam after the attack. Adam had taken pictures, which he'd shown me. I could have lived without seeing those pictures.

The containment center guards didn't much like Adam coming in there with me, but there wasn't much they could say about it. He outranked all of them. *I* didn't like that Adam pulled up a chair and held Dominic's hand while I laid out my candles. It made Dominic look too much like a victim, and me too much like the villain.

I tried not to think too much as I took up my place on the opposite side of the table from Adam. Dominic didn't even glance at me, his gaze locked with Adam's. "Take care of Dominic," Dominic said, and I blinked in momentary confusion until I realized it was the demon speaking, asking Adam to look after his host. The intensity with which they looked at each other made me think they were more than just friends, and the anguish in the demon's voice suggested he genuinely cared about his host. But I told myself to mind my own business.

The exorcism went smoothly. Dominic didn't scream or curse, and I dispersed the demon aura on my first try.

When I opened my eyes, Dominic, sans his demon, lay on the table crying, still clutching Adam's hand. The tears suggested that his brain might be functioning, but I questioned him anyway as the guards came to unlock the restraints.

"Do you know who you are?" I asked, leaning over him, trying to keep my voice soft and gentle. I'm not real good at soft and gentle. I know, you're shocked to hear that.

He looked at me with watery, miserable eyes and

nodded. "He didn't do anything wrong. All he wanted was to defend himself, and you killed him for it."

Oh yeah, he knew what was going on all right. And I had never felt so guilty for exorcizing a demon before.

"I'm sorry," I said, my throat tight and achy.

Dominic seemed about to say something else as he sat up, his upper body now free from the restraints. But Adam rose from his chair and sat on the edge of the table beside his friend. Or was Dominic just Adam's *host's* friend now? Too confusing. I decided not to think about it.

"She did what she had to do," Adam said. He did soft and gentle a lot better than me, which was kind of surprising considering he usually had a pretty hard edge to him. "We have to operate within the bounds of the law. Even when the law is wrong."

That last was directed at me, but I managed to swallow my natural retort. This wasn't the time or place to discuss the role of demons in American society.

Dominic gave a moaning sob. Adam wrapped his arms around him and rocked him like he might a heartbroken child.

I got the hell out of there and wished Adam had found someone else to do the exorcism.

My mood lifted when I met Brian for dinner. Of course, it's hard for your spirits not to rise when your boyfriend answers his door wearing nothing but a cute little bow tie and holding a long-stemmed white rose between his teeth.

I grinned at him as I slipped into his condo, closing the door behind me. "I see you got the flowers."

"Yes," he said around the stem in his mouth. "They're lovely."

I laughed and plucked the rose from between his lips. I held the bud to my nose and inhaled deeply. The scent was disappointingly faint, but sweet nonetheless. Out of the corner of my eye, I noticed that Brian was happy to see me and getting happier by the moment. I tossed the rose aside and gave him a visual once-over, finding that I was rather happy to see him myself.

He stood up straight, thrusting his shoulders back like a soldier at inspection. Once again I laughed, but even I could hear the lust in that sound. Moments before, I'd been standing outside his door wondering if I should try to beg off tonight. Now I could barely remember why.

I began to circle him, and he turned his head to follow my movement.

"Face front, soldier!" I barked. Well, I tried to bark, but my voice came out husky.

"Yes, ma'am!" He did better at the bark than I did, his head snapping back around to face front so fast it made me wince. With my luck these days, he'd get whiplash during some harmless sex play.

The rear view was spectacular. Brian has the tightest little buns I've ever seen. Made me want to get down on my knees and take a bite. I settled for smoothing my hands over his cheeks, feeling the quiver of his muscles as he struggled to stand at attention. My pulse drummed between my legs, and I caught myself thinking how lovely it would be to have Brian to come home to after *all* of my tough days.

I shoved the thought aside, not wanting to ruin the mood with thoughts of the future. There was no better way to get my mind off the distasteful exorcism than to drown my body in physical sensation, and, damn it, that was exactly what I was going to do. Absolutely no thinking allowed.

I pressed myself close against Brian's back, hands still cupping his butt, then trailed my tongue over his shoulder blade. He managed to hold still, but his breath hissed in and out of his lungs, and his skin tasted faintly of salt. Man, I loved making him sweat!

I took a long and leisurely tour of his back, pretending not to notice when he squirmed at my ministrations. His hands were fisted at his sides, and I could feel the excited thump of his heart under my lips.

"Morgan, please."

I smiled as my hand dipped between his legs from behind, my fingers just barely brushing his drawn-up balls. The only thing I loved more than making him sweat was making him beg.

"Please what?" I asked, then stood on tiptoe and lightly nipped his earlobe.

His Adam's apple bobbed as he swallowed hard. "It's been almost a week. My self-control has its limits."

Not that I'd been able to tell. My will always broke before his, but I couldn't pretend I didn't like it that way. My whole body felt warm, my senses hyper-acute. My nostrils flared as I picked up the mingled scents of sweating male, Old Spice deodorant, and arousal. The longer I made this last, the longer I could escape my less-than-enjoyable thoughts.

I slid around to the front. Brian was most definitely at full mast, the head of his erection shiny with pre-cum. I licked my lips, and he groaned. There was no missing how desperately he wanted me, and yet still he managed to keep the reins on his lust. Someday I was going to find a way to shatter that almost legendary self-control of his. Unfortunately, until *I* mastered the art of self-control, he was destined to win.

My limited patience at its end, I dropped to my

knees, steadying my victim with a hand on each of his hips. I could feel the intensity of his eyes on me. I loved knowing that he was watching. When my tongue flicked out for a quick taste, we both gasped. There was something so primally satisfying about taking him into my mouth. My every sense was alive and involved—tasting him, smelling his arousal, hearing the harshness of his gasps for breath. His hips rolled against my mouth, and I knew he wouldn't last very long if I kept this up. I also knew that if I let him come in my mouth, I'd have to give him some recovery time before I could have him inside me. If I gave him time to recover, my treacherous mind might click into gear and spoil things.

Reluctantly, I released him despite his groan of protest.

"Even *you* aren't that cruel," he complained, looking at me with lust-darkened eyes.

I climbed to my feet, my knees embarrassingly shaky. He opened his mouth for another protest, but then I started unbuttoning my blouse, and his protest died.

With a wicked grin and a crook of my finger, I began backing toward his bedroom. He followed like a stalking panther as I shrugged out of my blouse. I was nowhere near coordinated enough to take off my pants while I walked backward, so I settled for opening the snap and pulling down the zipper. By then I had crossed the threshold into the bedroom.

My timing was spot-on, my bra hitting the floor just as the back of my knees hit the bed. Brian flashed me a predator's smile, then bent to help me out of the rest of my clothes. He had to interrupt the flow a bit to grab a condom from the bedside table, but we were both way too far gone for that to spoil the mood.

When he slipped into me, it was pure heaven. I was

wet enough to let him bury himself in one thrust, and the feeling was like coming home. I pulled his head down to mine, and he kissed me with all the pent-up passion of a man who's been separated from his true love for months.

I drowned in the reality of him, in the natural fit of our bodies, in the dizzying rush of his desire, in the terrifying intensity of his love. I lost all power of higher thought, my body one big nerve ending, my heart near to bursting with more emotions than I could name.

We came at almost the exact same moment, both of us loud enough to no doubt embarrass the neighbors. Like we cared.

Brian cuddled me in the aftermath, my head cradled against his chest, our legs intertwined, both of us panting desperately for air. When the first rush of afterglow started to fade, I felt a flutter of panic in my chest. I loved Brian too damn much for my own good, especially when practicality told me it would never last. Yes, I knew he loved me, too. But I've never been a believer in the myth that love conquers all. Someday, he would run out of patience with me, and my heart would shatter into tiny, sharp pieces.

He wanted me to stay the night, but I didn't trust my mood. I didn't want to ruin the memory of our spectacular lovemaking. And I didn't want to risk the chance that my continuing fears might make me say something stupid to push him away. The really scary thing is, from the way he looked at me, I had a feeling he knew exactly why I was running away.

I got home a little after nine and watched part of the Temple basketball game. They were beating the crap out of some team I'd never heard of, so I turned it off and went to bed early.

I woke up in bed the next morning with that familiar

tired feeling in my system. The feeling like I hadn't really been sleeping all night. I tried to tell myself I was just tired, that normal people get tired even if they're not sleepwalking.

That comforting fantasy lasted about thirty seconds. Then I saw the sheet of paper laid out neatly on my bedside table. This note was almost long enough to be called a letter.

Reluctantly, I picked it up and read.

I am not a figment of your imagination. My name is Lugh. You invited me in two months ago. You were drugged. That's why you don't remember. It was the night Andrew hit you. I believe he hit you so that your memory of that night would be a little fuzzy.

They're using you to keep me captive. I would not have taken you voluntarily. They called me by name, and I had to come. Your mental shields are so strong I can hardly break through. You fight me even in your

That was all he wrote. All I wrote. Whatever.

I guess if I really *was* possessed by a demon, I'd managed to fight him off in the middle of his letter.

I shivered. All well and good to tell myself it was impossible to be possessed and not know it, but this seemed a pretty elaborate fantasy for my subconscious to dream up.

I mean, where did I get the name Lugh from? It's not a name I'd ever heard of before. It sounded masculine, and I was thinking of this demon as a "he." Which was just a little extra evidence that this was all my imagination. If I really *was* possessed, the demon should have been female. Not that it was impossible for a demon to possess a human of the opposite sex—it was just that they usually didn't want to. Of course, my imaginary demon claimed he was forced to possess me against his will, so perhaps his preferences meant nothing.

But no, I was being paranoid. This was a reaction to my last conversation with Andrew/Raphael. I was still pissed at him for hitting me, so I'd concocted a plot right out of some B-movie Hollywood horror script. Yeah, that was it.

Unfortunately, I wasn't doing such a great job of convincing myself.

I didn't destroy this letter, instead taking it with me into the kitchen and rereading it umpteen million times while I drank my coffee. I'd honestly never heard of a human being whose personality was strong enough to make the demon, rather than the host, the helpless passenger. But just because I'd never heard of it didn't mean it was impossible.

Wondering about the name I'd made up for my imaginary demon, I looked it up on the Internet. I hoped I'd find it was some kind of nonsense word. Unfortunately, I discovered it was a real name from Celtic mythology that roughly translates to "shining one."

By the time I'd finished my third cup of coffee, I decided I needed a second opinion. Val had looked at my aura in Topeka and declared me clean, but it wouldn't hurt to have her look again. And if she saw no sign of demon invasion, then maybe I could put this nagging fear to rest.

If not, I might have to bite the bullet and see a shrink, like Brian had suggested. *Not* an option I wanted to contemplate.

Val lives in a narrow, three-story town house on Delancy Street. The place always makes me feel outclassed. My house is nicely decorated and all, but Val's is a freakin' work of art. Everything's color-coordinated, and I'd never seen a place where a person actually lived that was so meticulously neat and clean.

She led me into her living room, sat me down on her spotless cream-colored couch—you tell me, how do you keep a cream-colored couch spotless if you actually sit on it?—and I spilled my guts.

"I know this is crazy," I told her before I started.

I could see her momentarily struggle not to smile, then give up the effort. "When is it *not* crazy when you're involved?"

I laughed at her quip, but even I could hear the nervousness. Val's brows drew together, the humor instantly chased away, replaced by a look of concern.

"What's the matter, Morgan?" she asked. "You look seriously spooked."

I ran a hand through my hair. "That's because I am." I huffed out a deep breath. "You know how I told you I've been sleepwalking lately?" She nodded. "Well, I've been writing notes to myself in my sleep."

Her eyebrows arched. "Wow. You mean, like, notes that actually make sense?"

"Depends on what you mean by sense," I muttered under my breath. "The first one was in Topeka. I wrote a note saying that the demon didn't take me because I was already possessed."

Val laughed at that. "*That's* what's got you spooked?" she asked. "I think you can relax. Aside from the fact that you don't act like a demon, I checked your aura in Topeka and you were completely human."

I rubbed my sweaty palms up and down my pants legs. "I know. I've been telling myself over and over that it doesn't make any sense, that it's just my imagination. But I can't help being freaked out." I pulled my latest missive from my pocket and handed it to Val. "I mean, Jesus, look at this! I don't have this good an imagination, so where is it all coming from?"

Val smiled indulgently as she took the note from my hand and donned her glasses for a closer look. I bit my lip as I watched her read, hoping she'd laugh at me some more and dismiss my foolish worries.

She didn't. In fact, I could have sworn she went a little pale, and her hand jerked as if she was startled.

"What is it?" I asked. "Does this mean something to you?"

She folded the note carefully, then shivered as if in a sudden chill. "I can see why it worried you," she admitted. "It would freak me out, too." Her face still looked pale, and whether she knew it or not, she was chewing her lower lip.

"But does it mean anything to you?" I asked again, wondering why she wouldn't meet my eyes.

She shook her head, staring at the folded note. "No. It's just creepy." She sighed, finally raising her eyes to mine once more. "Still, it's got to be your imagination. If you were possessed, I'd have seen it in Topeka."

I had the distinct impression there was more to it than she was telling, but if there was, I wasn't sure I wanted to know about it. "Will you take another look at my aura anyway?"

She frowned, then shrugged. "Hell, I guess it's no skin off my teeth. And if it'll make you feel better..."

"Thanks," I said, more relieved than I wanted to admit.

She flashed me an encouraging smile. "I'm sure there's nothing to worry about, Morgan."

I forced an answering smile. "Who me? Worry?"

Val laughed and gave me a quick hug. She knows

I'm not the hugging type, so she let go before I had a chance to complain.

"I'll go get my kit," she said. "I'll be right back."

For whatever reason, I felt unbearably antsy the moment she left the room. I stood up and paced, trying to work off my nervous energy.

What did I have to be nervous about? I *knew* Val wasn't going to find anything. But the nerves got worse and worse as the seconds ticked away.

Butterflies flapped in my stomach. My head started pounding, and I wanted nothing more than to run frantically out her front door.

What was the matter with me? I touched my fingers to the pulse in my neck to find it racing wildly. Sweat dewed my skin. Was I having some kind of panic attack? I'd never felt anything like this.

As I tried to psychoanalyze myself, I noticed something odd. Val's house is old and creaky. You can hear every step anyone takes. I'd heard her mount the steps to the second floor, and I'd heard her moving around upstairs. Now I heard nothing at all.

I stopped pacing as the inexplicable panic reached a crescendo.

Not knowing why I was doing it, I turned and faced the stairwell. And suddenly, there she was.

I hadn't heard a single creak out of the stairs. That's because she'd been sneaking. If it hadn't been for the creeping panic that made me look, I never would have gotten out of the way in time.

There was a loud pop, and I threw myself to the floor.

Taser probes rocketed through the space I'd just vacated, embedding themselves harmlessly into the back of a chair. Val cursed softly and ejected the spent cartridge.

I didn't have time for shock, or outrage, or even pain. She reloaded, and I snatched a cushion off the sofa. I ducked behind it just as the Taser popped again. I felt the impact of the probes hitting the cushion, but— thank you, Jesus—it was thick enough to insulate me.

I peeked over the top of the cushion to see Val closing in on me, Taser still at the ready. She was going to try to take me down in hand-to-hand combat.

It was a tactical error on her part. One, I'm six inches taller than her and I work out. Two, if your family is Spirit Society, you either learn to fight at a young age, or you spend your entire childhood getting the shit beat out of you. I'd opted for fighting.

Val jabbed the Taser in my direction, trying to sneak it in around the edge of my shield—er, sofa cushion. I blocked her easily but didn't notice her foot until it was too late.

Her heel made contact with my shin, and if she'd been wearing hard-soled shoes, I'd have been in trouble. As it was, she was wearing sneakers, and she didn't do any serious damage.

"Ow!" I yelled. "What the fuck do you think you're doing, Val?"

She didn't answer. Her eyes were fierce and focused on her goal. I'd never seen her look like that before. She grabbed the sofa cushion and tried to rip it out of my hands. Since I had two hands on it, and she had only one, I had a heavy advantage in our game of tug-of-war. I gave a particularly hard tug to wrest the cushion from her grip, and she let go.

I cursed as my own momentum felled me.

The impact with the floor knocked the cushion from my hands, and the breath whooshed out of my lungs. Val hurled herself on top of me, throwing an awkward punch with her left hand. The punch was just a diversion, though, as she tried to ram the Taser into my ribs.

I ignored her left hook and latched onto her right wrist with both my hands. I didn't let go when her fist contacted my face.

The blow might have been awkward, but it sure hurt.

I was seriously pissed now, and I let instinct take over. I rolled hard to my left. Val was too small and light to pin me, so I ended up on top, with her Taser trapped between our bodies so she couldn't zap me without zapping herself as well.

My punch was not awkward, and Val's body went limp. I almost hit her again, but stopped myself.

Panting, hurting, wondering what the hell was going on, I rolled off her inert body. I pried the Taser from her unresisting fingers and checked the battery indicator. Still plenty of juice left. I patted her down as she slowly came to, but didn't find any more weapons.

I stood up and moved away from her. My cheek ached where she'd hit it, and there was another ache, too. A deeper one. My eyes burned, and for a moment I thought I was going to cry. Val had been my best friend since high school. The only person I trusted enough to talk to about my mysterious problem. And she'd *attacked* me!

Val moaned softly, then opened her eyes to see me pointing her own Taser at her.

"Sister, you've got a lot of explaining to do," I growled. Anger and indignation helped quell the hurt.

Val looked up at me with wide, astonished-looking eyes. "I'm sorry," she said.

Not what I'd been expecting. About thirty seconds ago, she'd been at my throat like a rabid dog. Now she was apologizing?

She sat up slowly, eyeing the Taser. "I thought you really were possessed."

"What?" I cried. This had to be some weird-ass dream, right? I mean, come on! "The whole point of this exercise was for you to check my aura."

She didn't try to get up. I guess I looked like I had an itchy trigger finger, and she couldn't be sure I hadn't reloaded the Taser while she was out.

"And if you really were hosting an illegal demon, then that would have been the perfect moment to attack me."

"You have *got* to be kidding me. If I was possessed by a homicidal demon, what makes you think I'd need to wait for the perfect moment?" I shook my head in disbelief.

"I'm sorry," Val said again. "You were acting strange. Like you were hosting a demon who didn't quite know how to pass for you yet." She reached up and touched the bruise that was swelling along her jawline as I watched. "But if you really were hosting a demon and out to get me, you'd have hit me a lot harder." She gave me pathetic doe eyes. "I'm really, really sorry."

The doe eyes weren't doing much for me. Too much adrenaline still pumping through my system, I guess. Also, though I supposed what she was saying made a sort of sense, I wasn't sure I believed her.

Had I really been acting that strange? Strange enough to make her think it wasn't really *me* talking to her but a demon pretending to be me? Before I'd shown her the note, she'd even remarked on the fact that I didn't act like a demon.

Problem was, I couldn't think of any other reason she'd have come at me like that. This was *Val,* my best friend, my confidante. Why would she want to hurt me?

"I know you've got to be pretty mad at me right now," Val said, "but I was just doing what I thought was right. I had to subdue you so I could exorcize the demon." She laughed nervously. "Would have worked better if you actually were hosting one, you know?"

My hand was beginning to ache from clutching the Taser too tightly. I lowered it, but didn't lower my guard. I felt ridiculous suspecting Val, but it wasn't like I could just forget what she'd tried to do. And it wasn't like I could dismiss the creeping sensation that her story made no sense. The best thing I could do was get the fuck out of there and do some serious thinking.

Val let out a sigh of relief and started to stand when I lowered the Taser.

"Don't get up," I warned her, pointing the Taser once more. I wanted to put some distance between us. She sat back on her rump and held her hands up in surrender.

I backed toward the door. I don't know what I thought she could do to me as long as I had her Taser, but at that moment I didn't want her at my back.

"I'll leave your Taser in the doorway," I told her when I reached her front door.

"Okay," she said, still sitting on the floor, looking a lot calmer than I felt. "If you want to talk later, give me a call. I know you must think I'm the worst kind of bitch right now."

I shook my head at her in disbelief. "Val, telling me I dress like a biker slut would be bitchy. Trying to Taser me goes so far beyond bitchy I don't have a word for it yet."

She hung her head in shame. "I know." When she looked up at me again, there were tears in her eyes. "Please tell me I didn't flush twelve years of friendship down the toilet because of my stupid mistake."

But, of course, I couldn't tell her that, and the tears didn't particularly move me. I put the Taser down in the entryway, then stepped out the door.

The place between my shoulder blades twitched the whole time I walked from her house to my office.

Chapter 6

I'd been chewing over Val's actions all day, and I didn't have an answer that made sense. There were two choices: either Val had really thought I was demon-possessed, or she'd been after me for some other reason. I couldn't explain her being so convinced I was possessed that she'd try to Taser me into submission. But I couldn't come up with a reason she'd be out to get me, either. Stalemate.

I tried to go to bed, but just thinking about lying down in my bed and closing my eyes made my stomach clench with dread. I didn't know what my subconscious would make of today's drama, and I didn't want to find out.

I tried watching some shitty movie on HBO, thinking that might distract me at least for a little while, but my mind refused to stop running on the gerbil wheel. I switched the TV off with a grunt of disgust. If I didn't find some way to get my mind off Val, I would be ready for the loony bin by morning.

I paced through my house, looking for the perfect antidote to thinking. My wandering eventually brought me to the second floor—what there is of it. The Realtor had said my house had "one and a half" stories. Personally, I'm not sure how you can have half a story, but I apparently had one.

There's only one room on the second floor, and I have everything I need on the first floor so I rarely go up there. The second floor has turned into a rather civilized-looking attic. Anything I don't know what to do with eventually makes its way up there. Including several boxes of books I'd never bothered to unpack since I'd moved in. I'm one of those pack rats who can't get rid of a book, even if I hated it.

I don't know what moved me to do it, but I found myself on my knees in front of one of those boxes, digging through it until I found a dog-eared paperback I didn't even remember owning. Had I ever read it? I didn't remember, but *someone* had certainly read it. If it was falling apart from being read so often, it must be good, right?

Hoping a book would absorb more of my attention than the TV had, I started to read.

I woke up with a start, sitting in the same armchair I'd sat down to read in, though my book was nowhere in sight, and there was a pad of paper on my lap.

Val is not your friend!!!
Morgan, wake up. Fight me. Hurry. There's someone downstairs!

I'd say the note made a chill crawl up my spine, but that doesn't do the feeling justice. It was more like an ice age. My heart leapt into my throat, and I clutched the arms of my chair. I had about two seconds to try to convince myself once again that it was just my subconscious. Then I heard the distinctive sound of footsteps downstairs.

My alarm most definitely had not gone off, but I knew I wasn't imagining it.

You might think a tough broad like me would go pull an Uzi out of a closet and charge down the stairs to confront the bad guys like Rambo on hormones.

Well, I'm tough, but I'm not stupid.

Walking very quietly, I moved to the window that looked out over my minuscule backyard. Pulse pounding wildly, I eased the window up. From downstairs, I heard what sounded like a whisper. A whisper that was answered, so there were at least two of them down there.

I sat on the window sash and swung my legs out. My yard is bounded by hedge roses, but I've also got a trellis of climbing roses outside my bedroom, which is just below the second-floor storage room. I grabbed the trellis, hoping it would hold my weight, and eased the window back down.

I scratched the hell out of myself on the way down because I hadn't had the foresight to plant thornless roses. I dropped to the ground and peered around the corner of my house.

There was a black SUV with tinted windows parked in my driveway. I'd never seen it before.

I didn't see anyone sitting in the SUV, but there could be an army in there behind the tinted windows. Still, the intruders in my house would eventually check upstairs, and I didn't want to be squatting here in plain sight when they did.

I made a dash across the yard, a tight fist of fear in my stomach as my ears strained for the sound of a shout, but all was silent. I hurdled the hedge roses—sometimes being tall and leggy can be a real advantage—then kept going. My neighbor's son has a tree house, and I thought that was the perfect place to hide and watch. I briefly considered knocking on someone's door to use the phone, but it was some ungodly hour of the night, and by the time I convinced someone to come to the door—if I even could—the bad guys would be long gone. Or they would have heard me knocking and come to get me.

I was probably leaving bloodstains on the poor kid's tree house, but it couldn't be helped. I hauled myself up the rickety wooden slats nailed into the trunk and piled into the tree house. A small window faced my house, and I had a good view of the driveway and my front door. Holding my breath, hoping that staying still wasn't a piss-poor idea, I watched and waited.

I didn't have long to wait. Not three minutes after I'd put my face to that window, my front door opened and three black-clad figures exited. I clapped a hand over my mouth to stifle my urge to gasp. All three of them were wearing ski masks, so all I could see were eyes, noses, and mouths, and even that wasn't very clear in the dark from this distance. From their size and shape, I guessed they were all male, though looks could be deceiving in the dark. What *was* clear was that all three of them were armed to the teeth.

I'm not a gun nut, so I couldn't tell you exactly what weapons they were carrying, but each of them had one big-ass rifle or shotgun strapped across his back and a sidearm holstered at his waist. Whoever they were, whatever they'd wanted, they'd been damn serious about it.

They climbed into the SUV and drove away. The driver didn't pull off his ski mask until he'd backed out of the driveway. I caught a faint glimpse of short hair through the front windshield, but that was it. I couldn't even tell you what color his hair was. I sure as hell couldn't read the license plate.

I don't know how long I sat up in that tree house, shivering from a noxious combo of fear and cold. Eventually, I decided the bad guys weren't going to come back, so I climbed down and cautiously crept back to my house. I kept expecting someone to jump out of the bushes and grab me, but no one did.

They'd locked the front door behind them—what kind of ski-mask-wearing home invader locks up afterward?—but I had a spare key hidden in the bushes. Not under one of those phony rock things that any idiot would know to look under if he was up to no good. My spare was under a *real* rock.

After I let myself in, the first thing I did was grab my Taser and arm it. Feeling mildly less skittish that way, I stepped into the living room and dialed 911.

I spent the next fifteen minutes scoping out the house, trying to see if anything was missing. I wasn't terribly surprised that nothing was. If those guys were burglars, then I was Santa Claus.

Just before the cops arrived, I slipped upstairs and tore the note I'd written to myself off the notepad. I tore the next three sheets off, too, just to be sure. I didn't think the police were going to search my place that thoroughly, but I still didn't want them finding the note. It would be too hard to explain.

By the time the cops left, it was five in the morning. I'd told them everything I could remember.

The "burglars" had rearmed the alarm when they'd left the house, just like they'd locked up. I'm betting they were trying to make it look like no one'd ever been there. When I thought about it, I realized that not only was nothing missing, nothing'd been moved. Great. Stealth burglars.

Stealth burglars who didn't steal anything, who carried two guns apiece, and who got into my house without destroying the alarm. The cops said they probably had my security code and had simply turned the alarm off when they came in.

You can bet I changed my code the moment the cops were finished with me. You can also bet I didn't go to sleep afterward, tired as I was. I spent the wee hours of the morning sitting on my couch, glassy-eyed, scared, and confused as all hell. And there was no one I could turn to for help. Not Val, who according to my demon or my subconscious—take your pick—was not my friend. Not my brother, for the same reason. And not Brian. Because if my already fucked-up life was going to hell in a handbasket, I refused to take him with me.

By the time night rolled around again, I knew I had to back off my "don't involve Brian" stance.

I spent most of the day at my office, writing up my reports on the exorcisms of Lisa Walker and Dominic Castello. Paperwork usually takes me longer than it should anyway, but in my state of sleep deprivation, it was a miracle I got done in eight hours.

Usually, Brian and I don't see each other much on weekdays. He's often working late, and I'm often traveling, and when we both have to get up early the next morning, it takes some of the fun out of it. But when I thought about going home, I thought about watching those three masked men leaving my house, locking up behind them, and my blood ran cold.

What were the chances that was just a one-time deal? Break in, find she's not home, go away, stay away. Yeah, right.

Could I count on escaping a second time? No. I'd

been damned lucky last night. Even with my subconscious early-warning system in place, it could have gone much worse.

Yes, I was still clinging to the hope that the notes were from my subconscious. But my grip on the illusion was weakening, and some panicky part of me insisted I was going to have to let go eventually. Still, my motto is never do today what you can put off until tomorrow.

Yet I couldn't spend the night with Brian without telling him *something* about what happened last night. It was out of character for me to spend the night at his place, especially on a weekday. So I told him the official police interpretation of the story—some professional burglars broke into my house last night and were scared off by the noise I made climbing out the window.

I sure as hell didn't believe it, and I didn't expect Brian to, either. But I must be a better liar than I thought. Either that, or it just didn't occur to him that I might lie to him about something like that. Remember, he's got that Anne Frank, people-are-basically-good philosophy that puts him and me on opposite ends of the cynicism scale. I felt like a heel—a feeling I was getting familiar with—but I made it up to him in bed. He's always been impressed with my oral skills, and I practiced every trick I knew on him.

Afterward, he fell asleep spooning me, but I lay there awake for a long time, afraid to sleep despite my body's desperate urge to shut down.

I woke up in a blinding white room.

White walls, white ceiling, white floor. White everywhere.

I looked down at myself to find I was wearing a pair

of white jeans with a white sweatshirt. I'd have said I was dreaming, except I didn't *feel* like I was dreaming. I pinched myself on the arm, and it hurt.

There was a sound like a quiet exhalation from behind me. Slowly, I turned around.

He was a shocking patch of darkness in the white. About six-five, with straight, jet-black hair pulled back into a ponytail at the nape of his neck. Black leather bomber jacket decorated with silver rivets. Black leather pants that clung to his legs and tapered into knee-high black leather boots. Tanned skin just light enough to be Caucasian, just dark enough to suggest maybe not.

After I got over the shock of black, I felt a new shock when I got a look at his eyes. They were the color of dark amber held up to the sun, and they were fixed on me with such intense focus that I felt pinned by them.

He took a step toward me, and I lost my paralysis enough to take a step back. He came to a stop, still watching me with that startling intensity, and raised his hands as if to say: "See, no weapons, completely harmless."

I didn't know what the hell was going on, but one thing I did know—this guy was *not* completely harmless. Tall, muscular, imposing, with glowing eyes and a severe, angular face that made me think serial killer. No, not harmless at all.

I cleared my throat, wondering why I wasn't more scared under the circumstances. I mean, last thing I knew, I was cuddled up in bed with nice, safe Brian. Now I was in some creepy white room, trapped with one of the scariest dudes I'd ever seen. Yeah, my pulse was a little elevated, but I wasn't terrified like I should be. Maybe I was drugged?

"I suspect we don't have much time," Mr. Terrifying said. His voice went with his look, a deep, growling bass that made my knees quiver.

I looked around the empty, featureless room—where the hell was the door?—and wondered just where he thought I was going to go.

Then the psycho-killer smiled suddenly, an almost impish expression that changed everything. The aura of menace disappeared as if it had never been there. Nothing about him had changed. He was still huge, still dressed in aggressive black leather. His eyes still seemed to glow as if there were some kind of light behind them. But he'd gone from insanely scary to impossibly sexy in about one second flat. All because of a smile.

"Your ability to fight me is astonishing," he said, still in that James Earl Jones rumble.

I shook my head and tried without success to find my voice. It seemed to be jammed in my throat somewhere, and despite the bizarre circumstances, my eyes insisted on taking another inventory of tall, dark, and dangerous. He didn't seem to mind me looking. In fact, if that bulge in the front of his pants was any indication, he liked it rather a lot.

Heat crept up my cheeks, and I decided that no matter how real this felt, it had to be a dream. I wouldn't be caught dead staring at a stranger's crotch the way I was staring at this guy's.

He laughed, and the sound reverberated somewhere deep inside me, drying my mouth and wetting other portions of my anatomy.

"I see I've chosen a guise you find pleasing," he said, and his amber eyes sparkled with good humor.

"Uh..." That was the best conversation I could manage at the moment.

The humor faded from his face. I felt bereft.

"You are dreaming," he told me. "In a way. I'm trying my best to communicate with you. The notes are not . . . adequate. You keep waking up in the middle."

Oh, so that's what this is all about. Yeah, this guy was just the kind of messenger my subconscious would come up with. I tried to play it cool, just waiting for the dream to end. I crossed my arms over my chest and gave him my best tough-chick-with-an-attitude look. He seemed less than impressed.

"I know you're telling yourself I'm some kind of figment of your imagination," he continued. "But honestly, Morgan, has your imagination ever been this vivid?"

I lowered my eyes, not wanting to see the knowing look on his face. He was a stranger to me. He had no right to look knowing.

"Look," I said, my eyes fixed on one of the rivets in his jacket, "I don't know who you are, or what you want—"

"If you'd be so kind as to let me talk, I'll tell you," he interrupted.

Reluctantly, I raised my gaze to his face again. God, he was gorgeous. Lethally so. I made a zipping-my-lips gesture. He raised an eyebrow as if he didn't quite get it, then spoke again.

"I am Lugh. I'm a demon, and I'm currently in possession of your body." He frowned, the expression marring the perfection of his face. "In a manner of speaking, I suppose, since I seem unable to influence you except when you're sleeping."

I remembered the letter I'd written to myself, the one where I'd named my imaginary demon Lugh. "So you say I invited you in under the influence of drugs, right?"

He nodded. "My first memory when I awoke in the Mortal Plain was of lying on your bed. You'd been tied down. A man in a mask untied you. He didn't say anything, and I couldn't make you move or speak. I would guess the man was Andrew, though I can't be sure."

"And I don't remember any of this . . . why?"

"Because you were drugged. You didn't have any more success moving your body than I did."

I wasn't buying any of this—or at least, I was trying not to—but I figured even in a dream, it's best to humor psycho-killers who could squash you without even breaking a sweat.

"Why would anyone want to go through all that trouble to stick you in an unwilling host?" I asked. "There are plenty of volunteers available."

He frowned, and the light behind his eyes grew brighter. "I have enemies among my people. People who do not like my message. I would say someone wants to keep me quiet. Which means someone knew that I wouldn't be able to gain control of your body.

"Letting Valerie know I'm communicating with you was not a good idea."

"Now listen here, mister—"

"If they're trying to keep me quiet, then they don't want me talking to my host."

I threw up my hands in frustration. "Who the hell are 'they'?"

He took a step closer to me. Again, I backed away. He might be the studliest guy I'd ever laid eyes on, but I didn't trust him as far as I could throw him.

"I don't know. Just be careful. Whoever they are, they're not going to leave you alone."

He flickered. Just like one of those old black-and-white movies.

"Damn it!" he said. "You're fighting me again. Please,

try to relax and let me talk to you. We have to figure out what to do."

I shook my head. I didn't know what I was doing to fight him, but whatever it was, I wanted to keep doing it. I'd had enough of this dream, thank you very much.

He flickered again.

Then he was gone, and I was alone in the white room.

Seconds later, I awoke to find myself cuddled safely in Brian's arms.

Chapter 7

I left Brian's before he woke up the next morning. Cowardly of me, I suppose, but I couldn't see myself calmly discussing my situation over coffee. I knew I wasn't a good enough actress to pretend nothing was wrong.

I'd spent the night at Brian's just often enough to warrant having a change of clothes there, though I was stuck using his Old Spice deodorant. I didn't realize how much I'd come to associate that scent with him until I'd left. The scent was faint, and I kept thinking he was right there with me. Maybe I should have stopped by a Rite Aid and bought some of my own stuff.

I made it to the office by seven. I'd finished the reports on my exorcisms yesterday, but there was still plenty of paperwork waiting for me, accounting details and such. I wasn't being what you'd call productive. I kept telling myself that Lugh was nothing but a vivid dream. Okay, I'm the queen of denial. So sue me.

At around eleven, someone banged on my office

door. I'd have said "knocked," except this sound was far more authoritative and I practically jumped out of my chair. Before I had a chance to invite anyone in, the door swung open, and a pair of plainclothes detectives stepped in. I vaguely recognized one of them. When you're an exorcist, you deal with the criminal element on a regular basis, and that means getting to know cops.

They were a bit of an odd couple, the two of them. The one on the left, whom I'd never seen before, looked too skinny to be a cop. He had the build of a man who could eat five-course meals on a regular basis and never gain any weight. I'd have said he couldn't scare a five-year-old on Halloween if it hadn't been for his eyes. They were the iciest blue I'd ever seen, and the expression in them wasn't much warmer. The eyes alone would be enough to keep most sane perps in line.

His partner, the familiar one, looked like the kind of guy who dressed up as Santa Claus for Christmas. He wasn't fat, exactly, but he had a definite beer gut, and his cheeks were rosy. Not a wholesome rosy, actually, more of an I-drink-too-much rosy, but stick a white wig and beard on him and I'm betting he'd have looked jolly enough.

There wasn't much ho-ho-ho in him today, though. Before I had a chance to ask if I could help them with something, he was flashing his badge.

"I'm Detective O'Reilly," he said. His voice surprised me. He looked like he should have a deep, growling voice, but it was on the high and reedy side. "This is my partner, Detective Finn."

Detective Arctic Eyes nodded a greeting. Neither one of them offered to shake hands.

I put on my most accommodating smile—these guys were making me nervous, and I didn't know why. They had to be here for a follow-up on the break-in at my house. I should be glad to see them.

"What can I do for you, Detectives?" I asked. Neither one of them returned my smile.

"We'd like to ask you a few questions," O'Reilly said.

I didn't like the way that sounded. "Sure. Please, have a seat." I motioned to the pair of chairs in front of my desk, but neither of them made a move to sit.

"I think it would be best if we did this at the station."

I blinked up at the two of them. "What's this about?" Surely they didn't need me to come to the station to talk about the break-in.

Finn took over talking. He had the kind of voice I'd expected from O'Reilly. "There was an illegal exorcism last night. Your name came up."

I shook my head. "What? Why?"

"Ms. Kingsley, please come with us," O'Reilly said. "You're not an official suspect yet, but we really do need you to answer some questions, and this isn't the place for it."

I chewed the inside of my cheek. I didn't want to make things difficult for our heroic men in blue. I have a great deal of respect for law enforcement officers—Adam White being one of the few exceptions to that rule. Still, this whole thing was making my skin crawl.

I glanced at my watch. "I can meet you there in half an hour." Just enough time to contact a lawyer—as long as I happened to be dating said lawyer. I didn't think I had time to find someone else. At least, not someone I trusted. I don't trust easy. Surprised?

O'Reilly leaned his hands on the chair in front of him while Finn tried to freeze my marrow with his eyes.

"We'd appreciate it if you came with us now," O'Reilly said.

But the vibe on these guys felt wrong. I didn't want to get into a car with them. I mean, I knew they were really police officers and all, but still, something was bugging me. I'd feel a hell of a lot safer meeting them at the station. Even if that would piss them off.

I was very calm and nonconfrontational when I responded. "I'll be happy to answer any questions you'd like. In a half hour, and with my attorney." I didn't ask if they had a warrant, because if they had, they'd have told me already. So far, cooperation on my part was entirely voluntary.

Finn looked like he wanted to say something nasty, but O'Reilly silenced him with a tiny shake of his head.

"We'll see you at eleven-thirty, then," O'Reilly said, looking at his watch. "I'm sure you won't keep us waiting. Right, Miss Kingsley?"

If he was trying to get a rise out of me, he had to do better than that. My fuse isn't *that* short. I smiled at both of them. "I look forward to it."

Finn snorted softly, but the corner of O'Reilly's mouth lifted as if he found me amusing.

The second they were out the door, I was on the phone, praying Brian wasn't in a meeting.

He wasn't in a meeting, but he wasn't overjoyed to hear from me, either. Apparently, he hadn't been happy to wake up and find me gone. I decided I'd apologize later, when I wasn't begging for a favor so it wouldn't sound so self-serving.

Brian's not a criminal attorney, but he's extremely competent. I figured as long as I wasn't officially under arrest, he'd be able to protect me from any major legal faux pas.

We met at the police station at right around eleven

forty-five. We weren't late on purpose, it just took Brian a little longer to tie up his loose ends at the office than I'd hoped. O'Reilly seemed to take it as a personal offense, though, and glared holes in my skull when I was shown into his office. At least Finn wasn't there to give me frostbite with his eyes.

"Where were you last night between three-thirty and five?" O'Reilly asked without preamble.

I glanced over at Brian, who raised his shoulders in a hint of a shrug. I took that to mean it was okay to answer the question.

"With my boyfriend," I said.

O'Reilly scribbled something on his notepad. "Name?"

My inner smart-ass wanted to say "Morgan Kingsley," but somehow I didn't think O'Reilly would find that funny. "Brian Tyndale."

O'Reilly wrote that down, then looked at Brian with narrowed eyes. "You her lawyer or her boyfriend?"

Brian's expression was mild, as if he didn't mind the cop's belligerence. *I* minded, but I kept my mouth shut. "Both," Brian said. "If you're going to press charges, I'll find someone else to represent her. Are you going to press charges, Detective O'Reilly? And if so, what are they?"

O'Reilly ignored the questions and asked one of his own. "Can you vouch for her all night?"

Brian opened his mouth as if to say yes, then fell silent. My heart sank to my toes. Brian was too much of a goody-two-shoes even to fib for me.

"Most of it," he said, and I couldn't help turning to look at him. I don't know if my face showed hurt, or anger, or both, but whatever it showed didn't seem to move him. "I don't know what time she left this morning."

Bastard. Asshole. Brutus.

These were just a few of the thoughts that ran through my mind. His face looked completely impassive while he slit my fucking throat. I was clenching my hands around the arms of my chair so hard I lost feeling in my fingertips. If O'Reilly had asked me a question at that moment, I wouldn't have been able to answer if my life depended on it.

The betrayal tasted sour on my tongue.

"So you can't account for her whereabouts between three-thirty and five," O'Reilly said, just to hammer in the point.

"Not unequivocally, no." Brian sounded like he might be discussing the weather, that's how much emotion was in his voice. And he didn't even look at me. "Now would you care to tell me what this is all about?"

O'Reilly ignored me and focused on Brian. "Sometime early this morning, there was an illegal exorcism." He glanced at his notepad. "A Mr. Thomas Wilson. He's a legal, registered demon host. Someone broke into his house last night, Tasered him, tied him up, then cast out his demon against his will."

"And why do you think it was my client?"

His "client." That made my stomach turn over.

"The exorcist used vanilla-scented candles for the ritual. Your *client* is known for using vanilla-scented candles."

"Oh for God's sake!" I burst out, indignation now taking over for the hurt. "Lots of exorcists use scented candles! And—"

Brian reached over and grabbed my arm in a grip so tight it hurt and startled me out of my anger. He turned those impassive eyes to me. "Let me handle this, Morgan. That's why you brought me along."

"Yeah, you've been a big help so far," I snarled.

His grip on my arm tightened even more. If he squeezed any harder, he'd leave bruises. In my state of mind, it should have made me go ballistic. Except it was such unusual behavior for him that I had to stop and think. He was still wearing his lawyer face, and there was no special boyfriend-to-girlfriend look in his eyes. But his fingers were crushing the hell out of me. I realized suddenly that he was gripping my arm from behind—so O'Reilly couldn't see how hard he was squeezing.

I swallowed hard and shut up, hoping this meant he was still on my side and was trying to keep O'Reilly from seeing it. Brian let go of my arm with a self-satisfied little nod.

"Detective O'Reilly," Brian said, "I'm sure if my client had performed an illegal exorcism, she wouldn't have left her candles behind to be found."

Oh yeah, *that* was a rousing endorsement.

"Maybe she was interrupted."

"That's hardly enough—"

There was a knock on the door, and Finn stuck his head in. I didn't like the smile on the detective's face as he motioned to O'Reilly.

O'Reilly rose. "If you'll excuse me for a moment. Please, make yourselves comfortable."

I whirled on Brian the moment O'Reilly was out the door.

"Be quiet, Morgan!" he snapped in a low, urgent voice. He'd lost the impassive lawyer look, his face now intensely earnest. "If I'd lied about your where-abouts and they'd found out about it, things could get very, very bad for both of us. Please keep your temper under control and let me handle this. We can fight later."

I was eager to get to the fighting right away, but O'Reilly stepped back in at that moment. He looked way too happy.

"Very sloppy, Miss Kingsley," he said. He uncurled his fingers to show that he had something in his hand. They were little pieces of brightly colored paper like confetti.

Only it wasn't confetti. Whenever you fire a Taser, it leaves a literal paper trail—anti-felon ID (AFID) tags, up to forty of them, with the cartridge's serial number on them. I had a nagging hunch I knew whose Taser cartridge these had come from. I also had a nagging hunch that when they downloaded the data from my Taser's data port, it would claim it had been fired between three-thirty and five.

I'd have said now I knew why the intruders had broken into my house—to switch out my Taser and frame me for murder—except you don't need three masked men to steal a Taser, and you certainly don't need two guns apiece. No, they might have switched Tasers on me, but that hadn't been their primary mission. A backup plan, maybe?

I suppressed a shudder. The attack on Wilson's demon had occurred *after* the break-in at my house. Which suggested the bad guys had paid another visit to return my original Taser after they'd used it at the crime scene.

I was going to have to get a new alarm system. Mine apparently was a piece of shit.

"Miss Kingsley, you're under arrest for the murder of Thomas Wilson's demon. You have the right to remain silent."

I didn't hear the rest of the Miranda spiel. I was far

too shocked. Brian didn't say a word as they cuffed my hands behind my back. I didn't like the way he was looking at me, like he thought I might actually be guilty. That realization was going to hurt somewhere down the road, but I wasn't ready to deal with it yet.

"Brian!" I said as they tried to lead me out of the room. "You know I'm not that stupid."

Both O'Reilly and Finn raised eyebrows at that. I guess they thought I should've been telling Brian I'd never do such a horrible thing. I wasn't sure Brian would believe that. I was *pretty* sure he'd believe that I wouldn't be dumb enough to leave my candles and Taser confetti behind.

I didn't have time to test the theory, though, because the detectives hustled me out of there before I could say anything more.

Chapter 8

Later that afternoon, there was another lovely round of questioning. This time, it happened in an actual interrogation room, and Brian wasn't serving as my lawyer. He'd referred a colleague of his—a very sharp, very lawyerly woman who'd hardly let me speak a word. The cops seemed especially interested in the fact that I had a bruise on my face. I'd have to remember to thank Val for that later.

Some remnant of misguided loyalty made me tell them I'd gotten the bruise during one of my sleepwalking adventures. They obviously didn't believe me, but then they were stuck on the idea that I'd exorcized what's-his-name's demon and gotten the bruise during a struggle.

My attorney promised me she'd arrange bail, despite O'Reilly's dark suggestions that I wouldn't get it.

Either way, I was spending the night in this lovely facility. At least in my jail cell, I had a cot and a toilet. A big step up from the containment center in Topeka.

However, I sure hoped being locked up for the night wasn't going to become a habit.

There was definitely a part of me that was scared. If the DA could make the charges stick, there was a very real possibility I'd go to prison. Maybe even for the rest of my life. But honestly, I had a hard time believing I'd get convicted.

I'm not some kind of Pollyanna who thinks that the innocent never get convicted. But I figured without a motive or a witness, even the most convincing circumstantial evidence wouldn't be enough.

At around five in the afternoon, the guards came for me again and led me to the interrogation room. They left me there alone, in handcuffs, and my stomach felt a little queasy. Was this the part where they tried to beat a confession out of me? I really, really didn't like that my lawyer wasn't there, and that the guards had completely ignored me when I demanded they call her.

I had about ten minutes to stew and sweat before the door opened and Adam White came in.

I wouldn't say he was the *last* person I expected to see, but I was definitely surprised to see him. I raised both eyebrows as he unlocked my handcuffs and took a seat across from me at the table.

"You're a little out of your jurisdiction, aren't you, Adam?"

He leaned back in his chair and stared at me. I didn't like it, but I refused to squirm. When he still didn't say anything, the pressure was too much and I had to break the silence.

"I'm not saying a word until my attorney's present."

He blinked as if surprised. "That won't be necessary."

"Like hell!"

He held up both hands. "I mean it, Morgan. This is

an unofficial visit. Like you said, I'm out of my jurisdiction."

"Then what do you want?" I sounded a bit snarly, and he hadn't said anything to deserve it, but being in jail didn't do good things to my overall attitude.

He folded his hands and put them on the table, leaning forward as if to keep it just between him and me.

Yeah, him, me, and whoever was watching and listening through the fake mirror behind his head.

"I want to know what's going on," he said, keeping his voice low but not quite whispering. His eyes locked on mine as if he could read everything he needed to know if he just gazed at me intently enough.

I leaned forward, mirroring his position. "When you find out, let me know."

The corner of his mouth twitched, and those caramel-colored eyes of his warmed with good humor. His expression was so friendly that for half a second I almost liked him. Then I reminded myself what he was, and the temporary insanity evaporated.

"Either get my attorney in here, or stop wasting my time," I said, and watched that good humor leak away.

He sat back in his chair, ditching the whole conspiratorial act. "I know you didn't do it, Morgan."

I had to laugh at that one. "Yeah, I know that, too."

He ignored the jibe. "I read up on your case, and about your 911 call the other night."

"Why? What do you care? You're a demon hunter, not a policeman."

If Adam has a temper, I have yet to see it. A normal guy would have taken offense at the suggestion that he wasn't a real policeman. Adam just ignored it.

"This is a demon-related crime. And you're obviously

being set up. That begs the question of why, don't you think?"

It did, but I couldn't come up with any logical explanation. I mean, my sunny disposition meant I had plenty of people who didn't like me, and maybe even some honest-to-God enemies. But I couldn't imagine anyone who hated me enough to try to frame me for murder.

"I'd like to help you, if you'd let me."

I shook my head, confused. "Why the hell would you want to help me? I kill your kind for money, remember?" That made me sound more mercenary than I really was, but I guess I was still trying to get a rise out of him.

"And I hunt my kind when they break the law. I know you have issues with me being a demon, but we're on the same side, whether you like it or not."

"That doesn't explain anything." Hell, I didn't even know why he was so convinced I wasn't guilty. He certainly knew how I felt about demons.

He cocked his head at me. "You think I need an ulterior motive to try to help someone I know is being framed for a crime she didn't commit?"

"When that someone is me, yeah."

He leaned forward again, reaching across the table to grab my hand in a firm, warm grip. It shocked the hell out of me, and of course I tried to pull away. Fat lot of good it did me. He clasped my hand between both of his.

"I'm trying to be your friend. I don't hold your profession against you, and I think you are a very honorable woman. That's why I came to you Monday to help with Dominic."

If I didn't suspect Dominic had been more than a friend to him, I might have thought he was coming on to me a bit. There was something in his eyes, a kind of softness, I'd never seen in him before. But I'd have understood a come-on better than this sudden bid for friendship.

"Let go of my hand, Adam."

He did, but he didn't lose that intimate look in his eyes. "I think you're in trouble. And I think you need help. And I think you're too stubborn to ask for it."

I figured he was right on one and three, but the jury was still out on two. And if it did turn out I needed help, Adam wouldn't be the one I'd turn to.

"It's very nice of you to try to rescue the damsel in distress," I told him. I tried not to be overly sarcastic, but I think I failed because he lost the bedroom eyes, or whatever it was he'd been giving me. "I'm a big girl, and I can take care of myself just fine."

The look he gave me then wasn't quite so friendly. "We'll see." He pushed his chair back from the table and grabbed the handcuffs. I wasn't stupid enough to resist, so I passively held out my wrists to him while trying to read the look on his face.

"You know, Adam, that sounded suspiciously like a threat."

The cuffs closed around my wrists. He met my eyes for a moment, and I couldn't read a thing. He'd wiped his face clean of all expression. That blankness disturbed me more than anything else I could have seen, and I dropped my gaze.

He left without another word, and the guards took me back to my cell.

When I woke up in that blinding white room again, I was kind of shocked. I hadn't thought I'd sleep a wink in that jail cell. It wasn't exactly the Hilton, and I wasn't what you'd call relaxed.

I blinked a couple of times, and Lugh was standing in front of me. He'd ditched the bomber jacket and wore a skintight black T-shirt instead. The rest of the outfit looked about the same as last time. The clingy shirt showed off a broad, powerful chest tapering into a lean waist that I'd bet anything featured a six-pack in the ab area.

I considered throwing a temper tantrum because this was *so* not what I needed right now. If I was actually getting some real, honest-to-God sleep, I wanted it to be peaceful like it's supposed to be. I *didn't* want to have a chat with my own personal demon.

I put my hands on my hips and glanced around the empty white room. Then I faced Lugh again.

"Love what you've done with the place," I said, faking a nonchalance I certainly didn't feel.

He smiled, showing movie-star–white teeth. I'm pretty sure smiles like that are against the law in some states. My dream-self got a severe case of jelly-knees, and I had to look away.

"I thought I'd focus on the important things first," he said.

That got me to raise my eyes back to his. "You mean like yourself?"

The smile widened. I was so glad I amused him. "Yes, I suppose I do. But I think I'm getting better at this, so I'll try for a little more flourish."

A sofa, coffee table, and love seat appeared out of nowhere. The sofa and love seat had spare lines and bland, cream-colored upholstery, and the coffee table was a piece of unvarnished lumber on legs. I'd have said I wasn't impressed, but *I* can't make furniture appear out of thin air.

"Shall we have a seat?" Lugh asked, gesturing to the couch.

I crossed my arms over my chest. I didn't like the idea that I might be here long enough to sit down for a cozy chat.

"Sorry, can't stay," I said. "I've got a bail hearing in the morning, you know."

He nodded gravely. His hair was unbound today, and I found myself admiring the blue-black shine of it. I rolled my eyes at myself the moment I noticed myself noticing.

"I know about your troubles, Morgan. I may not be able to control you, but I am still with you at all times."

My dirty little mind conjured up pictures of rolling around in bed with Brian. Had Lugh been a conscious passenger through all that? My cheeks heated and I wished I'd wake up right this moment.

"Please don't fight me now," Lugh said, interrupting my spiral into humiliation. "We need to talk, don't you think?"

I forced away the image of giving Brian a blow job while Lugh rode along. It wasn't easy, and I had a feeling I'd go back to it later. But Lugh was right, and we needed to talk.

Reluctantly, I dragged my feet toward the sofa and sat down on the middle seat, taking up as much room as I could. I might be willing to talk to Lugh, but I didn't want him sitting on the same couch as me.

My first thought was that he moved with the grace of a dancer as he strode to the love seat. But that image was all wrong for someone who practically radiated danger, so I amended the mental image to one of a martial artist. That worked better. He folded himself into the love seat, stretching long legs out in front of him and crossing them at the ankles. His skin looked almost golden against the creamy fabric, and his long, silky hair was raven's-wing black. I reminded myself of nice, wholesome Brian and told my hormones to get a life.

I leaned back against the sofa cushions, affecting a casual pose, though I was uncomfortable on so many levels I couldn't count them. "You wanted to talk," I said in my blandest voice. "So talk."

For the first time, a hint of uncertainty crept into his expression. He licked his lips like he was nervous. My hormones suddenly noticed how full and sensual his lower lip was. I pulled back the reins and tried to focus.

I didn't have the patience to wait for him to decide what to say, so I decided to hurry him along.

"Tell me again why you decided to move in uninvited."

His eyes narrowed. "I was not uninvited. You were not in your right mind when you spoke the invitation, but you did speak it. What's more, you invited me in particular, not just any demon. And you invited me in such a way that I could not refuse the call. Believe me, Morgan, this is not where I wish to be."

Glad to know I was such a wonderful prize. "So what you're saying is that you were *forced* to possess me. I've never heard of such a thing." The subtext was *I don't believe a word of it,* but though I didn't actually say it, I could see in his eyes that he understood.

"It's not something that is supposed to happen," Lugh said slowly, as if choosing his words carefully. "It requires the host to summon me by my True Name, which is known to only my closest family."

I raised an eyebrow. "So Lugh isn't your real name?"

His smile was somehow softer this time, but my hormones liked it just as much as his other smiles. "It is my real name, but not my True Name. A True Name has power, and a great deal of ceremonial significance. Not everyone has earned one, but for those who have, it is their most closely guarded secret."

I salted that little tidbit away for later digestion. There were more important questions before me right now. "So you claim someone called you by name and forced you to possess me against my will. Why the hell would anyone do that?"

The smile disappeared as if it had never existed. The lines of his face seemed to harden and sharpen as I watched, and his eyes glowed brighter. I was guessing this was anger, and it scared the crap out of me. I swallowed hard and pressed myself deeper into the sofa cushions, thinking now might be a good time to wake the hell up.

Lugh saw my reaction and visibly calmed himself. When he spoke, his voice was mild, though the glow in his eyes hadn't diminished.

"It isn't you I'm angry with," he said. "It's . . . whoever's done this."

That slight hesitation made me think he knew exactly who had done it, but I didn't want to piss him off by insisting he tell me. I didn't know if he could actually harm me, but I didn't want to find out.

"As I told you before, I am a reformer among my people," he continued. "Reformers are often unpopular. I believe I was called to you to silence me. Which means someone close to me betrayed me by telling my True Name, and which may also mean that someone knew you'd be able to suppress me."

"Uh-huh." How someone could know that was beyond me, since as far as I knew it was impossible for a human being to remain human when possessed. "And what else could it mean?"

The look he gave me was very grim. "It could mean that they summoned me here to kill me."

I didn't like the sound of that at all, because I suspected baddies of that caliber wouldn't do it by just exorcizing him—they'd do it by burning me at the stake.

Lugh met my eyes and some of the grimness left his face. "But that's probably not the case," he said gently. "Otherwise, they would have killed me that first night."

I thought about Val and about the masked men who'd broken into my house. "Maybe they were happy to let you live as long as I was in control. But when I showed Val that letter and they knew you were communicating with me, they shifted to Plan B." Plan B, which probably involved him being burned to death in my body. Oh, joy.

I tried to imagine Val being party to a plan to kill me, and my mind balked at it. She was my best friend, goddammit! She wouldn't hurt me.

Except she *had* hurt me, and she'd tried to Taser me, and her explanation for why just didn't ring true, no matter how much I wanted it to.

My throat tightened and for a moment I thought I might cry. I rarely let myself cry, and when I do, it's not in front of other people. Certainly not in front of sexy, terrifying demons who just happened to be cohabiting with me in my body.

"That does seem like a very real possibility," Lugh said.

He'd moved over to sit next to me on the couch. I hadn't seen him do it, so I supposed he just poofed from one place to the next. I jumped about a mile into the air and scrambled away from him. His hand closed around my arm to keep me still.

"You have nothing to fear from me, Morgan. I am

not your enemy, and I couldn't harm you even if I wanted to."

Yeah, *that* was real reassuring.

"Let go of me." I said it in a very calm, steady voice, even though my heart was jackhammering. It wasn't all fear, either. His hand felt wonderfully warm and solid on my arm, and his body seemed to radiate a comforting heat. His hair spilled over his shoulder and brushed against the skin of my arm, and it was like a brush of warm silk. Up close, I could smell the leather, along with an exotic, musky scent I couldn't put a name to.

He did as I asked, but he still crowded my personal space on the couch.

"Give me some room, will you?" I asked, a hint of desperation in my voice.

To my intense relief, he moved away. My hormones put up a feeble protest, but I shut them up with a mental snarl.

"What should I do?" I asked, because I frankly was clueless.

"Find the strongest exorcist you can and have him try to exorcize me."

My jaw dropped open in shock.

My expression seemed to amuse him for a moment, then he sobered and put that grim face back on. I didn't like his grim face.

"I'm a reformer for human rights, Morgan. One of my most important causes is to prevent my kind from possessing unwilling hosts. I think whoever has done this to me has a cruel sense of humor. And he also knows that I will not willingly be party to such a plan."

He leaned forward and took my hand. For reasons I didn't want to examine, I let him. "I won't lie to you," he said. "I suspect even your strongest exorcist won't be able to cast me out. I'm very powerful among my kind, or my reform efforts would not have worried anyone. But you have to try it anyway, or you risk losing your own life in a most unpleasant manner."

A lump formed in my throat. As much as I hated demons, I wasn't sure I wanted this particular one to die in a heroic sacrifice to save my life. And having seen what happens to most hosts when their demons are exorcized, the idea didn't seem too appealing. Of course, if the alternative was him dying because I was burned alive, I'd take Door Number One.

"I'll see what I can do. Of course, I have to get out of jail first."

"I suspect that will happen rather quickly."

He flickered, and I realized I was waking up when I still had lots more questions I could ask. I opened my mouth to blurt one out, but the next thing I knew I was sitting bolt upright in my bed. That is, my prison cot.

A guard was standing outside my cell, looking impatient. "Lady, you sleep like the dead," she said.

I really didn't like that particular phrase at the moment.

The cell door opened. "Your lawyer's here," the guard said, unclipping her handcuffs from her belt.

Hoping that was good news, I peacefully held out my hands to be cuffed and tried not to think too much about my dwindling hopes that Lugh was just a figment of my imagination.

Chapter 9

I made bail, which was a relief. It didn't mean the murder charge would go away, of course. I trusted the justice system to some extent, but not enough to just sit back and let them handle the whole thing.

I'd been mulling over the question of who might hate me enough to frame me for murder, and a name had finally risen to the top of the list: Dominic Castello. He hadn't been very happy with me on the day I'd cast out his demon. And if Dominic was involved, that would explain Adam's mysterious interest in the case.

My first priority when I got out of jail was to get cleaned up and change into fresh clothes. I momentarily regretted that I'd chosen to live out in the suburbs instead of in Center City, because this little jaunt was going to cost me around three hours. Still, I felt too grungy to skip it.

I wasn't surprised to find my house had been thoroughly tossed by the police. It didn't look like they'd made any particular effort to be messy about it—it wasn't like on TV where they sweep the contents of bookshelves on the floor and leave them in a heap—but lots of things weren't where they belonged. But I was just going to have to live with it, because this wasn't the time for housekeeping.

They had, of course, confiscated my Taser. Normally, I wouldn't have minded so much. There were times I carried the Taser when going into the city, but it wasn't like it was glued to my hip. Right now, though, I kind of minded because I was about to do something that might be a tad on the stupid side. I was going to pay a visit to my good friend Dominic.

Since he wasn't demon-possessed anymore, you might think I didn't need the Taser for self-defense. However, he was still considerably larger than me, and if he blew a fuse, I'd be at a distinct disadvantage. But that wasn't going to stop me.

I looked him up in the phone book, and, sure enough, he was listed. He'd made it real tough for God's Wrath to find him. He lived in South Philly, in a largely Italian neighborhood. I wondered if he had Family connections, in which case visiting him might be even stupider than I'd originally thought.

I took the train into the city, then took a cab to the address. I stood on the front stoop for a moment, gathering my wits. On the stoop next to Dominic's house, an old man wearing an undershirt sat on the steps smoking a cigarette and eyeing every woman under the age of fifty who passed by. When I felt his attention lock onto me, I decided it was time to get moving.

I rang the doorbell, keeping a watch on the geezer out of the corner of my eye. He was definitely giving me the once-over. As long as he was just looking, I was fine with that. I wasn't dressed particularly sexy today, thank goodness.

I had just decided Dominic wasn't home when his door opened. He didn't look happy to see me.

"What do you want?" he asked. It wasn't quite a snarl, but it wasn't much friendlier. Oh yeah, this guy was holding a grudge, all right.

I tried to look sympathetic even while I moved him a little higher up on my suspect list. "I wanted to check up on you, see how you were doing. You were pretty broken up the other day." I shrugged and looked abashed. I think. "I feel terrible about it. You got a raw deal."

He didn't seem to know what to do with that. I could see the belligerence drain from his eyes, and his posture relaxed, though he still looked wary.

"You came all the way out here to check on me?" he asked.

Ah-hah! I thought. How did he know how far I had to come to check on him? Maybe he knew where I lived because he'd had to look it up so he could break in and jack with my Taser.

I smiled at him. "I've been having a rough couple of weeks. I figured I could use the good karma."

He actually smiled back, which made him feel less like a suspect in my book. He opened his door a little wider.

"Would you like to come in, have a cup of coffee? Since you came so far."

Well, how friendly of him! Unless he was just trying to allay my suspicions. Or trying to lure me into his house so he could beat the crap out of me.

"I'd love to," I said, and walked into his house as if I trusted him implicitly.

The place was tiny, narrow. The whole first floor consisted of a living room, dining room, and kitchen that all blended into each other, no doorways or anything.

Dominic apparently shopped a good deal at Goodwill and the PTA thrift store. Nothing matched, not even the four chairs that surrounded his dining room/kitchen table, and everything was just a little worn and faded.

He pulled out a chair for me—a red vinyl number with a slash in the seat through which stuffing peeped out—and moved the two steps it took him to get into the kitchen.

"So how are you holding up?" I asked as he busied himself starting a pot of coffee.

He shrugged with his back still turned to me. "I'll live." He started the coffee brewing, then turned around to face me, leaning his butt against the counter and crossing his arms over his chest. "But someone very close to me just died, and it's going to take a long time for me to recover."

His eyes shimmered with unshed tears, and I wondered if I was being the world's most insensitive bitch to come here and interrogate him—under the guise of friendship, no less. But I considered him my best suspect, so I soldiered on.

"I'm sorry about that, Dominic," I said in my gentlest voice. "I really am. What happened to you and your demon wasn't fair. But at least you survived, and your mind is intact. It could have been much worse."

He blinked away the tears and glared at me. "You don't know what you're talking about. You can't imagine what it's like."

No, I couldn't. I couldn't imagine having my own free will and personality restored to me and being distraught about it. Then again, I couldn't understand volunteering to give it all up in the first place.

Dominic stepped forward to put his hands on the back of the chair across the table from me. His knuckles turned white as he met my gaze. "Last week, I was a hero. I made a difference in this world. I saved lives that no ordinary human being could have saved." His eyes glowed with fanatic intensity. "My life *meant* something. Now I'm just another guy."

My hands clenched into fists and I ground my teeth. I tried to moderate my response, I really did. But he'd hit a nerve, big time. "Just because I'm not hosting a demon doesn't mean my life is meaningless!" I snapped. Okay, forget for a moment that I *was* hosting a demon. I was still trying very, very hard not to think about that. "My life means a hell of a lot to me. Why should yours mean any less to you?"

The coffeemaker gurgled to a stop. I'd have ignored it in his shoes, but he shoved away the chair he'd been gripping and turned to the kitchen. I couldn't believe he was actually going to serve me coffee after that little exchange, but he opened a cupboard and pulled out a pair of mismatched mugs. When he reached for the coffeepot, a red stain spread across the back of his white button-down shirt. A stain that grew as I watched it, forming a long stripe across his shoulder blades.

My mouth dropped open, but Dominic was oblivious as he poured the coffee. It wasn't until he'd set the mugs on the table that he noticed my expression. His eyes widened.

"Why are you looking at me like that?"

I swallowed hard, wondering if that stain could possibly be what it looked like. "Your back," I whispered.

To my surprise, a rosy blush colored his olive-skinned cheeks. Not the reaction I'd expected.

"Did that happen when the God's Wrath people came after you?" I asked, though I already knew the answer.

He shook his head, his blush deepening as he stared

at the scarred tabletop instead of at me. "Uh, no. Saul—my demon—healed those wounds long ago."

I like to think of myself as this tough chick who has seen everything, but in some ways I still had a core of naiveté to me. I honestly didn't know what to make of what I was seeing, didn't understand his blush.

"Did they attack you again?"

He looked at me, and his expression changed from embarrassed to bemused. "Are you for real?"

I think maybe at this point, some little corner of my mind was making sense of things, but it wasn't a conscious corner. "Why are you bleeding?"

He blinked, then laughed. "Yeah, you're for real." He pulled out the chair he'd been standing behind and sat. He'd lost all his righteous indignation. And all his embarrassment, apparently.

"I'm bleeding because my lover got too rough with the whip."

It was my turn to be embarrassed. My face practically glowed with it, and my gaze dropped to my coffee cup. I hadn't taken a sip yet, and right now I didn't have any inclination to change that.

"Oh," I managed, and wished Scotty would beam me up.

"Another disadvantage to being without my demon," Dominic continued. "Before, my lover could hit as hard as he wanted, and Saul would heal the damage. Now he has to learn how to be careful of my fragile human flesh."

Yeah, I still wanted to get the hell out of there. But I have to admit to a certain level of morbid fascination as well. This guy was so different from me, he might as well be another species! I risked a glance upward and found him watching me with a mixture of amusement and bitterness.

"So you actually *like* being whipped so hard that you bleed?" My stomach tried to roll over at the thought. I stopped it by sheer force of will.

But Dominic shook his head. "No, that was a mistake. It won't happen again."

"But you liked it when you had your demon to heal you," I persisted.

Again he shook his head. "I like a little pain, but not that much. It was Saul who liked the hardcore stuff. He stopped me from feeling it when it got too rough for me." A hint of a sad smile. "When the God's Wrath mob beat me, I didn't feel a thing. Saul took it all, until it was too much even for him and he struck back. But I'll never have that kind of protection again."

"Because of me."

But Dominic surprised me again. "No. I know it's not your fault. If you hadn't done it, someone else would." He met my eyes. "That doesn't mean you and I will ever be friends. I hope to God I never lay eyes on you again after today."

I don't know why, but that hurt. I shoved my untouched mug of coffee to the side, spilling some of it in the process. Then I pushed my chair back from the table and stood.

"The feeling is mutual," I told him. "You're a sick puppy, Dominic. Get help before you get yourself killed."

His eyes blazed as he surged to his feet. For a moment, I thought he would come over the table after me, but he just skewered me with his eyes.

"Don't you *dare* judge me! You don't know a goddamn thing about me."

"I know you let your lover whip you bloody! And I know if he enjoyed doing it before, he's going to keep enjoying it even when you don't. You need to get out."

"No, *you* need to get out, Ms. Kingsley. Get out of my house!"

I managed to shut myself up, but it was a near thing. If his lover had enjoyed ripping his back to shreds when his demon could heal him, then that meant he was a real sadist. How long would he be satisfied with the tamer pleasures that were all Dominic could now tolerate?

I didn't know this guy, and he hadn't given me much reason to like him. But maybe because I felt responsible for his being in danger, I genuinely wanted to help him.

He followed me to the door, I think so he could have the pleasure of slamming it in my face.

I turned to him before I stepped out. "Tell Adam that if he hurts you, I will personally hunt him down and exorcize his ass."

I think I kind of hoped he'd tell me Adam wasn't the sicko who'd done this to him. No such luck. He just ushered me out the door and closed it firmly behind me.

Chapter **10**

After my productive interview with Dominic, I took yet another train ride, this time to go back home and stay there. It was Friday night, which would usually be a date night, but I wasn't what you'd call in the mood. I figured eventually I'd forgive Brian for not giving me an alibi, but not yet. I called him when I got home just to let him know where I was, but our conversation was brief and tense.

When I got off the phone, I straightened up the house a little, then changed my alarm code yet again. I'd showered earlier in the day, but since I wouldn't be working off all my stress in bed, I figured now was a good time for a hot bath. I let Calgon take me away for about a half hour, and it helped.

I was just wrapping myself in my terry-cloth robe when my doorbell rang and shattered every hint of relaxation in my muscles. I cursed.

I should have known Brian wouldn't give me time to come to grips with what he'd done. He wanted me to get over it *now,* and he was going to get in my face about it. It's one of the things he does that drives me crazy. He can't just let me be angry for a while without trying to fix it. I think in his life, he's used to working things out on a short timeline. Arguments in his family are patched up before the sun sets on them.

I'm not that way. Never will be. It's not that I don't want to be. I mean, who wants to spend half of their life pissed off? I just wasn't raised in an atmosphere where I could learn to do it. You might think that because I was the rebel of the family, they had no influence on me. They did. It was just the wrong kind of influence.

I worked myself into one hell of a snit as I stomped toward the front door. I was going to chew Brian a new one then send him packing with his tail tucked between his legs.

Which would have been a perfectly good plan if it had actually been Brian at the door. Instead, it turned out to be Adam.

I groaned and wished I'd had the good sense to look through the peephole rather than letting my anger with Brian make assumptions for me.

"You know that old saying about a bad penny?" I asked, pulling my robe closed a little tighter. I tried not to think about the blood staining Dominic's back, tried not to imagine Adam with a whip in his hands. It didn't work.

I guess I hadn't disliked Adam as much as I'd thought, or I wouldn't feel so . . . betrayed by what I'd learned. How stupid is that?

Adam looked at me very closely. I had no clue what he was thinking or why he was here. His eyes lingered a long time on my cheek, and I wondered if I still had suds on it. I was too self-conscious to reach up and check.

"May I come in?" he asked.

I blocked the doorway with my body. "No." I was not inviting this sadistic bastard into my house. Especially not when I was all alone and wearing nothing but a bathrobe.

"I can push my way past you easily."

"And watch me file charges so fast your head will spin."

He laughed grimly. "I'm the Director of Special Forces. I think you'll need more than a trespassing charge to scare me."

"Get the fuck off my property, Adam. I mean it." I tried to slam the door, but he made good on his threat and pushed past me, into my house.

I was so unwilling to be alone in the house with him that I tried to make a run for it, barefoot and in my bathrobe.

Demon-quick, he reached out and grabbed my arm, yanking me back into my house and slamming my door. His fingers dug in hard enough to leave bruises, but I was afraid he might enjoy it if I complained. Of course, he might be enjoying my struggles, too. Didn't sadists get off on that kind of thing?

Against my will, my gaze dropped down to his crotch. Thankfully, there was no sign of an erection. Maybe he only got off on other men?

"Oh for God's sake, Morgan!" he snapped. "Are you checking me out to see if I have a hard-on from manhandling you?"

Since that was exactly what I was doing, I couldn't muster much righteous indignation.

He dragged me up against his body, bending his head so his lips almost brushed my ear when he spoke.

"It would have to hurt a lot worse than this to turn me on, love. And if you're getting ready to stomp my instep, I'd recommend against it."

I guess he must have felt the tension in my body, but I was surprised he'd been able to read it so well. I seriously considered doing it anyway, but I didn't want to know how he'd retaliate.

"Let go of me," I growled through clenched teeth.

He did, but the coiled tension in his body told me he was ready to grab me again if I made the slightest wrong move. My heart was trying to pound its way out of my chest, and a sheen of cold sweat broke out on my skin despite the half hour I'd spent in the tub. He could crush me without even trying. And the more it hurt, the more he'd enjoy it. Even *my* bravado wilted in the face of that threat.

His voice when he spoke was deep, and low, and full of menace. "I would like to hurt you right now, Morgan. I really would. Dominic's having a hard enough adjustment without you barging into his house and casting aspersions on his lifestyle."

His words scared the shit out of me, but when I looked up at his face, what I saw there wasn't so much anger as pain. "What do *you* care? Your demon pal isn't living in him anymore. He's just a puny human now, right?"

"Not that it's any of your business, but I told you his host and mine were friends before Saul and I came along. My host cares about Dominic, and *I* care about my host. Leave him alone, Morgan. Please."

"Let me get this straight. You whipped him until he bled, but you're mad at me for hurting his feelings?"

His expression hardened, the pain fading—or at least hidden. "Yeah, that's about it."

Maybe Adam really did care about Dominic, in his

own sick way. But for whatever reason, *I* found myself caring about Dominic, too. I glared up at Adam, despite my fear.

"I meant what I said to him. If you hurt him, I will hunt you down. I agree with you that he's had it hard enough already."

Adam eased down a bit. "You really mean that."

"You bet your ass I do." *And please don't ask me why, 'cause I know I won't be able to explain it.*

I wouldn't quite call the expression on Adam's face a smile, but it was approaching one. "Well, that's one thing you don't have to worry about." He fixed me with a penetrating look. "He bled on the first stroke. I gave him plenty more after that and didn't leave a mark on him. I learned."

I held up both hands. "TMI, Adam."

He laughed. "Don't you want to know how I comforted him afterward?"

I shot him my most vicious glare, but I knew I was blushing again. My mind glommed on to an image of Adam's naked butt—not that I'd ever seen it, mind you!—doing wicked things. The thought should have been icky, but that wasn't exactly how I reacted to it. My own reaction... Now, *that* was icky!

I shook the image off as best I could. "So are you planning to hurt me?" I crossed my arms over my chest, coincidentally pressing the edges of my robe more tightly together.

His smile was almost condescending. "I never hurt anyone for sport without their consent." The intensity came back into his eyes, and I had to fight the urge to take a step back from him. "I must admit, I'd really like to, though. There's only so much Dominic can take these days, and I've got plenty of excess...energy.

Maybe someday I'll find a way to persuade you to consent."

"Hah! Hell will freeze over first."

He grinned at me. "I'll start praying for an ice age, then."

I wanted to slap that grin off his face. "Are we finished here? Will you get out of my house now?"

"Oh, I don't think so."

"What if I asked really, really nicely?"

"You don't have it in you to ask nicely, love." He seemed to have gotten over his anger, or at least buried it under something else. Amusement, I guess. I liked it better than the anger, but only marginally.

I sighed. "Any chance I could get you to stop calling me 'love'?"

"Sure. Offer me some hospitality."

I didn't like the glint in his eye. "What kind of hospitality?" I couldn't have sounded more suspicious if I'd tried.

"A drink would be nice. I want to talk to you about the murder charge. I found out something that I think you should know."

Okay, he'd piqued my interest. "I'll go put some clothes on. You can wait in the living room." I gestured with my hand.

Adam's grin was pure mischief with a lust chaser. "You don't need to dress up on my account."

I thought of any number of snappy comebacks, but I figured they'd only make things worse. I pointed imperiously at my couch. "Sit. Stay. I'll be back."

I heard him chuckling to himself as I turned my back and made for my bedroom. Putting some clothes on and climbing out the window made for a tempting fantasy, but if he really had learned something important, then I had to know. Of course, considering how he felt about me right now, I didn't know why he'd want to share information.

Adam was turning out to be quite the little enigma, and I didn't like it one bit.

I dug out one of my old pairs of jeans, the ones I'd bought before the low-rise style came into fashion, and put on a baggy sweatshirt that I'd stolen from Brian one night when he'd wreaked havoc on my blouse. The combination made me as shapeless as possible, which I figured was a good thing considering how Adam kept looking at me. I wondered if Dominic would object to him looking at a woman that way. Then I wondered why he and Dominic still seemed to be an item now that Dominic's demon was gone. Then I wondered why I was wondering and pushed the subject forcefully out of my mind.

I regretted my choice of outfit as soon as I walked back into the living room. Adam took one look at me and started to laugh. I plopped onto the yellow love seat and allowed myself to sink into the cushions.

"You were afraid I'd jump your bones if you didn't dress like a bag lady?" he asked, the corners of his mouth twitching with humor. I noticed for the first time that he had laugh lines around his eyes. If he weren't a gay demon with a penchant for S&M—heavy on the S—I might have found that sexy.

I stuck my chin out. "You mean to tell me you don't know you've been looking at me like I was Little Red Riding Hood and you were the Big Bad Wolf?"

He sobered a little, but there was still a hint of humor in his eyes. "No, you're right. I've been laying it on rather thick." The last of the humor faded. "You don't have to be afraid of me, Morgan. I wouldn't hurt you without consent, and I'm not into rape."

"Yeah, you're just an all-around nice guy."

He shrugged. "I wouldn't go that far."

"You said you had information for me. Why don't we call a halt to the verbal sparring and get to that part."

"Fair enough. When Dominic called to tell me you'd stopped by, I knew it hadn't been out of the goodness of your heart." I winced, but he ignored me. "I figured it meant you suspected him of setting you up. So I asked him about it."

My eyebrows reached for my hairline. "You asked your lover if he'd framed me for murder? I guess I'm not the only one with trust issues."

He waved my snarky comment away. "I knew he didn't do it. But I also knew if anyone wanted to get you in trouble, they might reasonably think Dominic would want in on it. Why commit a crime yourself if you can manipulate someone else into doing it for you? So I asked him if anyone had asked any probing questions about you since the exorcism. He said no—at first. Then I asked who all he'd talked to since then, and a very interesting name came up. And when he thought about it a little more, Dominic realized this person had poked at him to see how he felt about you."

"You know, anytime you want, you can stop being coy and just spit it out."

"All right. I'm talking about your brother, Andrew."

I clenched my teeth. It shouldn't have been so painful to hear yet another piece of evidence that Andrew was my enemy. Lugh had pretty much tried and convicted him already. And he wasn't really my brother anymore, he was the demon Raphael.

Logic be damned, it hurt anyway.

"Just to be sure, I got hold of the 911 call. It was anonymous, made from the victim's house, and there were no fingerprints on the phone. The voice was muffled, but I'm pretty sure it was Andrew's."

I took a deep breath. "So why are you here talking to me? Why aren't you arresting Andrew?"

"My jurisdiction is violent crime. A 911 call isn't a violent crime."

"Performing an illegal exorcism is!"

"Is your brother an exorcist?"

He knew the answer to that, because there's no such thing as a demon exorcist. Of course, a few days ago I'd have said there was no such thing as a demon who could possess you without you knowing it, so what did I know?

"If he called from the house," I argued, "then he's at least an accomplice."

But Adam shook his head. "My evidence against him is that he talked to Dominic yesterday and I think I recognize his muffled voice on the phone. Not enough. Not even close. But it's enough for me to tell you to watch your back."

I cocked my head at him. His face radiated sincerity. "Why would you care? You hate me."

He rolled his eyes. "I don't hate you. I'm mad at you. If you don't know the difference between the two, then it's *you* who needs to get help, not Dominic."

Geez, did Dominic repeat our conversation word for word?

Adam stood up in one fluid movement. I had to fight my way out of the depths of the cushions. About as graceful and fluid as a hippo.

"I'll get out of your hair now," he said. "You have changed your alarm code, right?"

"Uh-huh."

He nodded his approval, and I walked him to the

door. I thought I was going to be rid of him, but he paused in the doorway and reached under his jacket.

"Oh, I almost forgot," he said. His hand emerged from his jacket, and he was holding a Taser out to me, butt first. "If you've got mysterious masked men breaking into your house at all hours of the night, you probably shouldn't be unarmed."

To say I was stunned is an understatement. I couldn't even begin to understand this guy. How could he go from threatening to hurt me to giving me a Taser to defend myself?

I hesitated a long time, looking at that Taser. For all I knew, it had been used to commit a crime, and Adam was even now setting me up, hammering another nail into my coffin. But as badly as he'd creeped me out tonight, my gut instinct told me he wasn't the one trying to frame me. So I took the Taser despite all my misgivings.

"Thanks." I cleared my throat. "And, uh, I'm sorry I upset Dominic. I didn't mean to, honest."

He nodded. I didn't know if that meant he accepted the apology, or if he was just acknowledging that I'd made one.

I started to close the door, but once again he stopped it with his hand.

"One more thing," he said, and there was that scary intensity in his gaze again. "The bruise that was on your cheek yesterday? It's gone."

Chapter **11**

I checked in the mirror before bed, just to make sure Adam hadn't been jacking with me. He hadn't. The bruise was gone.

The last faint hope I'd harbored that I wasn't possessed died. I'd had enough bruises in my life to know there was no way one would disappear overnight without help. I tend to heal fast, but not *that* fast. I thanked my lucky stars no one at the police station had noticed.

That led me to question why Adam hadn't arrested me just now. He knew I wasn't a legal, registered demon host. And now he knew I was possessed. And he'd just walked away. Yet another puzzle to add to the growing list.

Stress and confusion are an exhausting combo, and after chewing over the puzzles for an hour with no success, I climbed into bed and tried to will myself asleep. For the first time, I found myself *wanting* to talk to Lugh. Maybe he could tell me something more about Adam's demon, explain some of the mysteries of the universe.

It took me the better part of forever to finally drift off. I felt like I hadn't been asleep more than five minutes when I woke up again.

Lugh was getting better at manipulating my dreams. The room was no longer that solid, featureless white. The walls were a light, warm beige, and a thick, rusty-brown carpet covered the floor. The furniture was back, with a few flourishes. The top of the coffee table was coated with a shiny varnish, and a scattering of dark red velour throw pillows dotted the sofa and love seat.

Lugh stood across the room from me, looking proud of his achievement. When my eyes found him, I lost all interest in his decorating skills.

Black leather was still his weapon of choice, but he was wearing a hell of a lot less of it tonight, at least on his upper body. I wasn't even sure what to call the arrangement of straps that crisscrossed his mouth-watering chest. They might be a shirt of some sort, or they might just have been random leather straps. They hid very little.

His chest was smooth and golden, with only a smattering of night-black hair. His nipples, framed by the black leather straps, were the color of milk chocolate. And, yes, he had the classic six-pack.

The leather pants clung lovingly to his hips and legs, showing off powerful muscles. And other assets.

Was it a coincidence that I'd had a few inappropriate thoughts about Adam and Dominic, and now Lugh appeared to me dressed like the S&M poster boy? I really hoped so, but I had a queasy feeling in my stomach. Just how much of my head could Lugh see into? And did I really want to know what he saw?

Apparently, I was gaping like an idiot, for his lips twitched into a grin, and he turned a slow circle for me. The rear view was spectacular. I had to clasp my hands just in case I might give in to the urge to grab a double handful.

Shit. This wasn't me. I mean, yeah, I like a nice-looking man as much as the next girl, but I'd never fallen in lust at first sight like this. What was the matter with me?

But of course, this was a dream—a dream Lugh was manipulating. Maybe it suited his purpose to cloud my mind with sex.

That thought helped drag my mind out of the gutter. This guy had a frightening level of power over me. I couldn't let myself forget for a moment what he was, or what he could do.

"So," I said, "you made my bruise go away." I sounded almost accusatory, but he didn't seem offended.

"I thought you deserved to have at least *some* of the beneficial effects of being a host," he said. He watched me from behind thick black eyelashes as he took a seat on the sofa.

There was plenty of room beside him on the sofa for me. I sat on the love seat. He smiled at me knowingly. It pissed me off.

"Yeah, it would have been real beneficial if Adam had decided to arrest me as an illegal demon host."

The corners of his mouth tipped downward. "I hadn't thought of that. Please forgive me. I had no intention of endangering you."

I figured he probably hadn't, but it wasn't like I trusted him. Right now, there wasn't a single person—or demon—whom I trusted. That was one hell of a depressing thought.

"The sooner you get me exorcized, the better," he said.

Forgetting for a minute that I could end up

brain-dead—and forgetting my reluctance to destroy this manly work of art—there was a gaping hole in this plan. "Yeah, that sounds all noble of you and everything, but you said you weren't optimistic that there was an exorcist strong enough to cast you out. If I go to an exorcist, and they can't cast you out, then they're going to report me. I suppose if you have access to all my memories, you know this is an execution state." At least the state would anesthetize me before burning me alive—something I kind of doubted Lugh's enemies would bother with—but that wasn't high on my list of preferred outcomes.

He nodded gravely. "I know. I hadn't thought of that last time we spoke. For that, I apologize. It was...careless of me. But I believe your friend Adam provides us an option."

My back stiffened. "Adam is not my friend."

"Be that as it may," he continued smoothly, "he already knows you're possessed and he hasn't arrested you. Go to him tomorrow, as soon as possible. Ask him to exorcize me."

I blinked and shook my head. "Ask *Adam* to exorcize you?" As if I hadn't heard him right the first time.

"Yes. He may not have the power to do it, but he has the power to try."

"So a demon can exorcize another demon."

"Yes. As a general rule, we prefer not to. And we prefer humans not to know."

It made me wonder what else demons preferred humans not to know. I had a feeling it was a long list.

"And how would I explain to him that I'm a demon wanting him to exorcize me? I've never heard of a suicidal demon. Or would he know you're not in full control?"

"Probably not. Before this happened to me, I wouldn't have known it was possible myself."

I noticed he said "before this happened to me." As far as I was concerned, it had happened to *me,* but I decided to let it slide.

"Yeah, so how do I explain?"

"Don't."

I grabbed one of the red velour throw pillows and clutched it. "You think he'll just exorcize you, no questions asked?"

"He'll ask. You just don't have to answer."

"And you think he'll do it anyway."

Lugh nodded. His face was devoid of expression. For whatever reason, it made me think he was hiding something. I worked the idea over in my mind. I felt the frown lines forming between my brows but didn't bother to smooth them.

I stared at Lugh's gorgeous, blank face and had a sneaking suspicion. I clutched the pillow more tightly to me and leaned forward, meeting his eyes.

"Do you really die when we exorcize you?" His face didn't change expression. But he didn't answer me, either, which was answer enough.

Rage heated my blood, and without pausing to think, I hurled the throw pillow at him with all my might. The pillow blinked out of existence about halfway to its destination. Not that it would have hurt him, of course.

I was on my feet, so mad I wanted to kick something. All the damn guilt Adam and Dominic had been piling on my shoulders, and Dominic's demon wasn't dead! At that moment, I'd have been happy to kill them both.

"It is against our laws to let humans know this," Lugh said. He seemed unaffected by my temper tantrum, which just made me madder. I opened my mouth to say something scathing, but he cut me off before I got started. "Dominic really believes his demon is dead. And Adam is forbidden by our laws to tell him the truth. It is, no doubt, one of the reasons he is so angry right now."

I swallowed down my own anger as best I could. "Then why are you telling *me* the truth? Or are you above your laws?"

For some reason, that made him smile. "I told you nothing. You came to a conclusion on your own. I simply chose not to contradict you."

He had a point, but I wasn't about to admit it. "Why would demons pretend exorcism kills them?"

He arched one elegant, dark brow. "If you didn't think exorcism would kill a rogue demon, what other method would you use?"

"Oh. Right."

A lock of his hair slid forward, and he brushed it back behind his ear. My fingers itched to touch the silky strands. I bet they'd be soft against my skin.

"Stop that!" I snapped.

"Stop what?"

"Whatever it is you're doing to my hormones. And don't pretend you're not doing anything!"

His smile was as sexy as it was sinister. "Would you prefer me to look hideous for you? I can manage it if you like."

As I watched, his image wavered and blurred, then slowly came back into focus. The stud muffin was gone, replaced by something that looked like what you'd get if you crossed a Klingon with a warthog.

"Is this better?"

Great. A smart-ass demon. Just my luck. At least I'd lost the disconcerting urge to jump his bones.

"Much," I declared.

He raised his heavy brow ridges, and I think looked surprised, though it was hard to tell in that misshapen monstrosity of a face. Unfortunately, he shifted back into Mr. Gorgeous.

"Look, at least put a real shirt on, okay?"

"You don't like this one?" He smoothed his hands over his chest, his eyes never leaving mine.

I reminded myself that I was in love with Brian, and Brian looked damn good. But that didn't stop me from squirming. No doubt about it, Lugh was doing something to me. Maybe if I closed my eyes, I'd spoil his fun.

It was embarrassingly hard to force myself to do it, but I closed them. My arousal level went down a notch, and I breathed out a sigh of relief.

"This is just a dream, you know," Lugh said, and he was much closer to me than he should have been.

My eyes popped open. I was no longer sitting on the love seat, but had somehow moved to the sofa. Right next to Lugh, who'd removed the leather contraption that had posed as a shirt and was now spectacularly bare-chested.

"You're allowed to be aroused even when you wouldn't be in real life."

Yeah, I suppose technically it was a dream. But it didn't *feel* very dream-like, and Lugh was real. I don't think Brian would like me drooling over him like I was. Hell, *I* didn't like me doing it.

"I'm not in the market for a demon lover, so back off."

He leaned toward me, amber eyes going dark as that fabulous hair slid forward to brush against my bare arm.

Bare arm? Hadn't I been wearing a sweatshirt when this dream began?

I was afraid that soon I'd be wearing even less, because I didn't seem to be able to pull away. He licked his lips, and it was all I could do not to gasp at the tug of arousal in my center. I tried to think of Brian, but Lugh's face filled my vision.

Then two things happened simultaneously. I heard a strange ringing sound. And Lugh pulled back, his nostrils suddenly flared.

"Something's wrong!" he said, not looking at me anymore. "Wake up."

And I did.

The ringing came from my phone. Rubbing my bleary eyes, I reached over to the nightstand and fumbled for the receiver. I almost knocked it to the floor, but managed to catch it.

"Hello," I said, holding the phone to my ear as I turned on the bedside lamp.

A fax machine screeched at me. I muttered a couple of curses and slammed the phone down. The bedside clock showed it was three AM. Who sends faxes at three AM? And why did they have to pick *my* number?

I almost lay down and went back to sleep, but I remembered Lugh saying something was wrong. I didn't think he'd meant the ringing phone.

I swung my legs over the side of the bed, finding my slippers. And that's when I noticed it. The smell of smoke.

I moved away from my bed and saw a wisp of smoke seeping in from under my door. As I watched, the wisp thickened and grew, pouring in more aggressively.

Why wasn't my smoke alarm pitching a hissy fit?

I bit my lip and went to the door, tentatively touching the wood to see if it was hot. It was. The smoke came ever more heavily, and now I heard the distinctive crackle of flames.

Shit!

The heat told me I didn't dare open the bedroom

door, so I lunged for the window. I shoved it open, only to find a neat little bonfire blazing beneath it.

I went cold. Somebody had disabled my smoke alarm and cut off my escape route.

Someone wanted me dead.

The smoke in my room was now thick enough to make me cough, so I dropped to the floor and considered my options while my heart hammered.

There were only two options available—the door or the window. I didn't think I was getting through either one without getting burned. But better a few burns than death, right?

Flames licked under my door, drawn by the steady draft from my window. I had to get out of here, and fast!

I chose the window escape route, but before I leapt out, it occurred to me that I might need a little extra protection. My feet propelled me toward the bathroom before my brain caught up with me. Holding my breath, I turned the shower on and hopped in, soaking my PJ's with freezing cold water.

I hopped out, my lungs burning from lack of oxygen, then sprinted to the window.

The bonfire had grown, but I had no choice. I ducked my head down into the sopping wetness of my pajama top and jumped, trying for as much horizontal distance as possible.

Intense heat surrounded me, tried to eat me alive. I landed on the ground on my hands and knees, my feet still in the fire. I rolled away as fast as humanly possible.

I pulled the pajama top away from my face, trying to see if I was on fire anywhere. Nothing seemed to be burning. Nothing except my house, that is.

Panting, coughing, dazed, I watched the flames spread through my beautiful English cottage.

Chapter **12**

I escaped the fire with nothing worse than a few second-degree burns on my feet. My house, however, burned to the ground. Everything I owned, my books, my clothes, my furniture, even my car ... gone. One of the neighbors called the fire department, but by the time they started pumping water on it, it had a life of its own. The good news was they got to it before it spread to any of the neighboring houses. When the shock wore off, I'd try to be grateful for that.

The police followed soon after the fire department. Having escaped out my back window, I hadn't seen the burning cross on my lawn. God's Wrath and the KKK both agreed that the burning cross made for a neat calling card.

Now why, you might ask, would God's Wrath burn down the house of an exorcist? We're supposed to be on the same side, right?

Wrong, according to God's Wrath. They think that exorcists are soft on demons because we don't target the demon hosts. They're really, really into burning people alive, and we spoil their fun. Plus, they feel the human host is just as deserving of death as the demon—even hosts who were taken against their will. Because in the World According to God's Wrath, only the Wicked can be Possessed by Satan's Minions. They were the Crusades, the Spanish Inquisition, and the Salem Witch Trials all rolled into one.

The neighbors poured out of their houses to watch the show as I sat with the EMS folks, sucking down oxygen and wishing my burned feet would do me a favor and drop off the ends of my legs so I wouldn't have to feel them. When the paramedics finally let me take the oxygen mask off, Mrs. Moore, my next door neighbor, brought me a cell phone so I could call Brian.

If I'd had a choice, I'd have spent the night in a hotel. Not because I didn't want to be with Brian, but because I was scared to death I'd be endangering him. You see, although this had all the classic makings of a God's Wrath attack, it was just too damn coincidental. I mean, really, what were the chances my best friend would try to Taser me, armed men would invade my house in the middle of the night, I'd be framed for murder, and God's Wrath would just happen to pick that moment to burn down my house with me in it?

I hoped like hell whoever was out to get me only had one murder attempt in them for the night, because without a wallet, I wasn't getting a hotel room. Reluctantly, I called Brian. I let him think the police were right and it was a God's Wrath attack. Just for tonight. Tomorrow, I'd tell him my fears that someone was seriously out to kill me and that I didn't want him caught in the cross fire. I figured that would be a really unpleasant discussion, especially since I wasn't willing to admit why I thought it was happening. Honestly, I didn't think he would turn me in as an illegal demon host, but after his performance at the police station the other day, I wasn't one hundred percent sure.

I borrowed something that looked like a moo-moo—yes, I know that's not how you spell it, but I defy you to wear one and not feel like Bessie the milk cow—from Mrs. Moore. It was better than my wet pajamas, but not by much. It hung almost to the ankles on her, but it barely skimmed my knees. And there was no way I was getting my size-nine feet into her size-six shoes, even without all the bandages.

I looked like the Mummy's grandma when Brian arrived to pick me up. My knight in shining armor scooped me into his arms anyway and carried me to his car so I wouldn't have to walk on my raw, bandaged feet. He held my hand for the entire drive. We hardly spoke a word. I stared out the window at the first hints of dawn, trying not to think, as tears leaked out of my eyes and cooled my cheeks.

When we got to his condo, Brian carried me again. If I'd been anything like my normal self, I would have objected. Once inside, he got me out of the muumuu in record time, but for once seemed oblivious to the fact that I wore nothing underneath. He tucked me lovingly into his bed, then climbed in beside me, still fully clothed. I laid my head on his lap and fell asleep to the feel of his gentle fingers stroking my hair.

Annoyingly, Lugh didn't fix my French-fried feet during my sleep. I guess he'd learned his lesson, but when I finally woke up around noon, I wished he hadn't. Every step I took made my feet blaze. I had to keep reminding myself how much worse it could have been.

Brian was downright incredible. During the time I'd slept, he'd gotten me a new bank card, ordered me a new credit card, and had me added to his own credit card account to tide me over. Not only that, he brought me breakfast in bed.

I was ravenous, so I scarfed down the syrupy, delicious waffles in record time. Brian watched me eat with a satisfied little smile on his face. My heart swelled, and I came close to crying for the second time in twenty-four hours. How could I have allowed myself to have even the most fleeting lustful thought about Adam or Lugh when I had Brian? I was ashamed of myself, and when Brian tried to take the empty dishes back to the kitchen, I wouldn't let him.

"Just leave them on the nightstand," I said, my voice gone husky.

His eyes darkened with desire, but a concerned frown puckered his forehead. "Are you sure this is a good time? You've had a really rough night."

I grabbed the collar of his shirt and pulled him down to me. He has the softest, smoothest lips I've ever felt. They tasted like home and heaven.

It didn't take much to banish his concern for my welfare. At the first brush of my tongue, he toed off his shoes and climbed all the way onto the bed, cupping my face in his hands as our tongues danced.

He came up for air, licking his lips and grinning wickedly. "You taste like maple syrup."

"And how do you feel about maple syrup?" My voice was little more than a breathy whisper.

He pulled the covers down to expose my breasts. Still looking like quite the naughty boy, he dipped his index finger in a pool of leftover syrup on my plate, then rubbed that finger lightly over one nipple. My back arched uncontrollably and I moaned. He repeated the process with the other nipple, then gave me his finger so I could suck off the excess.

Our eyes were locked on each other as I took his whole finger into the wet heat of my mouth. The darkness of his eyes, the flush of his face, told me he felt the caresses of my tongue somewhere other than his finger. I imagined dribbling maple syrup over his hot, hard cock, then filling my mouth with him. Moisture dewed my core, and I wanted him inside me *now*.

For one brief moment, I thought about my unwanted guest, experiencing everything I experienced right along with me. Then I shoved the thought aside.

Unlike a lot of men I'd known, Brian loves the foreplay almost as much as he loves the main event. He could spend an hour, easy, on the sensual torture, so that when we finally gave in, the immense relief of it made the pleasure that much more precious.

Now, though, I didn't want the foreplay. This wasn't about physical gratification. This was that primal, life-affirming sex you have after a close brush with your own mortality. Brian, lover-extraordinaire, figured that out without me having to tell him. See why I'm selfishly holding on to him even when I think he'd be better off without me?

He played with me only long enough to get the worst of the stickiness off my nipples, then got down to business. Straddling my legs, he sat back on his haunches to open his belt and unzip his fly. He didn't bother to take anything off, just shoved his pants and shorts down far enough to be out of the way, then kneed my legs apart.

Normally, I would have insisted on a condom. I'm on the Pill, but I believe in practicing at least two forms of birth control at a time, just in case one fails. But after last night, I wanted no barrier between us—wanted to feel nothing but *him,* stroking me deep inside, loving me with his body and his heart.

When he slid into me, it felt so right I couldn't contain my moan. I pulled his head back down to mine and devoured his mouth. His hips started to pump—hard, jarring thrusts. I wrapped my legs around him and moaned.

He didn't make love to me, not this time. He *fucked* me. And it was perfect. I came so hard I screamed myself hoarse. I hope the neighbors weren't home.

When it was over, he was embarrassed by what he termed his lack of finesse. Still breathing hard, I reached up to stroke his sweaty cheek.

"There's a time and place for finesse. This wasn't it."

"Yeah," he said, and rolled off me. I don't know if he was convinced or not. But at that moment, the afterglow was so wonderful I didn't much care.

The problems started when I asked if I could borrow a pair of Brian's sneakers. He's bigger than me, but my feet are real gunboats, especially when wrapped in bandages, so I figured I'd be able to keep them in his shoes. He hadn't minded when I'd insisted on getting out of bed and getting dressed. This, he minded.

"What do you need shoes for?" he asked me suspiciously. "You need to stay off your feet."

I needed shoes because I had to visit Adam and see if he could exorcize my hidden demon. I planned to keep that little tidbit to myself. Not that I thought what I was about to say would go over any better.

I wished I could have gotten by without having this conversation, but it was inevitable. I sighed and patted the bed beside me. He crossed his arms and glared down at me stubbornly.

"You're not going anywhere, Morgan."

I begged to differ. "I have to."

"Bullshit!"

I jumped. I'm not used to him getting angry so quickly and easily. It made me think I was having a bad influence on him.

"You don't understand," I said. "I think someone's really trying to kill me, and I'm putting you in danger by staying here."

That got his attention. Color drained from his face. He didn't sit on the bed beside me, but he pulled over a chair and leaned his butt on its arm so his eyes were closer to my level.

"You mean someone other than God's Wrath."

I nodded.

"Who? Why?"

I sighed. "If I knew that, my life would be a hell of a lot easier."

Once I started talking about it, it wasn't hard to convince Brian that I was right. He had to admit it was unlikely all this shit was suddenly raining down on my head by sheer coincidence. I didn't even have to tell him about the mess with Val, which was a good thing, because I couldn't imagine how I could explain it without telling him I was possessed.

Brian is in many ways the quintessential modern, sensitive man. But that doesn't mean he doesn't have the same primitive instincts as other men buried deep under his civilized veneer. You can just imagine how much a man likes hearing that his woman is in danger and she's going to keep away from him for his own safety.

I don't actually remember much of the argument. I

think my subconscious is protecting me from the pain, because it got pretty nasty toward the end. Brian bellowed at me, his face red with rage. This from a man who almost never raises his voice. I, of course, bellowed right back. We were so angry at each other it was lucky we didn't resort to fisticuffs.

I slammed out of there, hardly feeling the pain in my tortured feet, at a little after three in the afternoon. I had a duffel bag with a change of clothes in it, Brian's credit card, and two hundred dollars of Brian's cash. He'd literally flung it at me when he realized that nothing he said or did short of tying me up was going to make me stay. Pride insisted I couldn't possibly take his money after this. Practicality told me my other options were limited.

Practicality won out, and I spent the next few minutes picking scattered twenties off the floor while Brian just stood there and glared. I expected him to say something like "and don't come back" when I walked out the door, but he didn't.

For a while, I thought I'd have yet another crying jag, but I managed to keep the tears inside. He'd taken it about how I thought he would, and I was just going to have to suck it up.

I checked into the Marriott at the convention center because it was conveniently located. Despite my agonizingly painful feet, I had to stop by the mall and buy some replacement shoes and clothing. I didn't try anything on. Somehow, I just wasn't in the mood for shopping. Go figure.

I couldn't get over the image of Brian yelling at me like that, of the raw pain that shone through his anger. Every time I thought of it, my eyes prickled again.

He was brought up in a world surrounded by loving, supportive family. They'd taught him that there was no problem too great to be solved, that love conquers all, that virtue shall be rewarded. It's not that he believes we live in a utopia, but he thinks it's worth reaching for.

Me, I was raised in a world full of anger, resentment, and bitterness. I'd learned how not to compromise from some of the best teachers in the world. I'd learned cynicism by the age of thirteen, and it was a lesson that would stay with me for the rest of my life.

I could never be a part of Brian's world. Once you've come over to the dark side, there's no going back to the light. But I could drag Brian down to my world without breaking a sweat. Today's fight showed me he was already starting to skid down that slope.

I couldn't let that happen. It would be like destroying a priceless work of art. I had to let him go before it was too late. Even if doing it would destroy a piece of myself.

At the hotel, I pinched my nose and forced down a rum and Coke on the off chance a little alcohol would make me feel better. It didn't. But whoever was after me wasn't going to call it quits just because I was feeling depressed, so I called Adam's office. Naturally, he wasn't there. I tried to convince the guy who answered the phone to give me Adam's cell phone number, but he flatly refused. My charm was slipping. I left an urgent message for him to call my hotel room, then lay on the bed and stared at the ceiling.

After fifteen minutes of that, I felt even worse than I had before and was seriously considering trying a little more booze. Lucky for me, the phone rang. I think if I'd drunk anything, I would have puked.

I refused to tell Adam what I wanted over the

phone—you never know who might be listening in—but he didn't press too hard. He'd heard about the fire, so I guess he was being considerate of my frazzled mental state.

He was at my door in twenty minutes. It occurred to me then that asking a good-looking guy to meet you in a hotel room might be considered a come-on in some circles. I hoped like hell that wasn't why Adam had agreed to come without asking any more questions.

He frowned when he saw me.

"You look like shit," he said.

I opened the door wider to let him in. "Thanks for the pep talk." I turned to look at him, remembering how I'd had impure thoughts about him yesterday, then remembering how I'd torn Brian's heart out of his chest earlier this afternoon. It was all too much, and I felt my eyes welling up yet again.

Adam's eyes widened. "I'm sorry," he said. "That was insensitive of me."

The last thing I needed was a good-looking, sadistic demon being nice to me for no earthly reason. Niceness could eat through my armor faster than anything.

I rudely ignored his apology, stomping over to the other end of the room to the pair of uncomfortable chairs. Well, I didn't really *stomp*, because my feet hurt too much, but I did a passable imitation. Adam must have noticed what the effort cost me.

"You haven't healed the burns?" he inquired as he sat.

I shook my head, not quite trusting my voice yet.

"Why on earth not?"

"Do you have an open mind?"

He made a sound between a snort and a laugh. "More open than yours, that's for sure."

I let that one slide, and told him about my hitchhiker.

I watched his face closely as I talked, looking for any sign as to whether he believed me or not. I couldn't tell, but I saw something else, something very interesting indeed. When I said Lugh's name for the first time, Adam started.

It was very slight. If I hadn't been watching so intently, I probably wouldn't have noticed.

Lugh's name meant something to Adam. It remained to be seen whether I could find out what.

He was silent for a long time after I'd finished. Deep in thought. At least, that's how I interpreted the faraway look in his eyes. He could have been wondering what to eat for dinner for all I knew.

When he finished thinking, he reached for me, grabbing my hand before I knew what he was going to do.

"Hey!" I protested, trying to pull away.

"Hush," he said, trapping my hand between both of his and closing his eyes.

I wanted to tell him exactly what he could do with his "hush," but figured it wouldn't do any good.

After maybe thirty seconds, he let go, opened his eyes, and shook his head.

"I can't find him," he said. "I believe you that he's in there somewhere, or your bruise wouldn't have healed, but your aura is overwhelming him." He stood up and started to pace. "How can a human be that powerful?" I think he was talking to himself, but that didn't stop me from answering.

"Are you asking how it's possible for me to overwhelm *any* demon, or this one in particular?"

Surprise, surprise, he didn't answer. Instead, he stopped his pacing right in front of my chair and looked down at me. I really wanted to stand up so I didn't have to crane my neck like that, but I knew how much it would hurt and I just wasn't up to it.

"So he wrote those notes to you while you were asleep, and he communicates with you through dreams, right?"

"Yeah."

Adam nodded, the look on his face saying he'd reached a decision.

"Sorry about this," he said.

Before I had a chance to get even vaguely alarmed, the back of his hand came out of nowhere and smacked into the side of my face with the force of a wrecking ball.

Chapter 13

I came to, lying on my back, ready to be miserable. That had been one hell of a backhand. I braced myself for the pain, maybe even some queasiness and blurred vision. Surely he'd hit me hard enough for a concussion.

I realized I was unusually clearheaded for someone who'd just been knocked unconscious. Then I realized my face didn't hurt. At all. I reached up and tentatively touched my cheek.

"Lugh healed it while you were out."

I turned my head toward the sound of Adam's voice. I was lying on the bed, and he was sitting on one of the armchairs, his legs stretched out in front of him, hands clasped over his belly. He looked damn proud of himself.

I pushed up on my elbows, still tensed for pain and nausea, but I felt nothing.

"He healed your feet, too, though you should keep wearing the bandages just for show."

Finally convinced that I would suffer no ill effects from Adam clobbering me, I sat up. I glared at him.

"You'd better tell me you exorcized him," I growled.

"Sorry, no can do. He's way out of my league."

I groaned and lowered my head into my hands. Panic welled from deep inside my chest. I wanted this...*creature*...out of me. I wanted my life back. My gorge rose, and I wondered if I had a concussion after all. I swallowed hard, trying to force it all down, keep calm, keep sane.

How long did I have before Lugh found a way around my defenses and took me over completely? It seemed I couldn't get enough oxygen into my lungs. I sucked air frantically, my heart racing as fear beat at me from all sides.

Adam was suddenly beside me on the bed. His hand fastened on the back of my neck and he pushed my head down between my knees. I tried to resist, but he was far too strong.

"Easy now, love," he said, still holding me down. "Breathe easy. Don't pass out on me."

Passing out seemed like a really good plan at that moment. Until I remembered that when I was unconscious, Lugh had free rein.

I forced myself to slow my breaths. I closed my eyes, concentrated, visualized taking the roiling panic, shoving it into a steel safe, and slamming the door shut on it.

I wasn't sure how long that safe would hold, but I seemed to be calming. Adam released his grip on my neck and rubbed my back vigorously.

"Stop that," I said as I slowly raised my head. My vision swam for half a second, then cleared. I was okay.

Yeah, everything was just peachy.

I hadn't expected Adam to obey me, but he stopped rubbing my back and moved back to the chair he'd originally been sitting in.

"Better now?" he asked.

"Yeah." Except for my overwhelming embarrassment at having fallen apart like that. Usually I'm a pro at hiding my feelings, delaying my reactions until I can have them in private. Then again, I'd never had to face my worst nightmare come true before. That can do funny things to a body's insides.

I cleared my throat. "So am I, like, stuck with him until I die?" The panic beat at the door of the safe, but so far, it held.

"Likely," Adam answered, and if I hadn't known better, I would have called his voice gentle. "He's very powerful, Morgan. I doubt there's anyone, human or demon, who could cast him out. Even when he's trying to cooperate."

"Great. Just great." I took a deep breath. "So who is he?" I looked up and locked gazes with Adam, whose expression gave away nothing. "Come on, Adam. I know you know who he is. You recognized his name when I said it."

Adam looked chagrined. "I'll have to work on my poker face."

"Cut the crap and tell me who the hell is hitchhiking in my body!"

He licked his lips. "Let's just say he's a VIP and leave it at that."

"Adam—"

He held up a hand. "All right—let's just say he *outranks* me and I'm not telling you unless he gives me the okay." He grinned and made a fist with his right hand, pounding it into the palm of his left. "Would you like me to ask him?"

I flipped him the bird and he laughed. I wondered if backhanding me like that had satisfied his earlier desire to hurt me. I figured probably not, since I hadn't actually been conscious long enough for it to hurt.

"Well, Adam, you've been a big help." *Not!* "Thanks a lot. You can go about your business now."

"Why do I get the feeling I'm being dismissed?"

"Um, because you are?"

His grin held a touch of evil. "Not that easy, love. There are people out there trying to kill you. Or had you forgotten?"

No, that's not something I was likely to forget. "Your point being?"

"My point being this isn't a good time to play Lone Ranger. I know how hot you are for independence, but you can't do everything alone. And you definitely need help with this one."

I sort of knew that, though I didn't like it. "Are you offering?"

"Yeah, I guess I am."

"Why? It's not like we're friends." Actually, we were closer to enemies, I figured, but we hadn't quite reached that stage yet. Though if he hit me again, that might be the last straw.

"No, we're not. But I wouldn't want anything to happen to Lugh."

For reasons I didn't want to examine, that stung. I hoped like hell it didn't show on my face. "So what's your plan?"

"First, we get you out of this hotel. This is not the place to go incognito."

"You got a better suggestion?"

The predatory gleam in his eyes told me before he spoke that I wasn't going to like the suggestion one bit.

"My place," he said. And no, I didn't like it.

"No fucking way."

"No one would think to look for you there. And Dominic and I can watch your back."

Bad enough to think about staying in a house with just Adam. Adam and Dominic together was just too much. *Way* too much.

"Which part of 'no fucking way' didn't you understand?" Okay, so it wasn't the most original comeback in the world, but my brain wasn't firing on all cylinders at the moment.

The wicked, evil grin was back. "Let me put it this way: you're staying with me, where I can keep an eye on you."

I stood up. He could overpower me easily, but I'd make one hell of a commotion as he dragged me through the hotel halls.

He stayed in his chair and smiled up at me. "We can do this one of two ways, love. You can come quietly..." He reached into his jacket pocket and pulled out a pair of handcuffs. "Or not." He dangled the cuffs from the end of his index finger. "Which do you prefer?"

Well, shit. In all my indignation, I'd forgotten the little detail about him being a police officer. I could make all the commotion I wanted. All he'd have to do is flash his badge, and no one would lift a finger to help me.

One thing was for sure: I didn't want Adam putting handcuffs on me. I'd have to put on a show of going along quietly. When we got to the lobby, I'd see if I could find a good opportunity to make a run for it. I wasn't sure where I would go, but anywhere seemed better than with Adam.

"I guess I'll come quietly," I said, grimacing.

He swung the cuffs around his finger, staring at me.

I guess I must be getting predictable in my old age, because he smiled and said, "I think not."

He stood up, and my heart lurched. I didn't like the look in his eyes, not one bit. I held up my hands in a protective gesture.

"No, really. I'll cooperate. You don't need the cuffs."

He cocked his head to the side. "You're actually frightened, aren't you? I would have thought it'd take more than a pair of handcuffs to frighten you."

I tried to reason with myself. Even if Adam wasn't a demon, he'd have a height and weight advantage on me. In reality, if he wanted to attack me, I'd be just as toasted with my hands free as with them in cuffs.

Reason wasn't helping much.

Adam raised his eyebrows. "What's the matter, love? Don't trust me?"

That pissed me off enough to put the fear temporarily to the side. "Not as far as I can throw you."

He nodded. "Exactly. And that's about how much I trust you, though I suspect I could throw you farther than you could throw me. So turn around and put your hands behind your back."

I shook my head and shivered. If he was going to put those damn things on me, he was going to have to work for it.

His voice and his expression softened. "Morgan, I'm not going to hurt you. I'm honestly trying to protect you."

"You mean protect Lugh," I shot back.

"Right now, it's the same thing."

"Please, Adam. I promise I'll come with you. Just don't—"

I guess he decided persuasion wasn't going to work. He was on me before I even knew he'd moved. He turned me around and shoved me face-first onto the bed, then put his knee in my back as he grabbed my flailing arms and slapped the cuffs on my wrists.

He moved his knee as soon as the cuffs were on, hauling me to my feet by my upper arm. My heart beat rabbit-fast, and cold sweat broke over my body.

Adam stood behind me, *close* behind me, holding both my arms. I felt his breath on my ear as he bent his head to mine.

"Remember to breathe," he said, his voice soft as a caress.

Once again, I fought my panic. I breathed in deeply through my nose, then let the breath out through my mouth. Some of the tension left me, so I tried it again.

After a couple more deep breaths, I felt almost normal. Plus, Adam had released one of my arms and given me some room.

"Let's go," he said, leading me toward the door.

I cast a longing glance at the shopping bags that held all my worldly possessions. He saw my glance and snatched them up with his free hand.

Still fighting the remnants of panic, I let him lead me downstairs to his waiting car and tried to ignore all the curious stares of the hotel patrons.

Adam had driven to the hotel in an unmarked police car, so I had the pleasure of riding in the back like a criminal. He didn't take the handcuffs off. It didn't improve my disposition.

The last of my fear faded, replaced by good, oldfashioned fury. I stared at the back of Adam's head and wished I could bore holes in his skull with my gaze. At the next stoplight, he adjusted the rearview mirror so he could look at me without turning his head. I met his eyes in the mirror and hated the laugh lines that crinkled the corners.

"Glad I'm such a source of entertainment," I muttered darkly.

He didn't say anything, which was probably just as well.

Apparently, being Director of Special Forces paid well. Adam's house wasn't huge, but it was a lot larger than mine, and it was that rarest of all city birds, a stand-alone, sharing no walls with any neighbors. I was impressed.

He parked in a tiny private lot right across the street, then opened my door and helped me out. He *still* didn't take off the handcuffs, but I knew how much good complaining would do.

"Hi, honey, I'm home," Adam called as soon as he stepped through his front door, dragging me along behind him.

A familiar voice answered. "Well, if that isn't the cheesiest—" Dominic came to a stop. His jaw dropped, but he recovered his composure quickly enough. "Morgan. This is a surprise."

I wanted to say something clever, but nothing came to mind. Adam led me farther into the house, and Dominic noticed the handcuffs for the first time. He gave Adam an inquiring look.

Adam shrugged. "Long story." He let go of my arm. "I'll be with you in a moment," he told me with a mischievous wink.

I had no idea what that wink meant. Until he stepped away from me and put his hands on Dominic's shoulders. Dominic spared me one uncomfortable glance, then stepped into Adam's embrace. Dominic is actually an inch or two taller than Adam, but something about the way Adam carries himself always makes him look like the biggest guy in the room. Even when Dominic had to lower his head to receive his kiss.

My face flamed. I wanted to look away, but I just couldn't. They were both so beautiful, each in his own way, and I felt as if waves of energy radiated out from them. Their lips moved restlessly against each other, and I was watching closely enough to see Adam's tongue slip into Dominic's mouth.

I don't know why, but it was one of the sexiest kisses I'd ever seen. I finally forced my gaze away, but I couldn't help hearing the contented purring sounds Dominic made as Adam Frenched him. My cheeks refused to cool down, and even though I wasn't watching anymore, I knew that image would stay in my mind for a long, long time.

I heard twin sighs of regret as they pulled apart. Adam's voice when he spoke was rough and smoky, unlike any sound I'd heard from him before.

"Let's get Morgan settled, shall we? Then we can continue where we left off."

I didn't hear Dominic's answer, but he must have conveyed his agreement somehow. I kept my gaze riveted to the floor as Adam unlocked the damn handcuffs. I refused to rub my wrists, though they were raw from my pointless struggles. As if I could break out of handcuffs!

Embarrassed and reluctantly aroused, I picked up the shopping bags and followed Adam up the stairs to the second floor. Dominic came up behind me. When Adam reached the top of the stairs, he turned to the right and started down the hallway. But as soon as he'd moved out of the way, I came to a screeching halt, because I could see into the room at the head of the stairs through its open door.

It was the blackest room I'd ever seen. The walls

and ceiling were painted black. The floor was a glossy black tile. A huge bed of black iron, covered with black sheets, rested against one wall. But that wasn't what made me take a hasty step backward so that I bumped into Dominic coming up behind me.

The recessed lights in the ceiling shone on the black wooden pegs that jutted out from the wall facing the stairs. At least a dozen of them. From each of those pegs hung a coiled monstrosity of a whip. And I realized the room was most likely a monochromatic black to camouflage bloodstains.

Dominic put his hands on my shoulders, or I might have knocked us both down the stairs in my hasty retreat. Adam stuck his head around the corner and fixed me with one of his creepy stares.

"Don't worry, love. That's not your room."

I swallowed on a dry throat and pulled away from Dominic's grip. Retreat wasn't an option, so I did my best to feign indifference as I walked up the last couple of steps. I'm a lousy actress.

I followed Adam down the hall and tried not to notice that Dominic was no longer behind me. I knew where he'd gone.

When I realized Adam was installing me in the room right next door, I balked.

"Huh-uh!" I said, stepping back again. "No way."

Adam flashed me a shark's smile. "It's the only room I have that locks from the outside. And you know I'm not going to trust you in an unlocked room."

I knew better than to ask *why* he had any room that locked from the outside.

There wasn't a chance in hell he was budging, but that didn't mean I couldn't try. "If you'd just put me somewhere else, I swear to you that I won't try to run away."

"Yeah, right. Come on, you know there's no point in fighting this. And you will be safe here."

I considered making a run for it—Dominic was no longer blocking my escape route, after all—but some shivery, cowardly part of me feared that if I ran, Adam might drag *me* into that black room instead of Dominic.

"Could you at least do me the courtesy of not..." I found myself too prudish to finish my own sentence, so I made an indistinct hand gesture instead.

Oh, did my discomfort ever amuse him!

"Of not fucking in the room next door?" he finished for me. "I made Dominic a promise, and I'm not a tease. Now, much though I enjoy shooting the breeze with you, I've got other business to take care of. Get in the room before I lose my patience."

Almost sick to my stomach with dread, I stepped into the room. Adam slammed the door shut behind me, and I heard the lock click. I pressed my back against the door and slid down until my butt hit the floor, then hugged my knees to my chest.

Chapter **14**

At first, I didn't hear anything. I sat with my back against the door, every muscle in my body tense, my ears straining for a sound they didn't want to hear. When the silence stretched for a few minutes, I forced a couple of deep breaths into my lungs and tried to relax.

Maybe Adam was just giving me a hard time. Maybe he and Dominic weren't doing anything in the room next door. Or maybe the room next door was soundproofed. I remembered those neatly coiled whips and hoped to God it was.

Strangely enough, though the room was scary as hell, I hadn't noticed any signs of chains or restraints of any sort, like I'd assumed you'd find in an S&M dungeon. Maybe it was just for show?

That faint hope faded when I heard what could only be the crack of a whip. I gasped and hugged myself, retreating as far as I could to the other side of the room, where a platform bed rested against the wall. I climbed onto the bed and squeezed myself into the corner, covering my ears with my hands.

And still I heard it. One lash after another, going on for what felt like forever.

Then it got worse. Dominic started to cry out after each lash. His voice sliced through me. I wanted to crash through the wall and tackle Adam, make him stop hurting him. How could he do that to someone he'd kissed so tenderly not so long ago? How could Dominic let him? How could Dominic *like* it?

I was crying, and I hadn't even noticed the first tear falling. I wished I hadn't been so fucking noble about trying to protect Brian. If I'd just let him win our argument, I could be cuddled in his warm, safe arms even now. My heart ached, and I hated myself more than a little.

Words can't describe how relieved I was when the whip finally fell silent. I hoped Dominic was all right.

Soon I heard evidence that he was just fine.

In some ways, pain sounds and pleasure sounds are almost alike. But there was no way I could misinterpret the sounds Dominic was making now as pain.

The walls might as well have been made of paper. Either that, or Dominic was just that loud. Adam hardly made a sound, though every once in a while I heard a grunt of pleasure that sounded too deep for Dominic's voice. Their bed was against the wall between our rooms, the headboard thumping rhythmically as the bedsprings squeaked.

My fear and revulsion leaked away. My hands slid away from my ears, and instead of just hearing, I *listened*. And in my mind's eye, I built an image of the two of them, both naked, both beautiful. Adam, pale and powerfully built, Dominic with his olive skin and his almost lanky frame. Dominic bent over that black, black bed, with Adam riding him.

I pressed the heels of my hands against my eyes, but that didn't make the image go away, didn't stop the arousal that dampened my panties against all logic. It had never occurred to me that I might find the image of two men going at it erotic. Maybe there were parts of myself I'd never dared explore. That I never *wanted* to explore.

I fought my arousal as hard as I could, but as long as Adam and Dominic kept fucking so loudly, it was a battle I couldn't win. Fighting myself every step of the way, I slid my hand between my legs. And then I couldn't fight it anymore.

My hand moved to the rhythm of their thrusts, and I lost myself to the forbidden, erotic images. I was going to be mortified when this was all over. And I didn't give a shit.

I clapped my other hand over my mouth as the pleasure mounted. I couldn't bear the thought that they might hear even the slightest sound from me, though logic said they wouldn't hear anything over the racket they were making.

Dominic cried out in release, Adam's cry coming a heartbeat later. My back arched and I bit the inside of my cheek so hard I tasted blood as those sounds burst through the last of my resistance and I came.

Afterward, I walked on shaky legs to the bathroom. I'd originally thought the door led to a closet, or I might have hidden in there instead of huddling on the bed. Would the sound of running water have drowned out the sounds from the next room? I didn't think so.

I stared at myself in the mirror for a long time. My

face was flushed, my eyes and cheeks sticky with tears. I took a shuddering breath then turned on the taps, washing my hands then splashing cold water on my face.

Adam had been deliberately toying with me, and I was letting him win. That pissed me off.

When in doubt, get angry, that's my motto.

The anger actually helped me feel better. Yes, I was still embarrassed by how I'd reacted to the sound of them having sex. And yes, I was still freaked out and vaguely sickened by what had come before. But I felt steadier, calmer.

I turned my energies toward thoughts of escape. Not that I felt I was literally in danger here. I'm not the trusting sort, but I believed Adam really wanted to protect Lugh. I just thought the price I'd have to pay for Adam's protection was too steep.

Unfortunately, there wasn't any way out except through the door I'd come in. The windows were shielded by decorative iron grilles, a not-uncommon safeguard against thieves. I messed with the door a bit, but I'm not a locksmith.

About forty-five minutes after the festivities next door had halted, a key slid into the lock on my door.

I'd been pacing the room, frustrated and trapped, but I stumbled to a halt. I tried to brace myself, but I wasn't sure my nerves were up to another sparring session. If Adam goaded me, I'd give him far more satisfaction than I wanted.

Only it wasn't Adam who stepped into my room a moment later, it was Dominic. He shoved the door closed with his foot, and I saw that he carried a tray. Seconds later, the aroma of garlic and green peppers hit me, and my stomach reminded me I hadn't eaten since noon.

He didn't meet my gaze as he laid the tray down on an antique writing desk that faced the window. As I watched, a flush crawled up his neck. I wasn't sure which one of us was more embarrassed.

"Are you all right?" I asked him.

He looked at me for the first time, and though he was still blushing, there was a hint of a smile on his lips. "I'm fine." He cleared his throat and stared at his feet. "And I'm sorry about...all that." His cheeks reddened further. "Adam does enjoy his mind games."

He pulled out the chair in front of the desk for me, every inch the gentleman. I was way too hungry to ignore the invitation, especially when the scent made my mouth water like Niagara Falls. I was, however, still in a pretty bitchy frame of mind.

"Sounded like he wasn't the only one enjoying it," I said, then wished I hadn't. First, it was snarky. Second, I really didn't want to talk about their sex life.

To my surprise, Dominic didn't take offense. He grinned at me, a surprisingly sweet, boyish expression. "He can be a jerk sometimes, but he sure knows how to make up for it."

I sat and examined my plate, which featured chicken smothered with peppers and onions and tomato sauce over a mound of spaghetti. It smelled heavenly. There was also a glass of dark red wine, which I ignored. I sampled a bite of the chicken, and I think my taste buds had an orgasm.

Dominic plopped into a recliner and looked at me expectantly. I licked my lips to catch the last drip of sauce while I cut off another hunk.

"Did you make this?" I asked with my mouth full. My mom would have had a conniption fit over my table manners.

"Yes," he admitted modestly, though I could tell he was pleased with my reaction.

"It's delicious," I told him, just to make sure he got the message. "You were wasted as a firefighter—you should have been a chef."

His smile fell away, and I wished I'd kept that little gem to myself.

"Sorry. That was insensitive. I was just trying to give you a compliment." I tried a wry grin. "I'm not very good at it."

He laughed at that, and it made me feel a little better. The laughter faded, and he rubbed his chest absently.

"It's only been five days," he said. "Sometimes it feels like it happened an hour ago. Sometimes it seems more like a year. I don't quite know what to do with myself. If it weren't for Adam, I think I'd have gone crazy by now."

I wondered if I would ever come close to getting this guy. "How can you be so close to him when you've only known him for five days? I mean, only known him as yourself. Er..." I couldn't think of how to phrase my question so it made sense, and I really wished I hadn't tried.

Dominic gave me a funny look. "I was still me when I was hosting Saul. It's not like I ceased to exist just because I wasn't in the driver's seat." He smiled faintly. "Saul was very fond of Adam, but *I* was the one who always loved him." The smile turned sad, the pain in his eyes enough to make me wince. "And I loved Saul, too. He deserved so much better than he got."

I really hated seeing his pain, and I thought about the secret Adam was keeping. Lugh told me they weren't allowed to tell humans the truth. But there was nothing stopping *me*.

"Did Adam tell you my . . . situation?" I asked him.

Dominic shook off his melancholy with a visible effort. "He told me you were hosting someone who can't control you."

"Did he tell you who it was?" I didn't get my hopes up, which was a good thing.

Dominic shook his head. "No. He just said that it's someone who outranks him in their world. Someone important."

"Yeah, well, my uninvited guest told me something I think you should know." I tore myself away from my plate, because this wasn't something you told someone while you were casually stuffing your face.

"The whole thing about exorcism killing demons is apparently a myth. Your demon isn't dead."

For a long, frozen moment, Dominic stared at me in shock. Then he burst into tears.

It startled me for a moment. I'd seen him cry before, right after the exorcism, but that hadn't been as shocking. Yeah, I know gay guys are supposed to be more sensitive, more in touch with their feelings, yada, yada, but Dominic just looks too much like your typical manly man. I hadn't the first idea how to deal with his tears.

He moaned Adam's name, and the tears turned into wrenching sobs that tore at my heart.

Well, shit. I might have just given Dominic the good news that his demon wasn't dead, but I'd also given him the bad news that Adam had known and hadn't told him. Although I hadn't done it consciously, I think there was a small, spiteful part of me that wanted to stick it to Adam for what he'd done today. But sticking it to Adam by hurting Dominic was just low and mean.

"He couldn't tell you," I said, wondering if it was

even possible to heal the wound I'd just made. "It's against their laws."

It sounded lame, so I shut up. I was pond scum. Yeah, I thought Dominic should know his demon was still alive, but this sure as hell hadn't been the way to go about it.

The door to my room slammed open. I jumped and let out a startled yelp. Dominic didn't even look up.

Adam looked from me, to Dominic, then back to me. The look on his face was deadly.

"What did you do?" His voice sounded calm, but he wasn't anything like calm.

I felt awful, but I wasn't going to admit it to Adam. I held my chin up and met his angry gaze. "I told him his demon isn't dead."

If looks could kill...

"Fuck!" Adam shouted. He strode forward.

I thought he was coming after me, so I leapt out of my chair, but he was going to Dominic, who still hadn't looked up. His sobs were loud and heartbroken, and he was rocking back and forth in his chair.

Adam knelt in front of the chair, putting both hands on Dominic's shoulders.

"Dom," he said softly, gently. "I couldn't tell you. I'm so sorry."

Dominic stopped rocking and looked up with tear-reddened eyes. "How could you let me believe he was dead? *How?*"

"Because I thought I had to. If I'd known Lugh had lifted the injunction against it, I would have told you in a heartbeat." He drew Dominic off the chair and onto his knees, then wrapped his arms around the still-sobbing man.

Cradling Dominic's head against his chest, Adam glared at me with such malevolence my skin tried to crawl away and hide. I considered making a break for the door, but I wasn't sure I'd live through the escape attempt.

"If you weren't hosting Lugh," he growled at me, "I'd kick your ass out the door and hang a big bull's-eye on your back."

A chill snaked down my spine. The humanity had disappeared from his eyes and his demon shone through. Literally. His eyes were glowing, like Lugh's did in my dreams.

Usually when I know I'm in the wrong, all my defenses go up and I go into full-out bitch mode. I always regret it afterward, but that's how I react in the heat of the moment. This time, I felt too shitty to mount even the most pathetic of defenses. It wasn't just because I was scared of Adam, either, though I was. Big, strong, fireman Dominic brought out something in me I hadn't known I'd had—a protective instinct that I might almost have called maternal.

I met Adam's furious glare. "I'm sorry. I didn't think before I spoke."

He didn't say anything, just kept staring at me with those glowing eyes until I had to look away.

I heard him stand, heard him urge Dominic to come with him so they could talk. Their feet passed in front of my field of vision on their way out, but I was too ashamed of myself to look up.

The door closed behind them with a deafening slam.

Chapter 15

There was another round of whipping later that night. Only this time, it was Adam's voice I heard crying out in pain—not even a hint of pleasure—and there were no sex sounds afterward. My guess was that Adam had done penance for keeping that crucial secret. I hoped it was cathartic for Dominic.

I hadn't bought any PJ's on my shopping trip, and I wasn't about to sleep naked in this house, so I curled up in bed fully clothed. I don't think I'd ever felt so miserable about myself in all my life. My mind kept going over and over how I'd treated Brian and the rift I'd caused between Adam and Dominic. Asking myself when I'd come to be so hateful. Wondering if it was too late for me to change.

I must have drifted off eventually, because the next thing I knew I was in Lugh's living room—or whatever it was.

I was sitting on the sofa, and Lugh sat on the love seat facing me across the coffee table. His right ankle was propped on his left knee, his arms spread out across the back of the love seat. He'd backed off from last night's aggressive outfit. Black leather pants and boots seemed to be a uniform for him, but tonight he topped it with a plain black T-shirt. He still looked good enough to eat, but I didn't feel an unbearable urge to fling myself at him. That was a plus.

My native defensiveness made an appearance, and before he had a chance to speak, I asked, "So are you going to tell me what a miserable bitch I am for what I said to Dominic?"

He smiled faintly. "Should I?"

I sighed. "Probably."

"You're too hard on yourself." His voice was rich and dark as molasses. "You meant well."

I sank into the sofa and crossed my arms over my chest. "Did I? Adam sure didn't think so."

"Adam barely knows you."

"And you know me better?" Dumb question. He probably knew me better than I knew myself, even though he was a total stranger to me.

He just smiled. "Your technique could use some work, but your heart was in the right place."

I suddenly remembered something Adam had said, something I hadn't paid much attention to at the time. *If I'd known Lugh had lifted the injunction . . .*

Lugh had lifted the injunction? Just how "I" was this VIP?

"So," I said, "Adam seems to think you're worth protecting."

Lugh slid his ankle off his knee and put both feet on the floor. "As I happen to be inhabiting your body, I should think you'd agree." He smiled at me. It was a friendly, disarming smile. But I'm not that easy to disarm.

"Wanna tell me who you are?"

"Not particularly. You haven't shown yourself to be the soul of discretion."

He scored a hit. I tried not to let it show. "Considering all the shit I've gone through because of you, I think I deserve to know anyway. I was almost burned alive last night, if you remember."

I think I scored on that one, though Lugh's expression didn't change much. He leaned forward and propped his elbows on his knees, looking at me as if trying to puzzle me out. His gaze was disconcertingly intense.

"Stop looking at me like that!" I snapped.

One corner of his mouth lifted, but he didn't let it become a full smile. "I suppose you do have the right to know how high the stakes are."

I kinda thought the stakes were pretty high already, what with people trying to crispy-critter me, but I kept that opinion to myself.

"I told you I'm a reformer," Lugh continued.

I made a "keep talking" motion with my hand.

He seemed to brace himself. "I frighten my own people because I have the power to make my reforms come to pass. You see, I've just ascended to the throne. I'm their king."

Well, that was a stunner, no doubt about it. I was possessed by the king of the demons? Hell, I hadn't even known they *had* a king. Then I realized he said he'd just ascended to the throne, which suggested that beforehand, he'd been a prince. Named Lugh.

I think for a moment, my heart stopped beating.

Lugh laughed at me. "No, I'm not Lucifer," he assured me. Either he'd read my mind, or my face gave away my thoughts. "Although I suppose it's possible some of the mythology is loosely based on me." I probably didn't look any less alarmed. He rolled his eyes. "Remember, this is the same mythology that says demons live in the fires of Hell. There have always been segments of the human population who find us frightening and therefore vilify us. That doesn't make the stories true."

He had a point. Much as I disliked demons, I'd never subscribed to the hellfire-and-brimstone point of view. There was no reason to change that now. I nodded to indicate I was over my moment of superstitious dread.

"My brothers have taken the first step to start a war of succession," he continued, "though I suppose if they succeed in killing me, it will not be much of a war."

"Brothers..." I made the word halfway a question, though I would have liked to come up with something more eloquent and intelligent-sounding.

Lugh nodded. "Two of them. Dougal is the elder and will succeed if something happens to me." He met my eyes grimly. "My youngest brother is named Raphael."

Shit on a stick! I swallowed hard. "That would be Raphael, as in the demon Andrew is hosting?"

"So it would seem."

I frowned. "But if this is a war of succession and Raphael is in on it, why didn't he just kill you the moment you possessed me? You make it sound like I was too out of it to put up much of a fight."

"True." His lip curled in distaste. "Raphael and I have a long history of bad blood. Dougal and I disagree on matters of policy, but with Raphael, it's always been personal." The hinges of his jaws stood out in stark relief, like he was grinding his teeth. "I suspect he found the prospect of a swift death...unsatisfying. And I suspect Dougal's other supporters are rather annoyed with Raphael right now."

He looked at me and shook his head as he spoke. "I always wondered why there was only one person there on the night I was summoned. I would bet my kingdom Raphael acted on his own to use you as a host. Since Dougal's quarrel with me is political, not personal, he wouldn't have let me live a moment longer than he had to. But Raphael is determined to make me suffer first."

And I thought I had troubles with *my* brother!

"So if Adam and I can get hold of Andrew, would you be able to cast your brother out of him?"

Lugh smiled at me. "Not unless you'd be so kind as to let me take control when you're conscious."

I shuddered.

"But even then, I don't know if I could do it. Raphael and I are evenly matched. I have no way of knowing who would win if we fought."

I narrowed my eyes at him. "What about me? Can I toss him out on his ear?"

Lugh sighed. "I'm afraid not. You are obviously a very skilled exorcist, but Raphael is beyond you."

That tweaked my pride. "You never know until you try. I've kicked some serious demon ass in my time."

He looked amused. "I regret to inform you that the vast majority of demons who walk the Mortal Plain are of far less exalted—and less powerful—lineage than Raphael and myself. You have not faced a demon of anywhere near our rank before."

Just what I wanted to hear. "And what about Adam? Did you ever really believe he could exorcize you?"

His shoulders lifted in a hint of a shrug. "No. But I hoped to speak with him. I need an ally."

"Other than me, you mean."

His amber eyes crinkled with amusement. "Are you my ally?"

"Well, duh! I don't have much choice, you know."

He inclined his head, causing a lock of that fabulous black hair of his to slide forward across his cheek. My hormones took notice, but didn't go nuts.

"Point taken," he said. "But I suspect Adam has skills and contacts that we might find useful."

"And you trust him?" I sure as hell didn't.

"If I didn't, I wouldn't have delivered myself into his hands."

My heart thudded. "This was *your* idea! You told him to kidnap me and lock me up."

Lugh laughed. "No, not in so many words. I asked him to help and protect you. He decided on the manner in which he would do so."

I had a few colorful things I wanted to say, but Lugh kept talking.

"Truly, Morgan, he is a good man, and he'll keep you safe to the best of his ability."

"A good man? Excuse me, but were you napping earlier this evening?"

Lugh's shrug was elegant. "I didn't say he was a *nice* man."

"Sorry, in my book, good men don't whip their lovers." Judgmental? Maybe so. But also heartfelt.

His stare pierced me. "Even if their lovers enjoy it?"

"Even if."

Lugh looked disappointed in me. "If you could inhabit another's skin as we do, your mind would be less narrow."

I wanted to tell him to go fuck himself, but I didn't know him well enough. Yeah, I actually have to know someone pretty well to be vulgar with them. I settled for willing myself to wake up from my dream.

I didn't expect it to work, but almost immediately my eyes opened and I found myself curled into a protective ball in bed. The room was still pitch black, my body heavy with exhaustion and interrupted sleep. I stretched and turned over, and before I had time to wonder if I'd now be awake the rest of the night, I was asleep again.

I woke up the next morning to the sound of someone clomping around my room. I blinked bleary eyes and turned away from the wall.

The clomping was the sound of Adam's biker boots impacting the wooden floor. I sat up cautiously, keeping my eyes fixed on him, but he had his back to me and didn't seem inclined to look in my direction.

He dropped a tray onto the writing desk, rattling dishes and silverware. It was just a wild guess, but I thought he was still pissed at me. I slid my feet out of bed, studying the tension in his broad shoulders. He must have heard me stirring, but he didn't look my way.

After putting the tray down, he made a beeline for the door. I gathered he planned to leave without once speaking to me or even looking at me. But, sad to say, he was the closest thing I had to a friend right now, and I needed him. I swallowed my fear and my pride.

"Adam, wait," I said as he jerked open my door.

He froze with the door halfway open, his hand still on the knob. Still, he didn't turn toward me, though I had a good view of his profile. His mouth was set in grim lines, his eyes narrowed, but it didn't look like anger. It looked more like pain.

"Did I cause irreparable damage?" I asked. I had to keep my voice fairly low so it wouldn't wobble. Despite Lugh's pep talk last night, I still felt really bad about the trouble I'd instigated.

He hesitated a long time in the doorway, then pushed the door closed and turned to face me. A muscle at the corner of his eye ticked, and his face looked paler than usual. For about half a second, that puzzled me. Then a sneaking suspicion crept into my mind.

"Are you hurt?" I asked him. He didn't answer. He didn't have to. I remembered what I'd heard last night.

I raised my eyebrows. "You've had plenty of time to heal the damage."

He shrugged, but the movement made him wince. "If I were so inclined, yes."

It offered me an unwanted glimpse into his psyche. "Would Dominic have any objection to you healing yourself?"

His chin jutted out stubbornly. "Doesn't matter."

Yeah, I knew what I was looking at, all right. Self-loathing: an emotion with which I was intimately familiar. It meant it wasn't so much me he was pissed at as himself. I found myself in reluctant sympathy.

"Dominic's demon could have told him the truth, too. It's not all on your shoulders."

His eyes closed and he heaved a sigh. "I still should have told him. To hell with our laws. It's not like Dom would have told anyone else." He opened his eyes and looked at me. "I might never forgive you for the way you did it, but I'm glad he knows the truth."

I accepted that as gracefully as I could. I wondered how Adam had managed to get so attached to the real Dominic so quickly, but I wasn't nosy enough to ask.

I was, however, fond enough of meddling to ask, "So is Dominic enjoying this whole martyr bit you've got going on?"

Adam's sensual lips twisted into an ugly snarl. "I'd be very careful what I said if I were you." His demon glowed in his eyes.

Oh yeah, I'd hit a sore spot, all right. A smart

woman would have done exactly what he suggested. I guess that means I'm not that smart.

"I know you mean to punish yourself, but I can't see Dominic as the kind of guy who—"

He took a menacing step in my direction. "Shut. Up."

"I would if I didn't need your help and all, but you're not much good to me—or to Lugh—if you're wigging out. So I'm asking you to ask yourself who you're hurting more by not healing yourself. My money's on Dominic. So I suggest you cancel the pity party and heal."

Both Adam's fists were clenched at his sides, and the glow in his eyes was almost too bright to look at. "Damn you!"

I shrugged, trying to look casual and unworried while my insides quivered. Adam in a rage is one of the scariest things I've ever seen. "Some would argue that I already am."

I watched him struggle with himself for a long time. If the struggle went the wrong way, I had a sneaking suspicion he was going to forget his scruples about needing consent to hurt someone. I felt almost as bad about this whole mess as he did, but not enough to martyr myself for it. Which begs the question, why did I set myself up for it? But some questions I don't want to ponder.

Finally, the glow in his eyes died. His shoulders sagged, and he shook his head with what looked like disgust.

"You're right. I'm being a self-absorbed idiot."

"So you'll heal yourself?"

He nodded.

We both jumped at the sound of clapping hands. I guess we'd both been so focused on our staring contest, neither one of us had noticed Dominic opening the door. His eyes were brighter, more alive than I'd ever seen them.

"Brava!" he said, still clapping as he looked at me. "I never thought I'd see anyone best Adam in a battle of wills."

"Fuck you," Adam said, but there was no heat in his words.

Dominic grinned wider. "Any time, handsome."

Apparently, he'd forgotten to be bashful around me. I'd have been embarrassed, but it was actually kind of cute—especially Adam's chagrin. Offhand, I'd say Dominic had forgiven him, which made me feel a hell of a lot better. I might not understand or approve of their relationship, but I didn't want to be the one to break it up. At least, not like that.

Dominic peeked over at the tray Adam had set down forever and a day ago. He frowned theatrically. "I see I slaved over a hot stove for nothing." He looked at Adam. "Why don't we invite our guest to join us downstairs for breakfast? We can discuss strategy."

Adam hesitated only a moment before agreeing. "If you want to shower and change before you come down, we'll wait," he said. "We'll be in the kitchen, down the stairs and to your right. Just follow the smell of food."

"I'll see you in a few," I said.

I can't tell you how much better I felt when they left and didn't lock the door behind them.

The door to the black room was closed when I made my way downstairs about twenty minutes later with my hair damp and no makeup. I thanked God for small blessings.

At the foot of the stairs, I had a brief, almost

overpowering urge to make a run for it. I managed to overcome it. I didn't want to stay here a minute more than was necessary, but if nothing else, Adam could give me a lot of information. That's assuming he was even willing to give me the time of day.

I found the kitchen easily enough. Adam was seated at the head of a rectangular butcher-block table, watching Dominic cook. There was no question of the fondness in Adam's expression, and once again I wondered at it. One week ago, Dominic had been to all intents and purposes a different person. Why was Adam still carrying on a relationship with his lover's host? I might have thought it was out of pity, but that wasn't at all what it looked like.

When Adam caught a glimpse of me, the expression on his face cooled considerably. He sat up straighter in his chair, losing that relaxed, comfortable look. It made me feel oh-so welcome.

Dominic held no such grudge. He smiled over his shoulder at me. "Have a seat. Food is almost ready, and there's coffee over there." He pointed with his elbow, his hands busy at the stove.

I gratefully poured myself a mug of coffee, but couldn't decide where to sit. I wanted to be as far away from Adam and his thundercloud as possible, but that would mean sitting at the foot of the table facing him. I settled for leaning a hip against the kitchen counter and cupping both hands around my mug. The coffee was heaven. Expensive stuff, by the taste of it, and freshly ground.

Dominic finished up at the stove, then set three plates on the table. He took the seat at Adam's right, and I no longer had to decide where to sit.

An awkward, tense silence draped the room as I took my seat. Four wedges of French toast dusted with powdered sugar steamed at me invitingly. I caught the scents of vanilla and cinnamon, and my mouth watered obligingly. Too bad my stomach was clenched into a fist.

Adam drowned his French toast in maple syrup and started wolfing it down as if unaware of the tension. But the guarded look in his eye told me he was as aware of it as I.

"So," Dominic said, his voice just a little too cheerful as he tried to force everyone to be at ease, "where do we go from here, eh?"

He passed the maple syrup to me. I obediently poured it, but I still didn't think the knot in my stomach would loosen enough to let me eat.

"What do you mean?" Adam grunted. Most of his concentration was still on his plate.

"I mean, what's the plan? Hiding and protecting Morgan is all well and good, but it's not a long-term solution."

Adam let his fork clatter onto his plate, though there was still a significant portion of his food left. He fixed me with a distinctly unfriendly look.

"Just so everyone's clear," he said in a pleasant voice while the expression on his face remained unpleasant, "we're hiding and protecting Lugh, not Morgan."

I couldn't help but wince a little at that, even though I'd made the same point myself yesterday. It made me want to apologize some more, but I didn't. For one thing, I was too stubborn. For another, I didn't think it would do any good. I'm not sure if Adam actually *hated* me, but he certainly disliked me a lot.

"Don't be an ass," Dominic said, startling the hell out of me. I'd gotten the impression he was too deferential, too submissive to challenge Adam directly like that.

Even more surprising—Adam took it. "Sorry," he

mumbled, picking up his fork once more and digging into his French toast.

Dominic smiled at me. "Eat before it gets cold. Italians take it very hard when people don't appreciate our cooking."

The knot in my stomach loosened a bit, and I took a bite. That first taste was all it took. Tension be damned; this was too good to pass up. Maybe that's why Adam was so fond of Dominic.

"Wow," I said, savoring the delicate flavors. "This is delicious." Adam was still shoveling it in like a pig at a trough. I took my life in my hands and said, "You might want to slow down and actually taste it. You don't know what you're missing."

He froze with his fork an inch from his mouth, his eyes locking on mine in what I suspect was shock. Yeah, I had a lot of nerve poking fun at him at a time like this, but I couldn't help myself.

Finally, he rolled his eyes, and a hint of a reluctant smile pulled the corners of his mouth upward. He put his fork down and cut the massive bite he'd been about to shove in his mouth in half.

"Is that better?" he asked.

I nodded, and Dominic gave me another one of those fabulous smiles. He seemed to like me a hell of a lot more than Adam did.

"So," Dominic said, "let's try this again. What's our next step?"

I'd have rather just eaten breakfast in peace, savoring the delicious food, but I supposed making plans was more important. Now, if only I had some idea what to do ...

Adam looked at me. "I didn't have much time to talk to Lugh yesterday. Can you give me an off-the-record recap of everything that's happened?"

I still wouldn't say I exactly trusted him, but if I didn't tell him, he could just clock me again and have another conversation with Lugh. So I told him everything I knew, including the painful truth about Val.

Our plates were empty by the time I'd finished. Dominic cleared the table, then came back and refilled all our coffee cups. I wasn't comfortable letting him wait on me like that, but I had just enough people skills to know arguing over it was pointless.

When he sat back down, Dominic was frowning. "So why would Andrew frame you for murder? It would be damn hard to burn you to death while you're in jail."

I hadn't even thought of that.

Adam smiled grimly. "If Morgan mysteriously disappeared while she was out on bail, what would the police think had happened to her?"

"Oh," Dominic said.

Lovely. Glad to see my enemies were so thorough and organized. If I had to have enemies, I'd much rather have disorganized and stupid ones.

"So far," Adam continued, "we have Andrew, Valerie, and three unidentified masked men on our list of enemies. It begs the question, how many more of them are there? Just how big is this thing?"

I rolled that around my mind. "Lugh said this was about a war of succession. If that's the case, I'd say it's pretty damn big."

Adam nodded. "Yeah. And just taking out a couple of foot soldiers won't be enough. We have to find out who's in charge."

"Wouldn't that be Andrew? Raphael?"

"Maybe, but I doubt it. If he was in charge, he wouldn't have tried to hide that you were hosting Lugh. One of the privileges of being in charge, you know?"

The more I thought about this, the less I liked it. The fewer bad guys trying to kill me, the better, but here Adam was, telling me that there were likely more of them out there than we knew about. Not a comforting thought at all.

"Maybe you need to have a candid conversation with your friend Valerie," Dominic suggested.

"Just what I was thinking," Adam said.

My stomach twisted into knots again. I'd been doing my best to avoid thinking about Val's betrayal. I knew I'd have to face my feelings about it someday, but it was going to be a bitch.

"Why don't you give her a call," Adam suggested. "Ask her to meet you here."

I widened my eyes at him. "And just how would I explain that I was asking her to meet me at the home of the Director of Special Forces?"

"I'm sure you can come up with something." He leaned forward, putting an elbow on the table and propping his chin on his fist. "You could tell her you've decided to throw your boyfriend over for me."

Dominic laughed and shook his head. I resisted the urge to kick Adam under the table.

"Ha-ha, very funny. But all jokes aside, I think I'd rather meet Val in a public place." It occurred to me to wonder why Adam wanted her to come to his house. I didn't like any of the answers I came up with.

He sat up straight, his face gone neutral. "I don't think that's a good idea. We need to control the meeting place, make sure she doesn't have backup."

"She's not going to burn me to death in the middle of a public place, no matter how much backup she has with her. Besides, she might have nothing to do with any of this. She might have been telling me the truth." I didn't really believe that, but I tried to allow myself to hope.

Adam didn't challenge my delusion, though the look he gave me told me exactly what he thought about it. "If it's just you and her meeting in a public place, why would you think she'd tell you anything? She'll just claim innocence, and you might want to believe it enough to be convinced."

My temper tried to make an appearance, but I tamped it down. He was right, but I still didn't want to bring Val to Adam's house. I had a sneaking suspicion I wouldn't like his interrogation techniques.

"I'll ask her to meet me for lunch at Reading Terminal," I said. "If I can't get her to tell me anything, then we'll switch to Plan B."

Adam looked exasperated. "And after you've had your cozy little lunch and she knows you're on to her, what do you think the chances are that she'll come meet you here for further questioning?"

I figured it was time to be blunt. "I'm not bringing her here so you can torture information out of her, and don't tell me that's not what you have in mind. I'll either meet her for lunch, or we figure out another plan."

"You're a fool."

"Well, you're a—"

"Morgan," Dominic interrupted, reaching across the table and laying a hand on my arm.

I ground my teeth and glared at his hand until he moved it away. But he'd gotten his message across. I swallowed my opinion of Adam and crossed my hands over my chest in a classic I'm-not-open-to-your-suggestions pose.

Adam pushed away from the table with enough force to rattle the dishes.

"Fine! Do it your way. But when they catch you and burn you at the stake, don't blame me."

He stomped out of the room like a kid having a

temper tantrum. I really wondered what Dominic saw in him. It seemed to take about five minutes of conversation for me to want to put a bullet through his hard-as-rock head.

"Well," Dominic said with a little grin, "I'm glad to see you and Adam have patched things up."

I couldn't help laughing. "Yeah. We're best friends now."

"Do you want me to come with you when you go meet Valerie? If she might have backup with her, it wouldn't be a bad idea for you to have it, too."

His offer touched me, especially considering what I'd done to him. "That's very nice of you, Dominic, but I think this is something I have to do on my own." My throat tightened. "She's been my best friend since high school. I need to find a way to deal with what she's done, you know?"

He nodded. "Let me at least give you a Taser, just in case."

That made me raise an eyebrow. "Why do *you* have a Taser?"

He laughed. "I don't, but Adam does. I'm sure he won't mind you borrowing it, as long as he doesn't know."

I was really starting to like Dominic. If I could just forget that he had some pretty sickening tastes, I might even say we could be friends.

"Thanks, Dominic. You're definitely one of the good guys of this world."

That seemed to both please and embarrass him. He muttered some self-deprecating remark that I didn't quite catch, then slipped out of the kitchen to go steal a Taser.

Chapter **16**

Val was only too happy to meet me for lunch. When I called her, she practically tripped over her own tongue with all her copious apologies and pleas for forgiveness. I tried to seem open to it, because if I didn't, she might decide not to come.

Reading Terminal used to be a train station, until they converted it into an indoor version of a big open-air market. You can buy just about *anything* there. Cheesesteaks. Fresh flowers. Exotic spices. Produce. Baked goods. Meat, fresh from the flank of a living cow... Okay, just kidding on that one. The place is a total madhouse at lunchtime. The convention center is right next door, so the market fills with tourists as well as native Philadelphians.

I met Val at one of the Mennonite lunch counters, fighting my way through the throng to get there. Val was there before me, and had somehow managed to save me a seat at the counter despite the press of people. We greeted each other cautiously as I boosted myself up onto the stool. I ordered a turkey sandwich and coffee, having to shout to be heard over the echoing roar in the building. Then I turned my stool and faced Val.

She'd gone with her off-duty look today, her hair loose around her shoulders, contacts instead of glasses. A crisply ironed blue Oxford shirt tucked into a pair of tailored chinos. Her sneakers were sparkling white, fresh out of the box.

"I'll buy your lunch," she said to me, leaning forward so she didn't have to shout. "It's the least I can do."

My best friend tries to Taser me, and she thinks buying me lunch is going to make up for it?

I let that thought show on my face, and she had the grace to look embarrassed.

"I'm really sorry, Morgan." She looked down at her manicured hands, twisting her fingers around each other. "It was an unbelievably stupid thing to do, and I—"

"Let's just cut the crap, okay?" Her head jerked upward and she gave me those wide, innocent eyes. Maybe if all this other shit hadn't happened after she'd attacked me, I'd have fallen for it. But the shit *had* happened, and I wasn't buying what she was selling.

"You tried to Taser me because you recognized the name of the demon who'd possessed me."

Her eyes widened even more. "You mean you really *are* possessed?"

I was glad the market was so damn noisy. I'd have hated to have this conversation in a quiet little café. No one even looked our way, though Val had practically shouted that.

I leaned into her personal space, my hands clenched into fists to help me resist the urge to wrap them around her neck and squeeze. "And after you Tasered me, you were going to take me to your friends—whoever the hell they are—so they could burn me to death."

The color leeched from her face, and she couldn't meet my eyes anymore. "Morgan," she said, her voice hoarse and whispery, "how could you possibly believe something like that?"

She sounded convincingly hurt, but her facial expression was all wrong for it.

"If I'm being so unreasonable, then why do you look so guilty?" She didn't seem to have an answer for that. My food arrived, but I wasn't feeling in the least bit hungry. I'd told myself that I'd already abandoned the last vestige of hope that Val was still my friend, but the hurt that crushed my chest now told me I hadn't.

I shook my head in disbelief. "Val, how could you?"

She raised her gaze to mine again, and there was a sheen of tears in her eyes. She blinked them away. "It's nothing personal," she assured me. "Things...weren't supposed to happen this way." She took a deep, loud breath and let it out slowly, and it seemed to settle her some. Her eyes were no longer teary, and though misery still hovered over her, her expression showed a heavy dose of resolve. "I can't tell you how sorry I am that you got dragged into this."

"Tell me what exactly I've gotten dragged into," I demanded, but Val shook her head.

"I can't do that." She licked her lips and met my eyes squarely. The tears were completely gone now, replaced by grim determination. "If you take my cell phone away from me, I'll have to use a pay phone to call the police. That'll give you a bit of a head start."

I blinked at her stupidly.

"You're hosting an illegal demon. And there isn't an

exorcist in the world strong enough to cast him out. I'm afraid that leaves only one alternative."

A chill shivered down my spine. She was going to report me. Her little friends had failed in their attempt to burn me to death in my house, and now they were going to try to get the state to do it instead.

Damn it! If only I could be sure Adam would be the one to investigate her complaint...

Val slowly unzipped her purse, then stuck her hand inside to rummage for the phone. I snatched the purse out of her hand, and she made no effort to fight me for it.

"I'm sure it's no consolation under the circumstances," Val said as I rooted through her purse until I'd found her phone, "but it's for the greater good."

"Greater good my ass!" I snarled as I shoved her purse, sans the phone, back into her arms. "I don't know what the fuck you think you're doing, but one thing is for damn sure: you're not the good guys."

I slid off my stool, my food sitting untouched on the counter. I was so furious I wanted to punch her, so hurt I wanted to cry, but I wasn't about to do either one. Val threw some money on the counter.

"You'd better hurry," she said. "There's a pay phone right outside the market. I'll be making a call as soon as I reach it."

Without another word, she turned her back on me My heart was pounding in my throat as I watched her push through the crowd. How sweet of her to give me this generous head start! And she wasn't even heading toward the closest exit. Maybe she thought her conscience would rest easier if she gave me something resembling a fighting chance. I started hurrying in the opposite direction, my mind frantically considering then rejecting various avenues of escape.

I was shaking and distracted, so when I bumped into a guy blocking my path, it took me a moment to realize who it was. When I looked up into Dominic's expressive hazel eyes, I suffered a moment of serious confusion.

"Dominic? What are you doing here?"

My now-hyperactive paranoia came to a hasty, terrifying conclusion. "You're one of *them*!" It came out a shout, and I took a hasty step backward.

"What?" he said, brow furrowed. Then he seemed to figure out what I meant. "No!" He took hold of my arm. "Adam thought you needed backup, after all. We followed you here."

I'm sure I still looked very, very suspicious. "We? Where's Adam?"

Dominic looked grim. "Following Valerie. Don't worry—he won't let her make a phone call."

"What's he going to do to stop her?" I had a sneaking suspicion I knew the answer. When Dominic didn't respond, I knew my suspicion was correct.

I'd never thought of myself as gullible before, but I'd sure been getting fooled a lot lately. "He just *pretended* to let me win the argument. He figured he'd use me to flush her out, then he'd grab her and take her to his place."

Dominic gave me a shrug and a sheepish smile. I narrowed my eyes at him.

"You knew what he was going to do, didn't you?"

Another shrug. "I've known Adam a long time, so yeah."

And here I'd thought Dominic and I were starting to become friends. He was just one more in a long list of liars.

"Thanks for helping me 'sneak' the Taser out, asshole," I said.

He ignored that. "Let's go, okay? I don't think you want Adam to be alone with Valerie for too long. Not if you object to what he plans to do."

I didn't like the sound of that one bit. "It's not like I can stop him."

"No," Dominic said gently, "but you may be able to . . . temper him."

I didn't want to participate in what was apparently going to become a good cop/bad cop interrogation. But it was either that, or leave Val to the mercies of the bad cop. She'd gone from my best friend to my worst enemy, but there were some things I didn't want to happen even to my worst enemy. I had a feeling Adam was one of them.

"Let's go," I said, and let Dominic lead the way.

It seemed like Dominic had parked about three miles away. Or maybe I was just anxious. I hurried us both along as fast as I could.

We drove back to Adam's house in silence. My last faint hope that Val was my friend had finally died. There was a hollow ache in my chest. I wanted to know why she'd done it, why she was party to a plot to destroy the demon king. Then I wondered why I was so sure Lugh was the good guy in this scenario. I mean, I had only his word for it that he meant the human race well. Maybe he was Evil Incarnate, and Val was right to want to destroy him.

Maybe, but I didn't think so. If Lugh were the bad guy, and Val my friend, she would at least have explained to me why she was trying to kill me.

Dominic pulled into the parking lot across from Adam's house. He didn't pull into a space, though, instead slipping a key out of his pocket and handing it to me. I blinked at him.

"You're not coming in?"

He shook his head. "I'm going back to my place for a while." He motioned at the house with one hand. "I don't want to get in the middle of all that."

I gave him a cold look. "Ignorance is bliss, is that what you're telling me?"

He didn't answer, but I could see my words had hurt him. This time, I wasn't entirely sorry. If he was going to condone whatever it was Adam was doing, then he should be willing to face it head-on.

I slid out of the car without another word, closing the door with unnecessary force. Dominic drove away as soon as I'd crossed the street.

For one agonizing moment when I shoved the key in the lock, I was tempted to follow Dominic's lead and run away. I didn't want to face this battle, didn't want to see what Adam had already done to my former best friend. But I couldn't abandon her to his mercy, no matter what she'd done.

The house was still and quiet when I stepped inside. My palms were damp, and I wiped them on my pants legs as I dragged myself toward the stairs. I knew where I'd find Adam and Val.

A whip cracked. Val screamed.

I lost my reluctance and charged up the staircase. The door to the black room was closed, but not locked. I burst into the room, then skidded to a halt.

Val's hands were attached to the footboard of that huge iron bed by two sets of handcuffs, one for each hand, arms stretched to each side of her so there wasn't much wiggle room. Adam stood behind her, a long, vicious-looking whip dangling from his hand. The back of Val's shirt was ripped open, but I didn't see any marks. It seemed that so far, Adam had done no more than scare the shit out of her.

"Well, well," Adam said, turning to look at me, "how nice of you to join us, Morgan. I was just asking your friend Valerie to tell me who she's working with. She's been reluctant to answer. Perhaps you can convince her that I'm not bluffing."

He swirled the handle of the whip like he was stirring batter, and the leather thong circled like a mini-cyclone.

"Morgan!" Val said, looking over her shoulder at me. Her eyes were almost swollen shut with tears. Rivers of mascara smeared her cheeks. "Please help me!"

I swallowed down all my anger at Adam. He hadn't actually hurt her. Yet. And if I could get her to talk, he wouldn't have to—and I wouldn't have to try to stop him.

"I'm not really in a position to help you, Val," I said, hoping I sounded calmer than I felt. "I'm at quite a disadvantage against Adam in hand-to-hand combat. Your best bet is to tell him what he wants to know."

She sobbed. "I don't know anything! Please, Morgan—"

"You were on your way to report me as an illegal demon so I'd be executed, and now you're asking for my help?"

Adam grinned at me. "I thought *I* was supposed to be the bad cop."

"Shut up, Adam."

He was still twirling the whip. He moved it closer to Val, so that the circling leather brushed her pants leg. She yelped and tried to jerk away, but of course she didn't have anywhere to go.

"Val, please tell him what he wants to know.

He . . . gets off on hurting people. Don't give him an excuse."

Adam raised his eyebrows at me, then glanced down pointedly at his crotch. I followed his gaze even though I didn't want to. Apparently, he wasn't enjoying himself at the moment. Of course, he hadn't actually hurt her yet.

"I'd tell him if I knew anything!" Val said, sounding desperate.

"That would have sounded much more convincing before our little chat at lunch," I said, and Val had no clever response.

"I suggest you back up a bit," Adam said to me as he stopped his little twirling game. "I'm very good with this, but you're still better off keeping your distance."

"Morgan!" Val screamed.

"Don't do it, Adam. Please. Let's just—"

He didn't wait for me to finish. The whip sliced through the air. The crack was almost deafening in the closed room. Val's scream tore at my conscience, but I honestly didn't know how I could stop Adam unless I could talk him out of it.

An angry red welt rose on the skin of Val's back. She sobbed, sucking in great gulps of air.

"That was a warning stroke," Adam said. His voice was dead calm, no hint of emotion in it. "The next one draws blood. Tell me who your associates are, and there won't be a next one."

"Please," she begged in a tear-ravaged voice. "Morgan, don't let him do this to me."

I should have been content to see Val in pain after what she'd done, but she'd been my best friend for too long. I couldn't make myself stop caring about her, at least not this fast. My eyes pleaded with Adam to stop, or at least to slow down so I could think of some way out of this.

"If you're too squeamish for this, love, then I suggest you leave. The unpleasant reality is that people are trying to kill you, and if we don't find out who they are, they'll eventually succeed. Considering the manner in which they plan to do it, I think a few lashes from a bullwhip are rather inconsequential."

It was hard to argue his logic, though I wanted to. I decided perhaps I had a better chance of influencing Val than Adam.

"Val, please. I can't stop him from hurting you. How much of this do you think you can stand before you break? Why put yourself through this?"

She didn't answer me, but she looked at me through those tear-filled eyes, and there was a hardness in her expression that chilled me. I don't know what she was about to say to me, because at that moment, the whip cracked again.

Another scream tore from Val's throat. As Adam had threatened, this time he'd drawn blood. My gorge rose, and for a moment I felt sure I was going to be sick.

"I'm not playing with you anymore, Valerie," Adam said. "Talk now, or you'll regret it more than you can possibly imagine."

In desperation, I took a step closer to them, reaching out a hand toward Adam. The whip flicked casually, almost playfully, in my direction. I jumped back with a little gasp, though he hadn't come close to hitting me.

"I mean it, Morgan," he said, his voice still calm and devoid of emotion. "If you can't take this, then get out. There's more at stake here than just your life, remember. I'll do whatever I have to do to break her."

"Please, no more," Val sobbed. "I'll tell you what you want to know. Just ... don't hurt me anymore."

I hugged myself, wondering if Dominic hadn't had the right idea all along. But no, if this was happening on my behalf, then it was my duty to bear witness, no matter how much I hated it.

"Who do you report to?" Adam asked.

"Andrew Kingsley," she answered.

"No, you don't," Adam countered. "You just know we already suspect Andrew, so you're throwing out a name you feel safe giving us. Try again."

Val hiccupped. "I don't know his name," she said, and it was almost a wail. "I call him Orlando, but that's a code name, not his real name."

"Human or demon?"

"Human."

"Describe him."

She was still sniffling and hiccupping, so the description came in short little bursts. "About five-ten ... two hundred pounds ... blond hair, blue eyes. Looks like a good candidate for a host, but isn't one."

"And who else is in on this plan?"

"I don't know. They make sure us small fry don't know enough to give everything away. Andrew would know a lot more than I do."

"Why, Val?" I asked. I knew there were more important questions, but my broken heart needed to know. "Why did you do this to me? Why did you let Andrew force this ... *thing* ... on me, and then try to—" My voice cut off, because I was going to start crying myself if I said another word.

"I'm really, really sorry, Morgan." She looked at me over her shoulder, and her eyes were wide and oh-so sincere. "You weren't supposed to be the host. Andrew acted on his own before we were ready. He has his own agenda, and it doesn't always mesh with ours. I would never have let this happen to you if I'd known. I didn't even know Andrew was one of us until after you showed me that note. When I reported it, he paid me a visit, and that's how I found out. I'm just a foot soldier, not even close to a general."

I took a deep breath to steady my nerves. Not that they could possibly be too steady at a time like this. "So if you'd put Lugh into some other host and burned that host alive, it would have been all right?"

She raised her chin. "Sometimes you have to make sacrifices for the greater good."

"I notice you didn't volunteer to host Lugh for the weenie roast. What is it you're sacrificing exactly?"

"Let's talk about this greater good of yours," Adam said. Val tensed. "Do you have any idea what it is you're fighting for?"

"We're fighting to preserve the natural order." She sounded mighty proud of herself. "If Lugh becomes king of the demons, he'll cut off contact between the Demon Realm and the Mortal Plain. We'd lose the demons, lose everything they do for us, all their good works."

Adam snorted. "Do you actually believe that?" He looked at me. "Lugh wants to outlaw the possession of unwilling hosts. As of now, while it's against human laws, it's not against ours. Nice irony that they forced him into an unwilling host, don't you think?"

I turned my gaze from Adam to Val, thinking she was about to refute what he'd said. She didn't.

"If enough humans were willing to offer themselves, then demons wouldn't need the unwilling!" Her eyes practically glowed with fervor. "The human race *needs* them. They're so much more powerful, so much wiser than we are."

My mind couldn't even encompass what Val was saying. I stood there like an idiot, unable to think of any reply.

Adam snorted. "Dougal has about as much respect for the human race as a human has for a horse. You would make your entire race into slaves?"

"We need guidance!" she answered. "We're like children next to the demons. A child might be frightened of the dentist and unwilling to go, but a responsible parent doesn't let the child make that kind of decision."

Had Val always believed this bullshit? I mean, she was an *exorcist*, for crying out loud! True, she'd always been more pro-demon than any other exorcist I'd met, and exorcists only cast out the scum of demon society. But considering what she now admitted to condoning, I wondered just how many of the demons she'd "exorcized" were still hanging around the Mortal Plain. And I wondered how she'd been able to hide her true feelings from me so long. She was just another fanatic. Like my parents. Like my brother. It sickened and saddened me.

"You're a deluded fool, Valerie," Adam said. "What else can you tell us about your organization?"

She raised her chin. "I can tell you that we'll win in the end. We'll do whatever is necessary to stop your puny king from taking the throne and destroying centuries of accord between demons and humans."

Adam shook his head in disgust. He coiled the whip and hung it from one of the pegs on the far wall.

Once again, my naïveté reared its ugly head. When he approached Val, I assumed he was going to unlock the handcuffs and let her loose.

Before I had any inkling of what he was about to

do, he'd placed his hands on both sides of Val's head and twisted.

The sound was sickening. Val's lifeless body collapsed to the floor, at least, as much as it could with her wrists still cuffed to the bed. My stomach rebelled, and I vomited, over and over until I had nothing left in me. My whole body was wracked with tremors. I didn't look up when I saw Adam's feet approach.

I'd always known Adam was a hard-ass. And, truth be told, I'd always been just a little afraid of him. But nothing could have prepared me for the shock of witnessing his transition from legal, law-abiding citizen to rogue demon under an automatic death sentence.

He left for a moment, then returned with a handful of towels, which he threw on the floor. He handed me a damp washcloth. I didn't want to take anything from him, but I wanted to get my face clean, so I grabbed it. The washcloth felt cool against my blazing cheeks and forehead.

"I'm sorry, Morgan," he said. "But it had to be done. If I'd let her go, she would have tried to have us both executed by the state. And she might have succeeded. Lugh is an illegal demon, and after kidnapping and assaulting Valerie, I'm now officially rogue."

He moved away from me. I looked up and saw him finally unlock the handcuffs. When Val's body slumped all the way to the floor, I thought I might have another round of dry heaves.

"How could you do that?" I whispered. "You just murdered her in cold blood." My God, Adam was a *cop*! How could he just murder someone like that?

He sighed. "I did what I had to do."

I looked up at him. His face showed a hint of mild regret, but no more than that. I wondered how many people he'd killed before, because I couldn't imagine him being this blasé about it if Val were his first.

"It doesn't even bother you, does it?" I asked. Numbness crept through my limbs and mind. This couldn't be real. I couldn't have just stood by and watched while Adam killed someone.

No, not just *someone*. Val. The woman who'd been my best friend for a decade.

But also, the woman who'd planned to kill me.

Adam looked thoughtful. When he answered, it was clear that he chose his words carefully. "It bothers me that you had to see this on top of all the other shocks you've had lately. It doesn't bother me that I killed her."

I shook my head. "How could that not bother you?"

He left Val's body lying on the floor and came to squat in front of me so he could meet my eyes.

"I'm not human, Morgan. Demons are very similar to humans, on so many levels that it's sometimes hard for you to remember that we're not. My host is unhappy with me for what I've done, but that's a very human reaction. I did what I had to do. Demons don't beat themselves up for doing what they think is right, even when they've had to do something distasteful."

I shook my head, unable to absorb what he was saying.

"To put it into perspective—if for some unimaginable reason, I were put into a position where killing Dominic was the right thing to do, I'd do it."

I gasped. I could actually feel the blood draining from my face. Adam hammered his point home.

"I'd do it, and I wouldn't feel bad about it." He frowned at my look of absolute horror. "I don't mean I wouldn't grieve. I mean I wouldn't feel *guilty*. And that's not because of *who* I am, but because of *what* I am. Our ... psychology, I guess you'd call it ... is different from yours."

I tasted bile on the back of my throat. "Get away from me."

"Morgan—"

"Get the fuck away from me!" It came out almost a shriek. I wanted to have a fit of screaming hysterics, but I had to hold together just a little longer.

Adam's face hardened. "You can be as pissed at me as you want, but just ask yourself what you would have done differently."

"I wouldn't have killed her, you bastard!"

He stood up and moved away from me. "So you would have just let her go? You would have let her call the police and turn us both in?"

I was hugging myself, and my hand pressed against something hard in my jacket pocket. My heart almost stopped.

It was the Taser Dominic had given me. I'd had it all along, had had the means to stop Adam from torturing Val, had had the means to stop him from killing her. And I'd forgotten all about it.

In hindsight, I can't help wondering if my subconscious had agreed with Adam's methods and made me forget I had the Taser. Maybe for all my righteous indignation, I'd *wanted* him to do those terrible things. If I hadn't, wouldn't I have realized that Adam couldn't let Val go free? Wouldn't I have known what that had meant?

Wouldn't I have stopped him?

In a moment of perfect clarity in the midst of a raging storm of emotions, I realized one thing: I couldn't stay in the same house with Adam for another moment. He might be my only ally, but if today's events proved

anything, it was that sometimes you're better off without allies.

I knew Adam wouldn't let me leave without a fight.
If I gave him any clue what I was going to do, I'd find
myself locked in the room next door. So while he was
bending over Val's body, I armed the Taser and shot
him in the back.

Chapter 17

I left Adam's house in something of a daze. I think it was shock.

I took the Taser with me, as well as the shopping bags I'd left in the bedroom. Adam was starting to regain control of his limbs when I was ready to leave, so I shot him again. He tried to say something—no doubt something really complimentary about me—but the electricity had damaged his control too badly and all he could do was glare at me as I walked out.

By the time I hit the sidewalk, my cheeks were drenched with tears. I swiped them angrily away, then made an anonymous 911 call on Val's cell phone, which I still had.

I didn't regret that call until about an hour later, when I checked in to a cheap airport motel under an assumed name. When the door closed behind me, and I was finally able to let go of the reins, I threw myself onto the bed and sobbed, not even sure what I was sobbing for.

Grief over Val's death? Maybe. Guilt over my role in it? Certainly. Fear for my life? That was there, too.

When the tears had run their course, leaving me exhausted in body and soul, I finally let myself think about what I'd just done to Adam. Would my anonymous call be enough to get a search warrant? Would Adam have had time to hide the evidence before the cops arrived?

If the cops found Val's body and Adam was executed as a rogue demon, would I ever be able to live with myself?

My head started to pound fiercely. I hauled myself into the shower, hoping the hot water would soothe me, but of course it didn't.

This wasn't the first time in my life I'd acted first and thought later. But never had the potential consequences been so terrible. I prayed that Adam had hidden the body and the evidence well, prayed that I wouldn't have to face the consequences of my actions.

Yeah, technically it was Adam who would have to face them, if it came to that, but I'm really, really good at guilt, and I was practically choking on it. As far as I could tell, I hadn't done a single thing right since the moment I'd realized I was possessed.

Feeling maudlin in the extreme, I called Brian. I didn't know if he'd take my call after the way I'd left, but I desperately needed to reach out to someone. I'd alienated everyone who mattered, and I'd never felt so alone in all my life.

I got his answering machine. It tells you something about my state of mind that hearing his voice even on a recording made me feel just a little better. I waited a bit to see if he would pick up, but he didn't. I told him I was sorry, that I loved him, and that I would try him again later.

The headache got worse, the pain stabbing through my eye socket all the way to the base of my skull. I begged some aspirin from the desk clerk, but it didn't help. I wondered if I was having a stroke or something. I'd had stress headaches before, but never anything like this.

Moaning in misery, I lay down on the bed and clutched the pillow to my face, blocking out all the light, but the pain just wouldn't let up.

Until I opened my eyes to find myself in Lugh's place again. The pain was blessedly gone, but one look at Lugh sent my sense of relief scurrying for cover.

Black leather, as usual, but different this time. He looked like a Hell's Angel crossed with one of those professional wrestlers who always play the bad guy. Heavy loops of silver chain decorated his jacket. Fingerless gloves with silver-studded cuffs circled his wrists. And instead of his usually elegant leather boots, he wore heavy, cruel-looking shit-kickers.

The look on his face said *I* was the shit he wanted to kick. I tried willing myself to wake up, but—wouldn't you know it?—this time it didn't work.

Lugh advanced on me, both his hands clenched at his sides, his eyes glowing like beacons. I backed away. I had a feeling that even though this was a dream, he was perfectly capable of making me hurt in it.

He kept coming, and I kept backing up, until I hit a wall that was closer than I'd expected. Maybe it hadn't been there until that moment. I put my hands up in a defensive gesture as he closed the last little bit of distance between us.

I could no more hold him off than I could a tank. His chest hit my palms and pushed my arms back. He slapped his hands hard against the wall on each side of my head and leaned into me.

I'd thought Adam was scary-looking when he was mad. Lugh was the stuff of nightmares. The menace radiated from him in almost palpable waves, pounding against my defenses. Every nerve in my body demanded I run for my life, but I couldn't force a single muscle to move.

Not that I could have gone anywhere anyway. He'd parked himself in my personal space, and he wasn't leaving until he was good and ready.

I swallowed hard and closed my eyes, unable to bear the pressure of his gaze.

"Morgan Kingsley, you are a *fool*," he growled. And I mean *growled*. The sound of his voice was barely human.

I quivered in terror. And believe me, I'm not the quivering type. Bravado is one of my best friends, but I couldn't muster a drop of it.

"Just what are you planning on doing?" he continued, still in that awful, growling voice. "You have no home, you have no friends, you have no resources, and you've fled from the one man who can actually help you!"

He was so furious I felt little drops of spit pepper my cheeks. Talk about realistic dreams...

"Open your eyes and look at me!" he commanded.

But I was too damn scared. I guess I was hoping if I didn't look, he'd go away, kind of like the monster under the bed.

He didn't.

One hard, strong hand closed around my throat and squeezed.

I gasped, and my eyes opened of their own accord. Once I met his gaze, I couldn't look away. And I wanted to, believe me I did.

Still holding me by the throat and squeezing just

hard enough to make breathing difficult, he leaned forward until his nose almost touched mine.

"The instant you wake up, you will call Adam and have him come to pick you up. Assuming, that is, that he hasn't been arrested thanks to you."

I grabbed his wrist with both my hands and tried to break his grip on my throat. I wasn't surprised when he didn't budge.

"He might not let me come back," I managed to choke out with what little air I could suck in. Funny how I needed to breathe even in a dream.

"He will. Unlike you, Morgan, he's not childish enough to let his emotions rule his common sense. And he knows there's more at stake here than your life."

"You don't understand. I watched him kill Val in cold blood!"

"I don't understand?" He shook me, rattling my teeth. "I'm a passenger in your body. I can read your thoughts. I understand *exactly* what you did. I understand that you were angry with yourself for allowing him to hurt her, and that you took your anger out on him in the worst possible way."

I had to close my eyes again, couldn't face Lugh's anger, couldn't face what I'd done.

Because, of course, Lugh was right.

He let go of my throat, and even with my eyes closed I knew he'd moved away, though I hadn't heard any footsteps. My back slid down the wall until my butt hit the floor. Eyes still closed, I touched a hand to my throat to see if he'd left bruises. It seemed not.

When I gathered enough courage to open my eyes again, I saw that he'd conjured a wing chair out of nowhere and was sitting on the very edge of it about ten feet away. His eyes still glowed, and his posture was still stiff and angry, but at least he'd given me some breathing room.

My voice came out weak and breathy when I spoke. "If you know my thoughts, then you know how sorry I am for what I did. If I could take it back, I would. But I'm only human. And watching him kill Val, hearing him tell me that he could even kill Dominic and not feel bad about it, was one too many shocks to absorb. I cracked."

A little bit of the tension eased out of Lugh's shoulders, and I thought his eyes glowed a little less brightly. "Adam has not often walked the Mortal Plain," he said. Thank God he wasn't growling anymore. The sound had been more disturbing than I wanted to admit.

"He realizes that humans don't understand demons very well," Lugh continued. "He doesn't realize that the reverse is also true."

If psychoanalyzing Adam would have a calming effect on Lugh, I was all for it. "What do you mean?"

"What he said to you was foolish, a tactical error. And you don't entirely understand what he meant."

"And you do."

He shrugged. Yes, the glow in his eyes was definitely dying down. Hallelujah!

"I'm a demon, so yes, I do. I'll try to explain it, but I can't guarantee I'll succeed." He was feeling so warm and fuzzy toward me he even offered a hint of a smile. "Just like I couldn't guarantee to make Adam understand why a human might feel guilty over what he'd done.

"It's not that we are without emotions. And it's not that we don't feel guilt. You remember how Adam reacted when you told Dominic his demon wasn't dead?"

I nodded. How could I forget? And yes, refusing to heal himself had obviously been a sign of guilt.

"We are by our nature a very pragmatic people. We will feel guilt and regret over something we feel we should have done differently. But we are better than humans at accepting those things we cannot change."

I thought about that a bit, rolled the idea around my mind and tried to understand it. "So Adam could kill Dominic without remorse as long as he believed it was something he couldn't change? Even though he's very fond of Dominic?"

Lugh smiled gently. "He's more than just 'fond' of him, but yes, that's the point he was trying to make. When he's had more experience with human thoughts and feelings, he'll understand why that was the wrong time to make the point."

I wasn't sure there was a *right* time to make a point like that. For one thing, it showed me just exactly how much you could ever trust a demon. Knowing that no matter how much they cared about you, they'd be willing to kill you if the situation warranted was not a comforting thought. Lugh might think of it as "pragmatic." I wondered if "ruthless" wasn't a better word.

"I think there's something else you should know," Lugh continued. "Something that might help you accept Adam a little better."

If he thought I was going to "accept" Adam, he was deluding himself. Naturally, I didn't share my opinion, though I suppose he knew it anyway.

"Adam's enjoyment of causing pain isn't typical human sadism."

Typical human sadism?

I think Lugh heard that thought, because a hint of a smile touched his lips, then vanished.

"A human who enjoyed the excesses that he does

wouldn't be so scrupulous about how he found his gratification. A human wouldn't have tempered his tastes for his lover as Adam has for Dominic. There are many psychological traits that would accompany sadism of that level if he were human—a need to dominate and humiliate, for one—that aren't present in Adam.

"I mentioned that he has not often walked the Mortal Plain. In our homeland, we are incorporeal, which means we do not have the sense of touch. It is not at all uncommon for young, inexperienced demons to be fascinated by the novelty of touch, and therefore to enjoy even sensations that a human would consider unpleasant."

This conversation made me extremely uncomfortable—I try to be tolerant, but obviously I don't always succeed—and I wanted it over as soon as possible. Unfortunately, my mouth didn't get the memo and invited further comment.

"From what I can see, he enjoys giving it, not receiving it."

"I'm sure he finds both appealing and fascinating."

I remembered hearing his cries of pain when Dominic whipped him, and I remembered thinking it didn't sound like he was enjoying himself one bit.

Apparently, Lugh read my mind and answered the question I didn't want to ask.

"Even those who find the physical sensations fascinating usually have a limit to how much they can stand. I suspect Adam specifically instructed Dominic to pass his limits. No doubt it was the only way he could think of to atone for what he'd done."

I supposed that made sense. There was no way I could interpret what had happened as anything other than penance, and for it to be penance, it had to be unpleasant. I wouldn't exactly say I understood what Lugh was telling me. What I *did* understand was that I couldn't always interpret Adam's actions based on human psychology.

I guess it's better to *know* that you don't understand something. Prevents you from making incorrect assumptions, or at least lets you make fewer of them. I hoped.

"So now that you know all these things, will you go back to Adam's house?" Lugh asked.

My cowardly insides shouted a frantic "no!" What I said instead was, "I'll think about it."

The tension returned to Lugh's posture. "Don't think about it. Just do it."

I bristled. "You may be king of the demons, but you're not the king of me. I'll think about it."

Lugh stood up. The eerie glow returned to his eyes as he stared down at me. "I suggest you think very, very quickly."

"Or what?" I asked. I actually wasn't trying to give him attitude—I just heard the undertone of threat and wanted to know what the threat was.

"Or I'll have to resume my efforts to take control while you're conscious."

That brought me to my feet in a hurry. "Bullshit. If you could take control, you'd have done it by now."

"When I first succeeded in controlling your dreams, I stopped trying to control your body. You've seen evidence that my control of your dreams has improved. Why would you think I won't get better at controlling your body?"

My stomach really didn't like this conversation. "You're just trying to intimidate me into doing what you want. It won't work."

"Why do you think you had such a terrible headache this evening?"

That stopped me cold, but only for a minute. "Stress will do that to a person."

"So will fighting a demon."

I swallowed hard. "So you're saying you were trying to take over and that's why my head hurt?"

"Yes. I'd vowed not to interfere with your life any more than necessary, but when you flee the only person who can help you, I have to protect you from your own foolishness."

It was my turn to growl. "I can protect my own damn self! Stay out of it."

"Even supposing I could, I wouldn't. Must I keep reminding you that there's more at stake here than your own life? Are you so small-minded?"

"Yes!" I screamed, angry and scared and desperate. "I never wanted to be a fucking hero. If I wanted to be a hero, I'd have volunteered to host. I'm a small-minded, selfish little bitch who just wants to live her own small, unimportant life in peace. I never asked for fucking Raphael to torture the fucking king of the demons by foisting him on me!" I sucked in a great gulp of air—I'd said all of that so far without breathing—but before I could continue the tirade, Lugh closed the distance between us and enveloped me in his arms.

I tried to pull away, but he was far too strong for me. My face ended up pressed against his chest, his hand splayed on the side of my head to hold me there. The leather of his jacket was much softer than it looked.

His other arm wrapped around my shoulders in a solid, unbreakable grip. His chin rested on the top of my head. I inhaled deeply, trying to calm myself, and caught the delicious scent of him, that unknown, exotic, musky scent that was like nothing else I'd ever smelled.

"I'm sorry, Morgan," he murmured, his hand rubbing gently over my back. "I'm so sorry you were dragged into this. I can't tell you how much I wish it hadn't happened, and not just because of the threat to me. I'll do everything I can to make things better for you and to keep you safe."

He felt so warm and strong against me that it sapped all my will. I slipped my arms around his waist and let him hold me, and tried for just a few minutes not to think.

One thing I'll say for Lugh—he gives great hugs. By the time he let go, the hysteria that had threatened to overwhelm me was gone. I wasn't quite at the acceptance stage yet—way too much fight left in me for that—but at least I was calm, steady, and rational.

He cupped my cheeks in his hands, tilting my head up toward his. For a moment, I thought he was going to kiss me. I *wanted* him to kiss me, wanted to lose myself in sensual pleasure. But he didn't, and it was just as well. I still loved Brian, and if by some miracle I lived through all this and persuaded him to take me back, I didn't want to have betrayed him in even such a small way.

I took a deep, steadying breath. "If I can come up with a solid plan of action that doesn't involve Adam, will you let me do it?"

He raised his eyebrows. "I would be most interested to hear it."

Yeah, so would I. "Is that a yes?"

He gave me one of those searching looks I was learning to hate. Then he nodded slowly. "If the plan is good, then I won't try to take you over. But understand, as much as I regret that you've been dragged into this against your will, I have a duty both to my people and to yours. I will not let sentiment interfere with doing what I know is right."

Yeah, he'd made that point crystal clear. "I understand," I assured him. "Give me twenty-four hours to come up with something better. If I can't, and if Adam is still willing and able to help me, then I'll go back."

I don't think he was thrilled with the compromise, but he accepted it.

Now all I had to do was come up with a brilliant plan in twenty-four hours or less.

Chapter **18**

No brilliant inspirations struck me while I slept, and I woke up on Monday morning with no better idea what to do than I'd had when I collapsed into bed Sunday night. A long, hot shower and three cups of terrible coffee with fake cream failed to produce a solution out of thin air.

It wasn't like I had any investigative skills. By the time I'm pulled into a case, the demon has already been captured and convicted. Even if I'd *had* skills, Lugh was right about how few my resources were. I mean, my house with all my worldly goods had burned to the ground just a few days ago. I hadn't even begun to dig myself out of that mess. I suppose I needed to make sure I'd be alive in a week or so before I tried to rebuild my life.

It didn't leave me with many options.

Not to mention, there was still a murder charge hanging over my head. I checked in with my lawyer's office, just to let her know I hadn't skipped town.

After I got off the phone with my lawyer, I called Brian again. I tried him at his office, but he hadn't gotten in yet. I left another message, giving him Val's cell number. Yeah, I know it was stupid to give him the phone number of someone who'd been murdered yesterday, but I was too paranoid to give him the hotel number.

Still no brilliant plans.

I flipped on the TV, more because I wanted some background noise than because I actually wanted to watch anything that was on at nine in the morning.

God conspired against me so that as soon as the TV was on, the screen filled with Adam's handsome face. My throat tightened.

He was standing at a podium, a forest of microphones in front of him. *Special Report,* said the top left corner of the screen. Across the bottom of the screen, a headline scrolled: *Director of Special Forces, Adam White, accused of murder.*

I pressed the heels of my hands to my eyes, wishing I could make everything go away.

"Do you have any hard feelings toward your men for giving credence to the accusation?" one of the reporters asked.

"Not at all," Adam said. His deep voice and good looks gave good TV. "They were only doing their job. I'd have been upset with them if they hadn't been thorough. I'm not above the law. My only hard feelings are for whoever placed that call."

Those hot caramel eyes stared directly into the camera, seeming to look through it straight at me.

"I promise you, the perpetrator will be prosecuted to the fullest extent of the law."

I swallowed hard, instinct telling me it wouldn't be the law that prosecuted me but Adam himself.

The cell phone rang. I muted the TV but wasn't able to tear my eyes from the screen as I fumbled the phone open, praying it was Brian.

"Hello?" I said.

"Morgan, Morgan, where is your head, little girl?"

I shot to my feet, wishing I'd checked the number before I'd answered. "What do you want, Andrew?"

"Take a few mental leaps with me, dear sister. You called in a complaint to the police yesterday on Valerie's cell phone. The police investigated your claim and found it was a hoax. Adam White is now hell-bent on arresting you. And you're still carrying the cell phone. Should I give you a lesson in modern technology?"

I stifled a groan. Yes, I was a moron. But I wasn't used to being on the run, hadn't thought things through that far. Of course the police would be able to trace the cell phone. They could be converging on me any moment.

I started shoving my few belongings back in shopping bags, holding the cell phone to my ear with my shoulder. Yes, I should have hung up immediately and run for the hills, but I couldn't help myself.

"Why are you calling me, Andrew? Why do *you* care?"

He chuckled. "Let's just say it would be inconvenient for everyone involved if you were arrested and they revoked your bail. So get your ass out of wherever you are and dump the phone. And don't worry, sis—I'll still be able to find you when I need you."

He hung up then, which was just as well or I'd probably have wasted more time cussing him out.

I was out of my room within five minutes, but I took the cell phone with me. I didn't want to lead the police to the room, where they'd find my fingerprints all over the place and know for sure I was the one who'd placed the call. I turned it off and removed its battery, hoping that would be enough to stop the police from homing in on it.

A police car pulled into the hotel parking lot as my cab pulled out. I held my breath, but the police didn't come screaming after us. I had the driver take me to Front Street—so named because it fronts the Delaware River. I got out, then tried to look inconspicuous as I did my best to wipe every fingerprint off the phone and its battery, then tossed both in the river.

My head started hurting as I wandered aimlessly along the riverfront, trying to figure out what my next step was. I pinched the bridge of my nose and said, "Cut it out, Lugh. You gave me twenty-four hours, remember?" The headache went away, but it had been an effective reminder.

I found a pay phone and called Brian, talking to his voice mail again. I told him to ignore the number I'd given him before. I wished like hell he'd just pick up the phone. I longed for him in ways I'd never imagined I could.

I took a bus back into Center City and bought a prepaid phone. I worried that Adam with his police resources might still be able to trace it to me. But my delusion that I'd be able to take care of myself was fraying around the edges.

I felt so desperate, I actually considered calling my mom and asking for her help. Luckily, I had a few more functioning brain cells than that. My mom claims she loves me despite my copious flaws, but she practically worships golden boy Andrew. She'd turn me over to him in a heartbeat, wouldn't even consider the possibility that he might not be the Dalai Lama, Jesus Christ, and Mother Teresa all rolled into one.

At around three o'clock, I tried Brian yet again. And got his voice mail, yet again. For some reason, that bothered me, and I called the main office number. The receptionist told me Brian hadn't been in all day and that he hadn't called in sick. Everyone was worried about him.

I was worried about him, too. I assured the receptionist that I'd go over to his condo and make sure he wasn't lying unconscious—or worse—on the floor.

All my keys were buried somewhere in the rubble that had once been my house, but I had a spare set at my office. I didn't like going there, where people who wanted me dead might expect me to go, but I didn't think I had a whole lot of choice.

"Hey, Lugh?" I whispered as I walked, hoping people on the street would think I was talking into a cell phone. "Can you let me know if you see anyone or anything that should worry me when I get near the office?"

My answer was a brief stab of pain through my eyeball. Lovely. I took that as a yes and tried not to scare the crap out of myself by thinking about being able to communicate with him while I was conscious.

No headaches battered at me as I approached my office. Didn't stop me from constantly looking over my shoulder and starting at shadows.

Of course, with my keys lost, I had to find a custodian to open my office for me. The delay made me twitchy, but eventually I tracked someone down to let me in.

I made a beeline for my pencil drawer. I'd yanked it open and grabbed my spare set of keys before I noticed the padded manila envelope that sat on my chair.

It shouldn't have been there. When I'm not in the office, my deliveries go to the mailroom downstairs.

And no one but the custodial staff had keys to my office.

Nervously, I upended the envelope onto my desk. A videocassette and a sheet of paper fell out.

The note was short and to the point: *Morgan. When you've watched this tape, call me on my cell phone. Andrew.*

Words can't describe how much I didn't want to see whatever was on this tape. Unfortunately, not watching wasn't an option.

I didn't have a VCR in my office, and of course I didn't have a home to go to. But Brian's place was only a couple of blocks away. I hoped I'd let myself in and find out he was home sick and just hadn't bothered to call his office to let them know.

I wasn't holding my breath.

By the time I let myself into Brian's condo, my knees were literally knocking, and my stomach was in turmoil. I wondered if I was on the way to a nervous breakdown, then sternly told myself I couldn't *afford* a nervous breakdown.

Brian wasn't home, and there were a gazillion messages on his answering machine. Looked like he hadn't been home in a while. I looked at the tape in my hand and prayed it wasn't what I thought it was.

My hands shook when I stuffed it into Brian's VCR and hit play.

Static for a moment. Then the picture I'd been dreading.

He was chained to a wall, hands above his head, a ball gag stuffed into his mouth. They'd stripped him down to his tightie-whities and shackled his ankles together.

The wall he was chained to was of old-looking, rough stone blocks, no doubt to give the room its dungeon–cum–torture chamber atmosphere. There were plenty of other sets of chains hanging from those walls. The camera panned to show a collection of whips that would put Adam's to shame, then a brazier holding a set of glowing irons, then something that looked like it might actually be a genuine rack.

When the camera panned back to Brian, he wasn't alone anymore. A cloaked and hooded figure stood in front of him, weaving a scalpel dextrously through his fingers. Brian watched the show with wide, scared eyes.

I was shaking my head, hand clamped over my mouth to contain my scream of pain and outrage.

The hooded figure smiled into the camera and stopped playing with the scalpel. He stepped toward Brian. I tried to brace myself, knowing what I was about to see, knowing I should just stop the tape now, knowing I couldn't.

He removed the gag, letting Brian suck in a few frantic gasps of air. But he hadn't removed it for any humanitarian purpose. He'd removed it so I could hear the man I loved scream when that scalpel sliced through his pectoral muscle.

I screamed, too, hoping my hand over my mouth was deadening the sound so the neighbors wouldn't call the cops. Blood dripped down Brian's chest and belly, hitting the waistband of his briefs, then soaking in. His eyes were squeezed shut, his teeth clenched, trying not to make any more noise. But he screamed anyway when the torturer sliced again.

I wanted to hurl myself into the TV, magically transport myself across time and space to save Brian. The feeling of helplessness was a crushing weight on my chest and shoulders.

The torturer faced the camera again. All I could see of his face behind the hood were a pair of blue eyes with darkened pupils and his thin lips, raised in a smile. He was enjoying himself. My gorge rose, but I forced it back down. I'd go puke my guts out in a minute. First, I had to see this through to the end.

"This was just a small taste," the hooded man said, his voice digitally altered. Another hooded man came into view in the background to shove the gag back into Brian's mouth.

"Cooperate, and that will be his last. As you can see, we are wearing hoods so he can't see our faces. We have no reason not to release him when you follow our instructions."

The picture fuzzed to static. It was over.

I sprinted to the bathroom, barely making it in time.

Puking two days in a row when I wasn't sick was a new experience for me. Can't say as I was overly fond of it.

My mind kept trying to rebel, trying to say "No More! Enough! Just STOP it!" For a minute there, I seriously doubted my sanity. Anger made a feeble attempt to come to my rescue, but I was just too fucking terrified to go with it.

They had Brian. They'd *hurt* Brian! I'd desperately tried to protect him, and this is what happened. I wanted to scream, break things, curl up in a little ball and die.

But none of that would help Brian. I *had* to get him back. It was too late to keep him safe, but I was going to save him. Or die trying.

I had a sneaking suspicion the latter was more likely.

When I was stable enough to manage it, I grabbed

the nearest phone and sat down. I wasn't sure my legs would hold me if I tried standing up for this call.

I dialed Andrew's cell phone number, hating him more than I'd ever hated anyone in my life. More than I'd imagined it was *possible* to hate someone.

He answered on the second ring.

"If I ever get my hands on you," I said in response to his cheerful greeting, "I'm going to castrate you with a butter knife."

"That would be a neat trick if you could manage it. I don't think Andrew would enjoy it very much, though."

I stifled a sob. "Andrew invited you into this world, you son of a bitch, so he can go straight to hell right with you. Where's Brian?"

Raphael laughed. "What, you think it's going to be that easy?"

"Don't fuck with me, Raphael. I don't care if I have to come back from the dead to do it, but I'm going to make you pay."

"Would you like to discuss the terms for Brian's release, or would you prefer to continue hurling invective? I have plenty of time, so by all means hurl away. You're quite entertaining."

Pain stabbed through my head, making me gasp. It went away almost immediately. I had a feeling it had been unintentional, that Raphael was getting Lugh's goat almost as much as he was getting mine. I didn't want either one of us to give him that much satisfaction.

"Everything all right over there?" Raphael asked with a good imitation of polite concern.

I wished I had a zippy, smart-ass comment, something to prove that I wasn't scared of him. Maybe if I wasn't so scared of him, I could have thought of one.

"Just tell me what I have to do to get you to let him go."

"It's very simple, Morgan. A trade. You for him."

Nothing but what I'd expected. Still my stomach clenched with dread. "You want me to turn myself in so you can burn me to death."

His voice when he answered was almost gentle. "Not very appealing, I know. But your other choice is to leave him to our mercies. We'll send you a new video every day. I'll oversee it myself, make sure he isn't hurt enough to kill him. If his pain doesn't move you after a week or two, we can add some sexual molestation to the mix, see if that motivates you to change your mind."

"You motherfucking son of a—"

The phone clicked off. Hands shaking with fear and rage, I hit redial. He answered on the first ring this time.

"From now on, you'll speak to me with respect. That outburst will cost Brian another day of fun and games in our dungeon."

"Raphael—"

"You'll receive another video tomorrow. I'm sure you'll find it most entertaining."

"Please—"

"When twenty-four hours have passed, you may call me again and we will have a civilized discussion of your terms of surrender."

He hung up again. This time when I hit redial, my call went straight to voice mail.

Chapter 19

I don't know how long I sat there hyperventilating, trying not to think about what might be happening to Brian. It was probably a long time. Lugh snapped me out of it with another icepick-through-the-eye.

"Okay, okay," I said, "I'm going back to Adam's. Knock it off."

A comforting numbness stole over me, making everything seem temporarily unreal. I thanked God for small blessings, even though I knew I'd pay for it later when it all came crashing down on me again.

It was late in the afternoon, so I gambled Adam would be home from work by now, assuming the murder charge didn't interfere with his work schedule.

Dominic answered the phone. He wasn't happy to hear from me. "You've got a hell of a nerve calling here!" he snapped.

I sympathized with his feelings, but I was far too distraught to muster a good apology, and a half-assed one just wouldn't do.

"Is Adam there?"

"No. And don't call here again."

He hung up on me. I considered calling back, but decided against it. Odds were he wouldn't answer. Adam might still help me for Lugh's sake. Dominic wouldn't.

Hoping Adam would be there by the time I arrived, I left Brian's condo and took a cab across town. When the cabbie dropped me off, I glanced at the parking lot across the street and was relieved to see Adam's car there.

That relief faded quickly when I imagined facing him after what I'd done yesterday. Had it been only yesterday? So much bad shit had happened in my life in such a short time it felt like several years had to have passed.

I dragged my feet as I climbed the three steps of his stoop, butterflies flapping wildly in my empty stomach. Then I remembered what Brian was going through, remembered the fear in his kind eyes, remembered the horrifying sound of his scream. I had to do this.

I rang the bell and held my breath. The seconds ticked by like slow torture. Then Adam opened the door.

He looked at me like you'd look at a dog turd you'd stepped on in your brand-new Manolos, but he didn't slam the door in my face. He stepped back, giving me room to come in without brushing by him.

I stepped inside and tried to remember how to breathe.

Dominic stood in the entryway. If looks could kill, I'd have been dead before I took a step.

"How *dare* you!" he spat.

"Dom," Adam interrupted. "This is between

Morgan and me. Go home. I'll call you in a little while."

The dismissal seemed to hurt, though Dominic tried to cover up the expression immediately. He strode toward the door, shoving me out of the way with his shoulder.

Adam caught him by the arm as he reached for the door. They didn't say anything, but something passed between them, some communication that relieved the tension in Dominic's shoulders.

Then Dominic was gone, and I was left alone with a dangerous demon who had every reason in the world to hate my guts.

"They have Brian," I said, reaching into my bag and pulling out the hateful videotape.

Adam raised his eyebrows, a look of mild curiosity on his face.

"My boyfriend," I clarified, and my throat tightened up. "They're torturing him." My voice wobbled, but I wasn't about to let myself cry, not now. If I let go of the tight reins on my emotions, I wasn't sure my sanity would survive.

Adam didn't look particularly moved by my plight. Not that I expected him to be. I forced myself to meet his eyes.

"I'd say I'm sorry, but that's so inadequate..."

"Quite," he agreed. His was a cold, marrow-chilling anger, not like Lugh's hot rage of last night.

"But you're all right?" I asked. "They didn't...find anything?"

"No."

Okay, we were into monosyllabic answers today. I forced myself to soldier on. "They're going to keep torturing him, send me a new tape every day until I turn myself in."

"Which, of course, you're not stupid enough to do, though you're pretty monumentally stupid."

I couldn't help wincing, thinking I liked the monosyllables better. I shook my head. "I don't know what to do. I can't let them keep hurting him. I just *can't*."

"If the alternative is giving yourself up, then yes you can. If Lugh dies—if Dougal takes the throne—your people are doomed. Not immediately, because Lugh still has supporters who will fight for you when he's gone. But one day, Dougal will turn you all into empty vessels, with no purpose in life but to host whatever demon wants you.

"I'm a demon-hunter because I'm one of Lugh's lieutenants. I'm here to help send as many of Dougal's people back to the Demon Realm as possible. I'm genuinely sorry that an innocent civilian has to suffer for the cause, but the cause is more important than any one person."

Nothing there I could argue with, though I was tempted. However, I wasn't about to give up on Brian.

"Then I'm just going to have to find a third choice, aren't I?"

He just looked at me, a dead, ugly stare that told me he'd definitely made the transition from disliking me to full-out hating me. I deserved it, but that didn't make it easy to swallow.

"I have to find him," I said. "I have to find where they're keeping him and get him out of there."

"And just how do you plan to do that?"

"With your help."

He laughed, but it was a bitter, brittle laugh. "You think I'm going to help you after what you did? Woman, you've gone mad! I'll shelter Lugh and do whatever it takes to help him. You, on the other hand, can go to Hell."

He grabbed my arm and started dragging me toward the stairway.

"I promise I'll stop by every couple of days to feed you," he said as I stumbled along behind him. "Lugh won't let you starve to death, but I doubt he'll be able to do much about your discomfort. Such a shame."

"Adam, please—"

"Shut the fuck up, Morgan." We'd reached the stairs. He took them two at a time. I was practically airborne in my attempt to keep up.

"Brian doesn't deserve to suffer for my sins!" I cried.

Adam didn't answer me—why should he care what happened to a complete stranger when his king's life was at stake? Certainly he didn't care about the pain Brian's capture was causing me. We'd reached the top of the stairs. The door to the black room stood gaping open like the mouth of Hell. My stomach did a back-flip. Adam wouldn't help me out of the goodness of his heart, but I knew with a sickening certainty what might tempt him to change his mind.

"What if I gave you my consent?" I choked out as he dragged me past the black room.

He came to an abrupt stop, turning to face me. "What?"

"You said once you wanted to hurt me, and you said you needed consent." My voice shook, and I doubted there was a drop of blood left in my face. I had to focus on saving Brian. I couldn't let myself think about what I was offering. "So what if I consent? Will you help me find Brian?"

Adam's gaze filled with speculation, even as he played hard to get. "You think your noble sacrifice will move me? If I felt so inclined, I could play with you to

my heart's content and there wouldn't be anything you
could do to stop me."

Despite the dread that suffused me, I forced myself to meet his eyes. "But that wouldn't be the same,
would it?"

His eyes darkened noticeably, and my instincts insisted I should run for my life. Maybe I would have if
he hadn't still been holding my arm. A fine sheen of
sweat glowed on his upper lip, and I knew I had him.
He wanted what I was offering. And I think he would
have wanted it even if he didn't have so much anger to
work off. How often had he and Dominic indulged in
their sick "games" when Dominic's demon could heal
him? And how badly did Adam miss what they used to
have? I was betting it was pretty damn bad, judging by
the expression on his face.

"You're right," he finally said. "It wouldn't be the
same."

His gaze shifted to the black room, then back to me.
He smiled, but it was a predatory expression. "Lady,
you've got yourself a deal."

Oh dear God, help me! I prayed as, heart thunder-
ing, breath coming in gasps, I let him lead me into his
chamber of horrors.

Chapter **20**

Adam pulled me into the black room, then left me there with a terse "wait here."

He closed the door behind him, leaving me surrounded by the blackness. I shivered and crossed my arms over my chest, wondering how on earth I'd come to this. My mouth was parchment-dry, my heart thundered in my ears. I felt small, and weak, and terribly, terribly alone.

I'd never been so afraid in all my life.

After what felt like an eternity, Adam returned, carrying a large box. I didn't want to know what was inside. There was a flush to his cheeks. Anticipation radiated from him. I wracked my brain for any other way I could gain his cooperation. None leapt to mind.

Adam set the box, unopened, on the floor, then turned to me. I must have looked really pathetic. He blinked a couple of times, visibly trying to control his excitement.

"You're not in danger here, Morgan," he reminded

me. "This is going to suck, but there's nothing I can do that Lugh can't heal."

I guess he meant that to be reassuring, but I don't think anything short of an unequivocal reprieve would have reassured me at that moment.

"You'll need to take off your shirt and bra," he continued as he approached me.

I crossed my arms over my chest and swallowed hard, stepping back from him.

He stopped and raised his eyebrows. "Come now, love. You know I need bare skin for this."

But I just hugged myself more tightly, unable to bear the idea of being even partially nude in front of him. He cocked his head and regarded me curiously.

"I told you before I'm not into rape," he said. "If that's what you're worrying about. I'm sure your breasts are stunning, but I assure you I can resist the temptation."

Honestly, I didn't think my virtue was in danger. It was certainly possible that Adam liked women as much as men, but I strongly suspected he was faithful to Dominic. Don't ask me why I was so sure, but I was.

No, my reluctance was based on a core of prudishness and a terror of vulnerability. I didn't think he'd understand, even if my brain were working well enough to communicate the point to him. I figured I was doing damn well to stay upright and conscious.

He looked at me for another long moment, then started to unbutton his shirt.

That roused me from my shocky numbness. "What are you doing?" I gasped.

"I'm giving you my shirt. You can put it on backward and protect your modesty."

If I hadn't been so scared I had to fight not to wet my pants, I might have enjoyed the view when he slipped the shirt off his shoulders. He had a really nice chest. There was a part of me just woman enough to notice in the most offhand manner.

He dangled his shirt from his index finger and held it out to me. I took it.

"I'll give you one minute," he said, stepping toward the door. He raked me with a head-to-toe look. "If your modesty can handle it, you might want to take off your pants so you don't get blood on them."

The bastard winked before he slipped out the door.

Still shaking, wondering if I would ever stop, I took off my blouse and bra, then slipped my arms into Adam's shirt. It was still warm from his body. The warmth spread goose bumps over my skin. I hadn't realized I was cold until that moment.

There was no way in hell I was taking my pants off, so I just stood there and waited, trying to keep myself from thinking, from anticipating, from dreading. My eyes locked on the box Adam had set on the floor, but I wasn't remotely interested in taking a peek inside.

He came back in, glanced at my pants, and smiled, but he made no comment. I had to force myself not to back away from him as he came close, towering over me. He licked his lips, and I swallowed hard.

"Remember, love, Lugh can make it all go away. You're not in danger."

I so didn't get this guy. Why was he trying to reassure me? You'd think scaring the shit out of me would be part of the appeal of this little scenario he had going on here. He wasn't following the psychotic sadist script I'd mentally composed for him. Of course, he wasn't human. I remembered Lugh telling me Adam wasn't a "typical human sadist," and I didn't know if that made me feel better or worse.

"Having second thoughts?" he asked, the sharp edge back in his voice.

I shook my head. "I just don't understand you."

He made a sound between a snort and a laugh. "You're just figuring this out?"

He took me by the arm—a much more gentle grip this time than the last—and guided me toward the far wall. I'd assumed he'd take me to the bed, handcuff me like he had Val. I didn't like the association, seeing as Val had been dead when he was done.

But no. Either he'd made a new addition to the room since I was last in here, or I hadn't been very observant. A pair of black leather restraints hung from the wall, almost invisible against the matte black paint.

Adam hooked a low black footstool with his foot and moved it under the restraints. I must have looked puzzled, because, of course, he had to stop to explain.

"Dominic's taller than me," he said. "I need the extra height to secure him comfortably."

"TMI," I said, proud of myself for that small hint of bravado.

He laughed briefly. "Step up, please."

I was shaking so hard I might have fallen in a heap if Adam's hands hadn't steadied me. He stood on the footstool with me and stretched my arm up toward the restraint. The pull forced me almost to tiptoe, but he managed to get the cuff secured around my wrist. I closed my eyes while he secured my other wrist. The leather cuffs were soft and supple, closing with Velcro.

When he'd finished, Adam closed his hands over mine, wrapping my fingers around the chains that attached the cuffs to the wall. I could feel his quickened breaths against my hair.

"Hold on tight," he whispered in my ear.

There wasn't much room on the footstool. To reach

both my hands, he had to press his chest to my back. His skin felt scorching hot against mine. With him pressed so tight against me, I couldn't help noticing the telltale bulge in his pants. I tried to jerk away from him, but there was nowhere to go.

The asshole laughed at me. "Don't worry," he said. "I have no desire to fuck you." For reasons I didn't want to examine, that statement stung. "I suppose I've become conditioned by playing with Dom. Ordinarily, this would just be a rush, not a turn-on." He sighed, and his . . . enthusiasm waned. "When Dom could heal, it was both, but now I have to be gentle with him. With you, however, I can indulge myself."

He stepped down, and I had to suppress a whimper of fear. I forced myself to think of Brian. He didn't have a demon to heal what his captors did to him. And without Adam, I didn't have the first idea how I could save him. I had to do this, had to endure it no matter how scared I was.

Adam's hands skimmed my back. I flinched away from the touch, but he was just spreading the edges of the shirt wider, exposing more skin. He traced the outline of my tattoo with his finger, stopping at the waistband of my pants.

"Nice," he said.

I closed my eyes and rested my forehead against the wall, praying for strength.

I heard his footsteps behind me, heard cardboard sliding against cardboard, then the crinkle of tissue paper. I squeezed my eyes more tightly shut and swallowed hard on a dry throat. When I heard him coming back, my head spun for a moment. Unfortunately, I didn't pass out. I wondered what would happen if I did.

Would Lugh order Adam not to hurt me? I had no idea. All I knew was that Lugh didn't seem to have any interest in taking me over at the moment, which might have meant he was happy to let Adam have his fun.

"This one's a new toy," Adam said, and I heard the slithery sound of leather brushing over the floor. He was getting breathless again. "An eight-footer. I just barely have enough room to use it in here, and then only if I'm very careful. I special-ordered it before God's Wrath attacked Dom. I don't dare use it on him now. These long ones are a bitch to control."

I really, really didn't want to hear this.

"I probably won't make contact with the first couple of strokes," he continued. "I want to get a feel for it first. If I hit you, it's accidental. I'll let you know when I'm going to do it on purpose."

Wonderful. "Just do it and stop gloating," I snapped, my nerves too raw to contain the protest.

"I'm not gloating, love. I'm just telling you what I'm going to do. But I take your point. I'll get on with it."

I nearly screamed when the whip cracked the first time. It was so loud, so terrifying. I felt a brush of air over the skin of my back, but as he'd said, he didn't make contact. Sweat drenched my body, and I bit my lip until I tasted blood. I wished I could just hit fast-forward on this little part of my life.

The whip cracked again, and again wind whistled over my skin. Adam made a satisfied sound.

"Brace yourself, love," he said. "This one's for real."

My hands tightened convulsively on the chains. The whip sang through the air and drew a path of fire across my shoulder blades. I dragged in a frantic breath and tried to press myself into the wall, as if I could somehow escape through it.

Another crack, and this time I felt like a knife had sliced through the skin of my lower back. Something tickled, and I realized it was the drip of blood. Before I had a chance to process that thought, the whip struck again.

This time, I did scream. I couldn't help it.

I honestly don't remember much after that. It's one of those memories that my mind does its best to protect me from. I don't know how many times that whip cut through my flesh, though I know it was a lot. I screamed myself hoarse in no time flat, then was reduced to scratchy whimpers.

My knees gave out long before it was over, and I hung by my wrists, my shoulders shrieking in protest.

When it got so bad I was tempted to pray for death, Adam finally stopped. I willed myself to pass out, but I didn't.

Moments later, he was on the footstool with me again, one arm wrapped around my waist, holding me up as he freed my wrists. When I would have collapsed, he scooped me up and carried me to the black bed. He set me on my feet beside it, supporting me by my shoulders.

"Lie on your stomach, love," he said softly, and he guided me down.

The sheets were silk, I noticed irrelevantly as I buried my face in the pillowcase and tried to contain the agony. The world swam around me, a dizzy, nauseating mess.

Adam's voice came to me from what seemed like a great distance. "Don't fight it." His fingers stroked over my hair. "Let yourself go. Let Lugh fix things. It'll be over soon."

His voice was strangely soothing. I felt myself go fuzzy around the edges. With unspeakable relief, I let myself sink into the darkness.

Chapter 21

I awoke lying facedown on an unfamiliar bed. My back felt like it was on fire. I whimpered, and a gentle hand stroked over my hair.

"I'm healing it as fast as I can," Lugh said, and even in the short time it took for those words to leave his mouth, the pain lessened by a degree.

My face was buried in a wonderfully fluffy down pillow, and I didn't feel inclined to move or speak. Little by little, the pain faded. His hand slid down from my head to brush over my bare shoulders.

It was only then that I realized I was naked.

I raised my head, turning it just enough to see that a crimson silk sheet covered me from the hips down. But I could feel that silk against my bare butt, and nothing covered the top of me.

Lugh's hand continued down the center of my back. I'd have jerked away, except it's hard to do that when you're lying on your belly and you don't want to flash someone.

"Is it necessary for me to be naked?" I asked, trying for cool aplomb.

I expected either a flirtatious or a smart-ass comment in reply. Instead, I suddenly found myself wearing comfy cotton knit pajamas. The top was a barely-there camisole with spaghetti straps, but it covered everything important.

I cautiously pushed myself up and turned over. My back felt fine. Lugh fluffed a couple of pillows and laid them against the headboard, a quilted affair covered in the same red silk as the sheets. I took the hint and sat with my back resting against the pillows, hugging my knees to my chest.

The pain was gone, but my whole body felt weak and shaky. I had a feeling that evil black room would feature prominently in my nightmares for years to come.

"As long as you are hosting me," Lugh said, reading my thoughts, "you will have no nightmares."

I appreciated that more than I could say.

"That was a very brave thing you did," he continued.

I snorted. I'd practically peed my pants in terror, and I'd screamed my lungs out. Not exactly my ideal of courage.

"You can be afraid and still be brave."

I nodded my agreement, though I wasn't sure I was convinced. It wasn't like I'd had much of a choice, not unless I was willing to let Brian die a slow death without even trying to save him. I met Lugh's eyes.

"Was it brave, or just plain stupid? I mean, will Adam really help me? Because if I went through all that for nothing, someone's gonna die."

He didn't quite smile, but I could see his amusement nonetheless. "I think perhaps you understand demons a little better than either you or I realized. I don't know if there's anything else you could have offered that would have reached Adam. But you did reach him, and he'll keep his word."

Thank God! But I had to disagree with Lugh's assessment. I might have figured out how to reach Adam this once, but I couldn't say I came close to understanding him.

"Now," Lugh continued, "I believe you and I need to talk about this rescue attempt you'd like to make."

"Oh?" I sounded suspicious even to my own ears.

His eyes crinkled around the corners, but it was only a brief flash of humor. "It's going to be dangerous."

"No shit." He gave me a quelling look, and I held up my hands in surrender.

"I could stop you from trying. I could tell Adam to keep you under lock and key."

My stomach knotted and I sat bolt upright. "No! You wouldn't—"

"I said that I *could,* not that I would. But if I'm going to allow you to endanger us both, then I must set a condition."

Why did I think I wasn't going to like this?

"You mustn't be captured," he continued, his eyes boring into mine. "You know what will happen if you are."

I shuddered. Yeah, I knew. And if you'd asked me a couple weeks ago if I'd be willing to risk being burned at the stake in a rescue attempt, I probably would have said no. I'd have been ashamed of my cowardice, would have hated myself for it, but I wouldn't have believed I had it in me. There was some small sense of satisfaction in finding out I wasn't as much of a chicken-shit as I'd once thought.

"Adam is to accompany you on any rescue mission, and he is to stay at your side at all times. He will not allow you to be captured."

I let out my breath in a loud whoosh. "In other words, if it looks like they're going to capture me, he'll kill me?"

"Yes." He reached out and took my hand, prying my fingers loose from their tight fist. His grip felt firm, strong. More reassuring than it should. "It's a case of the lesser of two evils. And I am, perhaps, being an irresponsible king in even granting you the option. If I return to the Demon Realm without having defeated my enemies here, there is nothing to prevent them summoning me into another host, and I'm sure they wouldn't make the same mistake twice."

His thumb stroked over my knuckles as he held my hand. Maybe I shouldn't have let him, but I needed that lifeline. He peered at my face, his brows drawn slightly together in an expression that was almost, but not quite, a frown. I read concern and regret in his expression.

"Why would you take the risk?" I asked, meeting his gaze, trying to understand him. "Why would the king of the demons risk himself for a human pawn? Not that I'm complaining, mind you."

He smiled at that, but quickly sobered. "It's Dougal who holds human life so cheaply. I suppose I see myself as a defender of the pawns, so to speak. If I don't defend them, who will?" He laughed. The sound held no humor. "Or perhaps I'm just a misguided, self-important fool who deludes himself into thinking he can save the world."

He ran his free hand through that scrumptious black hair. This was the first time he'd seemed even vaguely human to me. It was good to know even demons suffered from self-doubt every now and again.

Before I knew what I was doing, I'd reached out to him, finally allowed myself the luxury of touching his face. Maybe he was using his understanding of my innermost thoughts and feelings to manipulate me. If so, at the moment I didn't care. I just wanted to give him comfort.

His skin was ever so smooth under my fingers, like he'd never had to shave. I almost giggled at the thought, for, of course, he never had. He closed his eyes at my touch, the corners of his mouth tipping up in a hint of a smile.

I finally gave in to the urge to touch his hair, running my fingers through the length of it. His hair was as soft and silky as it looked. I moved closer to him on the bed, and his arm slipped around my shoulders. Arousal tingled over my body, though the touch wasn't particularly sexual. I snuggled close to his body and laid my head against his shoulder.

We sat like that for a long time, taking silent comfort from one another. I realized that for the first time in my life, I actually *liked* a demon. And a demon who'd possessed me against my will, at that! Was this how Dominic had felt about Saul? If so, perhaps I understood a little better how Dom could have been so heartbroken over losing him. I still wanted Lugh gone, wanted my life back the way it was before. But I realized with a little squeeze in my heart that I would miss him.

Lugh turned and planted a soft kiss on the top of my head, then pulled away with every semblance of reluctance.

"I should let you sleep," he murmured. "You're

always tired in the morning when you've dreamed with me."

I shook my head. "I can't afford to sleep until morning. Brian needs me."

"He'll still need you in the morning. And you need your strength."

"But—"

He put a finger to my lips. "Adam will be working on the problem while you sleep. Rushing in headlong serves no purpose."

Tears prickled my eyes. "But they're going to hurt him again."

"I know," he said softly. "But they need him alive. If you mount an ill-planned rescue attempt, that won't be the case anymore. So sleep. Gather your strength. Be ready."

I took a deep, steadying breath. "Do I have any choice in the matter?"

He shrugged and his gaze slid away from mine. That was answer enough.

Accepting that I wouldn't budge him, I did my best to swallow my impatience. "I guess I'd better hurry up and sleep then."

The last thing I saw before sleep took me was a fond little smile on Lugh's lips.

The next time I awakened, I found myself in the guest room in Adam's house. Not the black room, thank you, Jesus!

I sat up tentatively, half-expecting the movement to hurt like hell, but Lugh had done a thorough job. I was even able to do a full-body stretch without a twinge. I sighed with relief.

My arms were still stuck through the sleeves of

Adam's shirt, though it had slid down so low I might as well have been topless. I pulled it off, then shuddered when I saw the dried blood that spotted the edges.

I threw the shirt across the room and slid out of bed. I didn't want to see what my pants looked like, but my skin felt the crusty texture of the waistband and I couldn't stand to wear them another moment. With shaking hands, I shoved them down my legs and stepped out, closing my eyes tightly as I tossed them, and my panties, in the same general direction I'd tossed the shirt.

I forced myself not to look as I hurried to the bathroom and turned the shower on as hot as I could stand. The water sluiced over my back and trickled down the drain, tinged with red. I fought another shudder and grabbed the soap, scrubbing frantically.

In reality, there wasn't that much blood. Adam must have cleaned me up when he brought me back to my room. I wasn't sure how I felt about him leaving me in the bloody clothes. On the one hand, it showed an admirable respect for my modesty, and I knew I'd have been pissed at him if he'd undressed me. On the other hand, it seemed a cruel reminder.

I didn't turn off the shower until the hot water started running out. Even then, I felt . . . unclean.

There had been nothing sexual about what Adam had done to me. Oh, he'd been aroused, but he'd made it crystal clear that had nothing to do with *me*.

So why did I feel violated?

I stood dripping in the shower, my forehead resting against the cool tile, trying to pull the scattered remnants of my sanity back together.

A knock on the bathroom door startled a shriek out of me.

"Morgan?" Adam asked. "Are you all right in

there? The shower stopped running twenty minutes ago."

God, had I been standing here in a daze that long?

"I'm fine," I lied. "I'll be right out."

"Come down to the kitchen when you're ready."

I made a sound he took for agreement, and I heard his footsteps retreat. I finally stepped out of the shower and dried myself off. I checked my back in the mirror, but there was no sign that I'd been whipped bloody the night before.

When I reentered the bedroom, I was grateful to see that Adam had taken the bloody clothes away. He'd laid the bra and shirt I'd worn yesterday out on the bed, along with a pair of police-issue sweatpants. I was grateful for them, since I'd left my shopping bags at Brian's yesterday.

The sweatpants were huge on me, but they didn't seem in danger of falling down, so that was okay. I didn't have any panties, but that wasn't an article of clothing I expected Adam to provide.

I realized I was stalling, so I forced myself out of the room and down the stairs. I'd gone through hell last night to secure Adam's help in rescuing Brian. Now it was time to see what my blood had bought me.

I stepped into the kitchen and was surprised to see Dominic. I guess after the way he'd reacted to me yesterday, I'd expected him to avoid me like the plague. I stood in the doorway, my feet rooted to the floor. I couldn't look at Adam. And I didn't want to look at Dominic.

Wordlessly, Dominic poured a mug of coffee and brought it to me, surprising me into looking up at him. His eyes showed nothing but sympathy, yesterday's hatred apparently forgotten. Or at least, pushed aside.

"You all right?" he asked as I took the mug and wrapped both hands around it.

"Yeah."

"Liar."

I shrugged. "The bad guys have my boyfriend. When he's safe, I'll have a nice little nervous breakdown. But I can't afford one now."

He smiled at that. "Come sit down. Adam has news for you."

By sheer force of will, I dragged myself across the room and sat at the kitchen table beside Adam. I still couldn't look at him.

"I watched the videotape," he said. He sounded completely normal, as if nothing had happened between us.

I couldn't manage that. I finally looked at him, and I know my expression was something ugly. "Did you enjoy it?"

Dominic started to say something outraged-sounding, but Adam cut him off.

"Give her a break, Dom."

Dominic shut up. I considered apologizing but decided against it.

Adam might be willing to let the smart-ass comment slide, but he wasn't about to respond to it. "I recognize the room he's in."

"What?"

"I know where they're holding him."

"How can that be?"

"Because I've been there," he answered in his best talk-slowly-so-the-moron-can-understand-you voice.

I'd never in a million years expected Adam to be able to tell me where Brian was off the top of his head. I'd assumed we'd have to mount some kind of massive search.

"So where is he?" I asked.

"He's in the basement of a private club on South Street, known as The Seven Deadlies."

My sluggish brain finally started to make sense of what I was hearing. "You mean it's an S&M club." My face must have shown my disgust.

Adam grinned, enjoying my squeamishness. "Not exactly. It caters to quite a variety of sins of the flesh. S&M is just one of them."

"And you've been there. Been in that room." I remembered the whips, the manacles, the freakin' *rack*.

He nodded. His glance slid over to Dominic, then back to me. "When Dom had his demon, we went there every once in a while. They have a wider array of toys than—"

I held up both hands. "Please, spare me the details."

He laughed. "Okay, okay. The important point is I know that room."

"And the important question," Dominic added, sitting down at the table with us, "is why would they hold him in a room that someone might recognize?"

I shook my head. "Certainly they wouldn't expect *me* to recognize it."

"No," Adam conceded, "but they most likely know you've been at my house. And the demons among them at least know I'm one of Lugh's lieutenants."

I remembered Raphael's phone call yesterday. He'd not only known I'd been with Adam, he'd also known I'd called the police on him. I didn't really want to remind Adam or Dominic about my less-than-noble behavior, but I did anyway.

"Raphael knew I was the one who phoned in the complaint," I said, then told them about my little conversation with my dear brother. "He'd have good reason to think you'd never see this tape. And I've got to admit, keeping him at an S&M club is an effective way to hide him in plain sight. No one there would worry if they heard screams coming from that room." The thought sickened me.

"You may be right," Adam conceded, in a voice that suggested he thought I was dead wrong, "but we still have to operate under the assumption that this is a trap."

If he thought I needed convincing that this was a dangerous situation, he was dead wrong. "Don't worry, I'm clear on that. Of course, you *are* the Director of Special Forces, and you have proof that a crime has been committed there. Can't you just, you know, storm the building or something?"

"That would be a very bad idea."

"Why?"

Adam and Dominic shared a look I didn't understand. Then Adam turned his attention back to me. It looked like he was picking his words very, very carefully.

"The owner of The Seven Deadlies is the demon version of a snitch."

"Huh?"

If I didn't know better, I'd have sworn Adam was uncomfortable. His eyes slid away from mine to focus on his cup of coffee.

"She's an illegal," he said, the corners of his mouth tight. "And the club caters to demons. *All* demons."

My wits weren't at their sharpest this morning, so I decided to test my understanding. "So you're telling me that not only is the owner an illegal demon, but the club is crawling with them?"

He shrugged. "*Crawling with them* would be overstating it, but, yes, I'm sure there are others who spend time there."

I didn't get this at all. "So basically you're just pretending to be a demon hunter. In reality, you don't give a shit about how many demons are out there preying on helpless, unwilling human hosts." My level of outrage was rising steadily, as was my voice.

"Not true!" he answered, and I could almost see his defenses going up. "Shae is an excellent informant, and thanks to her I've captured demons I'd never have found any other way. It's just that she won't give me all of them."

"Basically," Dominic interjected, "she gives him the ones she doesn't like. Luckily, it's easy to get on her bad side."

"And you don't haul her in because . . . ?"

Adam gave me the kind of condescending look you'd give a preschool child. "Because then my number-one informant wouldn't be on the street anymore. Letting her continue to operate is a necessary evil." He gave me a look somewhere between a grin and a sneer. "Besides, you should be damn grateful I don't haul in every illegal demon I meet, or I'd have arrested you the first night I knew you were possessed, and you'd be ashes by now."

I wanted to debate this some more, but managed to reel myself back in. I had more important things to think about right now than the morality of allowing police snitches to roam free. "Why does any of this mean we can't storm the club? And please don't tell me it's just because you don't want to offend your snitch."

"No, it's not that. It's just that she has other contacts within the police department. Contacts who will warn her if we try to orchestrate a raid on her club."

"And this necessary evil of yours would tell the people who have Brian and they'd, what, kill him? And she wouldn't have a problem with that?" My voice was rising again, along with my blood pressure. I reminded myself for the millionth time that I needed Adam's help and that yelling at him wasn't the best way to get it.

"Shae is a mercenary, through and through," Adam said. A tick in his jaw suggested I was getting on his nerves, but so far he seemed better in control of his temper than I was of mine. "Pay her enough, and she'll be happy to overlook just about anything. But believe me, she's a lot less malevolent than most illegals. And we're not debating this. The situation is what it is. If we try to mount an assault, she'll hear about it, and she'll take whatever precautions she feels are necessary, up to and including allowing Raphael's people to kill your dearly beloved. So no police support. What's your next idea?"

I thought it was a sign of my newfound maturity that I managed to let the subject drop. Not that it was easy when righteous indignation threatened to overwhelm me. But I had to keep focused, had to get Brian out of there. I could complain about the snitch thing later.

"If the frontal assault is out," I said, and only a hint of my anger showed in my voice, "then I guess we're just going to have to be sneaky."

"And you have a plan for this sneaky rescue?" Adam asked, giving me his best bland look.

"No. But I bet someone as intimately familiar with the place as you are can come up with one." My smile at that point was no doubt sickeningly sweet.

Unfortunately, Adam smiled back. His smile, however, was *not* sweet. "Oh, I think I can come up with a suggestion."

Why did I think I wasn't going to like this suggestion of his? "All right," I said, accepting the inevitable, "lay it on me."

Chapter 22

My suspicion that I wouldn't like Adam's plan was spot-on. Go figure. However, since I couldn't come up with a better one...

That afternoon, I had the unique pleasure of going shopping with a police escort. Adam, of course. Hoping that none of the bad guys would see us together, he drove me to New Jersey for this little expedition instead of taking me to any of the Philadelphia spots. He stole glances out of the rearview mirror every five seconds while we drove, but he said he didn't see any signs of pursuit.

Our first stop was at a dive of a salon, where I let a gum-cracking teenager with hair like roadkill bleach my hair a very white blond. She did the same to my eyebrows, then moussed my hair into sticky spikes. I looked wretched, but I also hardly looked like myself, which was the idea.

Next, we went to a dive of a clothing shop that specialized in biker-slut couture. Adam browbeat me into buying a black vinyl miniskirt, a black leather bustier that laced up the front and didn't close all the way, and black vinyl thigh-high boots with stiletto heels. When I looked at myself in the mirror, I didn't know whether to laugh or cry.

When I emerged from the dressing room to purchase my costume—I refused to think of these as clothes—I saw that Adam had added a pair of black leather wrist cuffs dotted with silver studs and a black leather dog collar with similar decoration.

I started shaking my head violently, but he tore the clothes out of my hands, piled them on the counter, and handed the amused salesclerk his credit card.

"If we're going to do this, love, we're going to do it right."

I imagined wearing that outfit out in public and considered the possibility that I might just prefer to die.

Our last stop was a shop that specialized in theater makeup, where we bought pancake makeup, obnoxious black lipstick, and obnoxious black eyeliner.

Well, okay, the eyeliner wasn't that obnoxious. It was just that I knew how much of it he was going to make me wear.

Late in the afternoon, Dominic called Adam's cell to let him know the expected videotape had arrived at my office. Delivered by messenger service, of course, so we couldn't track it to its source. I asked what was on the tape, but all Adam would tell me was that Dom said it was "what you'd expect." Maybe I was better off not knowing.

I called Andrew from a pay phone, seething with hatred. We began negotiations for Brian's release, discussing where we would do the trade, but my temper got the better of me again and he hung up on me. It was just as well—we needed to stall a bit anyway, because I wasn't about to turn myself in.

We met Dominic for dinner at what I would swear was a Family-owned Italian restaurant, then we rented a cheesy motel room. Adam didn't want any chance that the bad guys would see me within three feet of him with my new do, and he wanted to make sure we weren't followed when we showed up at the club.

On the theory that it would be easier to disappear into the crowd if the club was as crowded as possible, we decided to show up around midnight. At ten-thirty, we started getting me into costume.

Yes, it was a team effort. Not that I needed help getting into my clothes, what there was of them, but I definitely needed help with the makeup. I tried not to laugh hysterically while Dominic covered my all-too-recognizable tattoo with that thick, pore-clogging pancake makeup.

Adam sent me back to the bathroom three times to put on more eyeliner and lipstick, until I looked like a biker slut in clown makeup. Then Dominic took his turn in that bathroom. I hadn't seen what his costume looked like yet, but I figured it couldn't possibly be as hideous as mine.

Adam gave me a definite once-over when Dom disappeared into the bathroom. His grin was lascivious in the extreme and made me want to lace the bustier tighter. But I'd already laced it as tight as it would go if I still wanted to breathe. There was at least a one-inch gap between my breasts, and the tight lacing meant lots of cleavage.

Adam licked his lips. "Such a shame you insisted on buying panties," he said. "It would have been so much fun imagining you in that outfit without them."

I gaped at him. The look in his eyes was pure lust, and unless he'd shoved a cucumber down the front of his pants while I wasn't looking, it was genuine.

I cast a furious look at the bathroom door, but Adam just laughed.

"Don't worry, love. While I can't help admiring the view, this," he said as he ran his hand down the bulge, "is all for Dom."

My face flamed, amusing him even more. I wondered if maybe I should try to revive the awkwardness of this morning. I think I liked it better than when he felt comfortable with me.

At that moment, the bathroom door opened.

Dominic wasn't as tricked out as me, but he definitely didn't look himself. He'd slicked back his unruly hair with something that gave it a greasy shine, and he'd changed into a black mesh T-shirt and obscenely tight black leather pants. He also wore cuffs and collar, similar to mine.

"*What's* all for me?" he asked, eyebrows raised, but he must have picked up on the particular flavor of tension in the room because his eyes zeroed in on Adam's groin. I didn't think the color that rose to his cheeks was entirely embarrassment. "Oh," he mumbled.

His pants were easily tight enough to show he appreciated Adam's appreciation. I wanted out of the room more than I could say.

"Morgan," Adam said, and there was a hint of sharpness to his voice that made me look up. "You're going to have to at least *pretend* you're comfortable with us. The Seven Deadlies is not the place for prudishness, especially not when you're supposed to be our third."

God, please kill me now.

I'd been mentally shielding myself all day, trying not to think about this wonderful plan of ours. But I couldn't do it forever.

As plans go, it wasn't much. Not knowing how many people—and demons—were guarding Brian, and not knowing what condition he would be in, there wasn't a whole lot of advance planning we could do. All we knew for sure was that we had to find our way into that basement. Considering what went on down there, there was only one way to manage it.

My acting skills are lousy, and if I actually had to participate in any S&M sex games, I'd never be able to do it. So Adam had come up with a story for me. I was Adam's new human plaything-in-training because Dominic without his demon just wasn't satisfying enough. But I was being punished, so for tonight, I would be allowed to observe, but not participate.

"If it makes you feel any better," Dominic said with a nervous smile, "I'm not what you'd call comfortable with this, either. Saul had no qualms about performing in public. I do."

"Oh," I said, feeling vaguely ashamed of myself for not thinking about that. I'd seen evidence before that Dominic wasn't an exhibitionist. "I'm really sorry—"

"It'll be okay," Adam interrupted, closing the distance between himself and Dominic and putting both hands on his lover's shoulders. "I'll make you comfortable." His hands slid up Dominic's neck until they cupped his face and pulled his head down for a kiss.

My first instinct was to look away, but I fought it. They'd warned me what I might see at the club once we got into the basement, and if I couldn't handle watching a couple of guys kiss, I was in deep shit.

It didn't take long for Dom to get over his bashfulness. He abandoned himself to that kiss like there was no one else in the room, pressing his body tight against Adam's and making contented sounds in the back of his throat.

When Adam's hands slid down Dom's back until they cupped his ass, I honestly wasn't sure *what* I wanted to do. A part of me certainly wanted to look away, but I couldn't deny that another part—perhaps even a larger part—was wildly turned on by the sight. They were just so damn sexy, both of them. My inner slut would have loved to slip in between them right now, absorb the incredible sexual energy they exuded. I wanted to slide my hands over Dominic's ass, just like Adam did, and feel Adam's impressive erection digging into my belly. Or maybe even other places...

I shook my head to clear it, and the lust level lowered enough to let me tear my eyes away. However, my pulse still hammered in my throat, and I doubted I would ever get those images out of my brain.

I cleared my throat loudly. "Okay, boys, I got the point. Now could we just get on with it?"

They both laughed.

"I'd love to get on with it," Adam said suggestively.

Like a fool, I let my gaze slide over to them again, only to see that Adam's hand had moved. Now it wasn't Dom's ass he was stroking. Dom's eyes were closed, his mouth slightly open, his head thrown back in pleasure. As far as I could tell, he'd forgotten I was in the room. Or he just didn't care anymore.

I mustered my mental forces. "Look, the man I love may be getting tortured right this moment. Do you think you could forego the incredible pleasure of making me uncomfortable so we can rescue him?"

Adam sighed dramatically but let his hand fall away. Dominic opened his eyes and visibly swallowed a protest.

"All right," Adam said. "You have a point." He gave Dominic's hand a quick squeeze, then stepped away to put on his shoulder holster. Unlike Dominic and me, he wasn't wearing a costume. Since he was required to carry his sidearm at all times, he said he'd always found it easier

just to dress like a normal person and wear a jacket to hide
the weapon when he went to The Seven Deadlies.

I thanked God for small mercies. Adam was danger-
ously sexy in his street clothes. I'd hate to see what he'd
look like in some kind of bad-boy costume.

Just before we ventured out of the room, Dominic
handed me a cell phone.

"Here," he said. "In case we get separated."

"We won't!" Adam said, and it was clearly an order.

"We won't," I agreed. But I took the cell phone anyway, sticking it into a convenient pocket at the top of
one thigh-high boot, and Adam didn't object.

We arrived at the club shortly after midnight. The
nearest parking was two blocks away. I felt like everyone on the street was staring at me as we walked those
endless two blocks. It was all in my mind, of course—I
probably didn't look all that outlandish in a South
Street–after–midnight context.

I practiced taking slow, deep breaths, and reminded
myself that Brian's life might well depend on me keeping calm and collected.

From the outside, The Seven Deadlies didn't look
like anything special. The neon sign above its doorway
was actually rather understated, and the facade was for
the most part unadorned. I guess I'd expected the place
to scream out its nature from miles away, though Adam
and Dominic had reminded me repeatedly that it was
both more and less than an S&M club.

At a ticket booth right inside the front door, Adam
and Dominic showed their membership cards and
claimed me as a guest. Adam generously paid my ad-
mission, and a relatively demure-looking young
woman stamped the backs of our hands.

There was a good-sized crowd waiting to get into the depths of the club, and we had to wait in line to go through the doorway. I took the time to look around me and was surprised by what I saw. There were a number of other people dressed, shall we say, exotically, but there were also a large number of relatively normal-looking folks. The age varied from just barely legal to forties, maybe even fifties, with a high concentration of twenty-somethings. I'd estimate about half the crowd was drop-dead gorgeous, and I wondered how many of them were demons. I decided I didn't want to know.

We had to pass between a pair of bouncers to enter the main room of the club. They hardly spared me a glance as I stepped by them, but they both moved to block Adam's way.

"Sir, I'm going to have to ask you to check your weapon," one of them said.

I drifted a little farther away from the door, well out of Adam's reach. It didn't take a genius to figure out that if the staff confiscated Adam's gun, he'd try to abort our mission. I wasn't about to let that happen.

He reached for his back pocket, then flashed his badge. The bouncer didn't budge. Adam rolled his eyes.

"You've never had a problem with it before," he said. I think he was trying to sound calm and reasonable, but the distinct edge in his voice ruined the effect.

"We've had a policy change."

"I'm required to carry my sidearm even when I'm off duty!" Adam said, his posture radiating menace.

The bouncer didn't look intimidated. I wondered if that made him brave, or brain-dead. "Then I suggest you find a club that will let you keep it. This isn't the place."

The crowd behind Adam was getting irritated with him, but he ignored them. "Let me speak to Shae."

"I'm sorry, sir, but I'm going to have to ask you to either check your gun or step aside."

Adam looked like he was one step short of killing someone. He tried to glare me into coming back through the doorway, but I didn't think he was surprised it didn't work.

With a snarl, he ejected the clip from his gun and shoved it at the poor flunky. The flunky gave him a ticket and a dirty look in return.

I think he seriously considered grabbing me and dragging me out kicking and screaming. I also think he realized it wouldn't work. It would be kind of awkward and unconvincing to pretend he was arresting me when he'd escorted me in, and he didn't seem inclined to make a scene.

He shook a finger in my face. "You stick to me like glue, understand?"

"Sure."

He glowered at me a little more; then Dominic put a hand on his shoulder and the tension eased out of him.

"Let's go get a drink, shall we?" Dominic suggested.

I wanted to get on with it immediately, but Adam said we needed to blend in with the crowd.

When we pushed through the door to the main body of the club, I had to stop for a moment to adjust to the assault on my senses.

I'd heard the dull thump of music before we stepped in, but that hadn't prepared me for this wall of noise. I'd done plenty of club-hopping in my early twenties, but not so much lately. I'd forgotten how deafening these places could be. Worse, the so-called music had a heavy techno beat with a droning, repetitive melody and no vocals.

The place was dark as a pit, with multicolored strobe lights providing intermittent illumination. People packed a minuscule dance floor, bodies jerking to the rhythm of the music. The floor was so crowded, it was hard to tell who was dancing with whom, and bodies rubbed together with careless abandon. A sign over the dance floor said *Purgatory,* which I thought an apt description.

The second floor of the club featured a balcony that circled the dance floor. The balcony was crowded with people, some leaning against the railing to watch the action below, some waiting in front of a series of closed, numbered doors like you'd find in a hotel. A sign over the stairway leading up to the balcony declared *Heaven.*

The strangest thing of all was the pair of tables set up one on each side of the entrance. One table held headbands with cheesy devil horns on them, and the other held headbands with cheesy angel halos. Many of the milling crowd wore one or the other.

"I told you this wasn't just an S&M club," Adam said, practically shouting into my ear to be heard over the music. "If you're here looking for a partner for some vanilla sex, you wear a halo. When you find a partner, you go to Heaven." He pointed to the balcony. "And you rent a room. If you're looking for something more exotic, you wear the horns, and when you find a partner, you go to Hell."

My gaze followed his pointing finger until I found the sign saying *Hell.* It loomed over a heavy wooden door that looked just how you'd expect the mouth of Hell to look.

I swallowed hard. "And that's where we're going."

His answer was a curt nod.

We fought our way through the crowd toward the bar, Adam forging a path while Dominic and I struggled along in his wake. We hovered like vultures until a table opened up, then dove for the high stools. I wasn't sure if I could sit on one without flashing, but figured it was dark enough that no one would have much of a view even if I did. Adam sent Dominic to the bar for drinks, laughing when I ordered my trademark piña colada. At least he didn't insist I order something more in keeping with my costume. I was nervous enough I wasn't sure I'd be able to keep any alcohol down.

Dom returned with the drinks and pulled his stool over very close to Adam, their knees touching under the table. I immediately felt like the third wheel, which I supposed was okay since that was my role for the evening.

There wasn't a whole lot of chatter—the music was too loud for it—and I tried to concentrate on my drink as Adam and Dom got progressively...cozier. It seemed Dominic had forgotten his discomfort with public displays of affection. Good thing for him, seeing as Adam's tongue was down his throat most of the time. If only *I* felt more comfortable with it, this wouldn't be quite so hellish. I battled to seem nonchalant and sucked down my drink in big swallows, hoping the alcohol would soothe my nerves.

Dominic was practically on Adam's lap when an unfamiliar woman appeared seemingly out of nowhere.

She was tall, maybe even taller than me, and her skin was that deep ebony hue you associate with people from the heart of Africa. Close-cropped hair showed off the artistically perfect shape of her skull, and she had the longest, most elegant neck I'd ever seen. She looked Adam and Dom up and down with an almost proprietary expression, then looked at me and raised an eyebrow.

I didn't know what to say or do, so I settled for giving Adam a nudge with my elbow to let him know we were no longer alone.

He came up for air, his eyes dark as sin. He blinked a couple of times, as if he'd forgotten where he was; then his eyes focused on our visitor.

"Shae!" he said, sounding delighted. "Long time no see!"

She threw back her head and laughed like he'd said something really funny. I didn't get the joke.

"I hear you were giving my people a hard time, you naughty boy," she said. Her voice was as dark as her skin, and something about it chilled me. Or maybe it wasn't her voice. Maybe it was that predatory glint in her eye.

I reminded myself that she was an illegal demon, and that made it easier to understand my quick and comprehensive dislike of her.

Adam grinned. "You could get me in trouble, Shae. It's against regulations for me to go unarmed."

She grinned back. "I promise not to tell on you." Her gaze moved to Dom. "I hear you've had a spot of trouble."

He nodded, but didn't elaborate. I got the distinct feeling he wasn't terribly fond of Shae, though he hadn't given me that vibe when Adam had talked about her earlier.

Shae's eyes found their way back to me, and she raked me with a head-to-toe examination that felt invasive and not at all friendly. "And who might this lovely creature be?"

Adam's hand closed possessively around my wrist. For the moment, I didn't feel inclined to object. He smiled at Shae.

"She's my new pet-in-training," he said, his fingers tightening on my wrist in warning. Guess he knew I'd be tempted to object to that. Honestly, he didn't need the warning. I objected, but this was the role I'd agreed to play, and if it was what I needed to do to save Brian, then so be it.

Shae stuck out her lower lip. "But, Adam, you've been shamefully neglecting the poor creature. I've had my eye on you for a while."

He let go of my wrist. "That's because she's being punished. She needs to learn to control her temper around her betters."

I lowered my gaze, hoping I looked ashamed of my disgraceful behavior while I clamped my jaws together and fought the urge to retort.

"But you brought her out on the town anyway."

I could almost hear Adam shrug. "What better punishment than to be forced to see what she's missing?"

"My, aren't you the cruel one."

"Always."

"So you're planning to visit Hell tonight?"

My insides clenched, but I managed not to gasp or cringe. I was trying to take everything one step at a time, but my mind kept racing ahead of me, wondering what I would see down there, wondering if my rescue attempt was doomed before it began, wondering if I was going to get myself and Lugh killed before the night was over.

Thank God I wasn't expected to talk.

"Naturally," Adam answered.

Shae made a sound I might almost have described as a purr. "I've missed you. You always put on *such* a good show."

My stomach turned, and I couldn't help raising my gaze. Adam looked completely at ease trading quips with Shae, and she showed every evidence of enjoying it, too. Dom, on the other hand, sat rigidly straight on his stool, and his jaws visibly worked.

No, he definitely didn't like Shae. And he was not happy with where this conversation was leading.

Adam sighed dramatically. "I'm afraid my show-manship days are over." He reached over and put a hand on Dominic's knee. "He's too fragile for the dramatic."

Shae's eyes were razor sharp. "And yet you're bringing him to Hell." There was a challenge of some sort in her voice, though I didn't understand it.

"Testing the waters," Adam said. "You have a wider selection of toys. Mine are all for rougher games than Dom is up to handling these days. I figured I'd take some for a test-drive."

Shae's eyes seemed to gleam in the darkness. Maybe that was her demon shining through, or maybe it was my imagination. "Oh, I think this is going to be an excellent show. I think it'll be so good I'll take you down there myself. On the house."

Adam met her gleaming eyes with a gleam of his own. "You are the most generous of hostesses."

While they congratulated each other with unpleasant smiles, Dom's face went white, his shoulders so tense I wanted to massage them. But he didn't protest when Adam threw an arm around his shoulder and dragged him down off the stool. Guilt gnawed at my stomach. I hated that I was putting Dominic through this. I wished I'd realized in advance how uncomfortable this plan made him, but I'd been too absorbed in my own problems to notice.

The three of us followed Shae through the crowd toward the back of the club, where the door to Hell awaited us.

Chapter **23**

As soon as the heavy door closed behind us, completely blocking out the drone of the music, I heard the screams. I couldn't force my feet forward, so I stood hesitating at the head of the stairs as the others descended.

Real honest-to-God torches set in wall sconces provided the only lighting, and the walls were the same rough-hewn rock I remembered from that hideous video. The stairs were uneven and worn in the middle, as if this basement had existed long before the rest of the club. Maybe it had.

Dominic turned to look over his shoulder and saw me hesitating. He held out his hand to me, letting Shae and Adam get ahead of him.

Swallowing my fear as best I could, I forced my feet down first one step, then another. My knees felt a bit wobbly, and the uneven stairs and stiletto heels weren't helping. I was nervous enough to actually take Dominic's offered hand. His palm was clammy, and I wasn't entirely sure which one of us was giving comfort and which one was taking it.

The sounds got louder and clearer as we descended much deeper into the ground than any basement I'd ever been in. Screams echoed against the stone walls, but there were other sounds, too. The crack of a whip. The smack of flesh upon flesh. And lots of moans, not all of them pain.

I didn't want to take those last few steps downward, didn't want to see the basement Adam and Dom had described.

I didn't have a choice.

The stairway opened out into a long, wide hallway lined with doors. Down the center of the hallway were rows of padded benches, like you'd see in the middle of a museum gallery. Only it wasn't great works of art these benches were facing.

Each of the rooms in the pit of Hell was fronted by a huge picture window, kind of like you'd see in a natural history museum. But these dioramas were of a very different nature, and weren't exactly what I'd call "natural," if you get my drift.

A small crowd had gathered in front of the first of those windows. Some sat on the benches, some knelt on the floor, but all watched the window with eager, lust-hazed eyes. A shrill feminine scream emanated from that room. The cluster of watchers drew closer together, hands reaching and stroking, an amorphous mass that hardly seemed human. Of course, probably many of them weren't.

I wasn't surprised to see Shae and Adam stop in front of that window, but I wished to God they hadn't. Whatever was happening in there, I didn't want to see it. I swallowed hard. Dominic's hand squeezed mine. And together, we stepped up to the window, though we still hung back a bit. If anyone had been paying attention to us, they probably would have wondered what the hell we were doing here if we were so squeamish, but they were all far too absorbed in the drama in front of them.

I still didn't want to look, but the spectacle drew my gaze.

The room behind that window looked like a classroom, complete with blackboard and a couple rows of uncomfortable-looking chairs with attached desks. At the head of the "classroom" sat a huge teacher's desk, covered with books and papers.

My eyes found that desk just in time to see a large forty-something man pick up a screaming woman about half his size and slam her down onto it. She struggled and kicked so convincingly that for half a second I thought she actually meant it. Then my brain caught up with my emotions and I realized it was all for show.

She wore the pleated skirt and crisp white button-down of a good little Catholic schoolgirl, complete with knee-high socks and Mary Janes. She was small enough to make a convincing young girl. If the ridiculousness of the costume hadn't tipped me off, I'd have known she was acting when the flailing of her legs made her skirt ride up enough to show everyone she wasn't wearing any panties.

The "teacher" shoved books and papers out of his way, then pinned the "girl's" wrists above her head with one meaty hand. A rhythmic clicking sound told me someone in the audience was jerking off to the sight. I clenched my teeth and didn't let my eyes wander. Bad enough to be forced to watch this disgusting scene—I didn't want to see the orgy it was inspiring.

Of course, as soon as I thought that, I couldn't stop myself from glancing in Adam's direction.

He watched the scene with an impassive expression, looking neither excited nor disgusted. Shae clung to his arm, and there was no mistaking her pleasure at watching the simulated rape of a child. I let my eyes slide downward and was relieved beyond measure that there was no telltale bulge in Adam's pants. Which led me to wonder at myself. I mean, I already knew how unpleasant his tastes were. I'd experienced firsthand his cruelty. So why should I be relieved that this wasn't turning him on? Why the fuck did I care?

I glanced at Dominic and saw that his eyes were fixed on the floor. A bead of sweat ran down the side of his face, and instead of just looking pale, he looked positively green. How had he survived it when Adam and his demon had come down here in the past?

He must have read the question in my face, because he leaned down and spoke softly into my ear.

"I've always hated this place," he confided. "Saul always shielded me when we came here. He never let me see anything that would upset me."

I couldn't contain my retort. "But he had no problem with making you 'perform' in public, even though he knew you didn't like it."

Dominic shook his head. "He didn't *make* me do it. I agreed to come here, and he agreed to shield me whenever he wanted to do something I wouldn't like." A hint of a smile played around the edges of his mouth. "I definitely had some good times here when Adam drew the curtains."

For the first time, I noticed the black curtains that framed the inside of the window. I bit my tongue to keep myself from saying anything I would regret. Just what did Dominic mean when he said Saul "shielded" him? I had visions of the demon using his body in revolting ways while Dominic remained blissfully unaware, and I had to suppress a shudder. I couldn't imagine trusting *anyone* enough to surrender so completely.

Dom's eyes flicked to Shae, then away. "Shae and Saul never liked each other. She thought his being considerate of me was a sign of weakness." His Adam's apple bobbed as he swallowed hard. "I think she chose this particular time to come to our table because she knew what was going to be happening down here and knew how I'd feel about it."

Oh, ick! I'd disliked her already. Now I *despised* her. How could Adam let her continue to operate? I mean, yeah, I understand the concept of snitches, understand they're a necessary evil at times, but surely there's a limit to how evil they should be allowed to be!

The scene I was now carefully avoiding watching reached its climax—so to speak—and the "schoolgirl's" screams took on a very different tone. Moans and sighs from the audience told me some of them were going along with the ride.

When Shae turned to look at Dominic and me, there was no way I could hide my revulsion. Dom didn't even try. Shae briefly touched her tongue to her upper lip, then slid her arm through Adam's to lead him farther down the hall.

I wanted desperately to flee back up the stairs. Instead, I followed them into the heart of darkness.

The curtains were closed over one of the windows we passed. Dominic leaned over to whisper to me.

"That's the rack room," he said.

My heart clenched, and I had to force myself to keep moving, not pay special attention to the room. I strained my ears, but heard no screams from behind that curtain. I hoped that meant they were leaving

Brian alone. And I wished we could just hurry this little expedition up.

Shae and Adam stopped in front of one of the doors, and Shae dug a key ring out of her pocket.

"Shit!" Dominic hissed under his breath.

You can imagine I didn't like the sound of that. But I kept walking, and so did he.

Adam stood blocking the doorway while he and Shae tried to stare each other down. I peeked through the window and tried to keep my expression as neutral as humanly possible.

The setup was much less elaborate than the school-room. Then again, it was also much more blatant.

A padded, adjustable-height table, like an examining table at a doctor's office, sat in the middle of the room. Only this table had legs with thick leather restraints attached to them.

Along one wall hung an assortment of whips and paddles. It was reminiscent of Adam's black room, only more revolting due to its public nature. I eyed the restraints on that table, and it was obvious just what position the victim would be restrained in.

"Thank you for offering us free use," Adam said to Shae, still wearing his neutral face.

"Oh, the pleasure's all mine." Her grin was feral and unpleasant.

They stared at each other, neither one backing down, neither one speaking. I glanced at Dominic and saw his jaws working as he ground his teeth. I suspected he would have enjoyed the prospect of "playing" in that room with Adam in private. But not like this.

It was Adam who backed down from the staring contest first, which kind of surprised me.

"I'll be drawing the curtain," he said. "If you'd like to rescind your offer of a freebie, that's fine, but—"

Shae smiled up at him. "Let's talk inside, shall we?" she said, gesturing toward the room.

"Shae—"

"Inside, Adam. I know why you're really here, and I don't think we should discuss it in the hall, do you?"

It was all I could do to suppress my gasp.

For the first time I could remember, Adam looked unsure of himself. I'd have enjoyed the spectacle, if I wasn't sick to my stomach. Shae put her hands on her hips and raised an eyebrow.

"Let's hear what she has to say," Dominic suggested. He looked scared shitless, and I wished like hell I'd never dragged him into this mess.

"All right," Adam agreed, but I could tell he didn't like it.

He stepped through the doorway, followed closely by Shae. Dominic started to follow, but I planted my feet and tugged on his arm.

"Dominic—" I started, but he wouldn't let me finish.

"Anything that happens to me will be something I've consented to. The same can't be said of your Brian."

My eyes teared up at the thought he was willing to sacrifice himself to save a man he'd never met. Of course, he'd been willing to sacrifice himself to host a demon and save *lots* of people he'd never met. It must be in his nature somehow. Once upon a time, I would have scorned him for it. Now I saw him for the hero he truly was and wished I could take back all the nasty things I'd said to him.

I settled for squeezing his hand and saying, "You're a really good man, Dominic."

His smile was grim. "Wait until I've actually consented to something before you get too grateful."

I had to admit, he had a point.

Taking a last deep breath, trying not to hear the sickening noises that still echoed through the hall, I stepped into Shae's playroom. Dominic followed and closed the door behind himself. The three of us stood facing Shae, whose smile looked supremely smug.

"How lovely to have the tables turned for once in my life," she said, her attention fixed on Adam. "Year after year, you've bullied and threatened me into doing what you wanted. Now it's my turn."

"Shae—"

"Shut up, Adam." Her smile was sweet as a shark's. "It's only because I'm so fond of you that I didn't pick up the phone the moment I heard you were here. You are the world's worst fool for walking straight into a trap like this."

I'd thought my pulse was racing before. Now I found out what racing really was. If this was a trap, I was dead. Adam didn't need a gun to kill me, and I knew he'd do it without hesitation if he thought Lugh was at risk. I was grateful he hadn't already broken my neck. But he didn't even glance in my direction.

"*I'm* a fool?" Adam asked, sounding incredulous. "You're allowing a human to be held prisoner and tortured here, and you think *I'm* a fool?"

She shrugged. "It's a risk, I'll admit. But a risk for which I've been well paid. You know me—anything for a buck."

I'd been doing a pretty decent job of keeping my temper under control, but it struggled to the surface.

Adam must have known me too well by now, for he turned to me before I managed to say anything and quelled me with one fierce look.

"What are your terms?" he asked Shae.

"Twenty-five thousand dollars, and you put on a lovely show for me."

I practically choked, but Adam didn't even blink.

"And in return, I get . . ."

"The key to the rack room. The key to the back exit. And a ten-minute head start before I make my phone call."

He glared at her. "*Thirty* minutes! We need to be long gone before they start looking. And no show."

"Ten," she countered. "I want to live through this, you know. It can't be *too* obvious that I've helped you. And no way you're getting out of here without giving me that show." Her eyes flicked to Dominic. "I've been waiting a long time for this."

"Your beef's with Saul, not Dominic," Adam reminded her.

She laughed. "No, my beef's with *you*. You're going to enjoy this despite yourself, and you'll hate yourself for it afterward."

Adam looked like he was one heartbeat away from killing her, but somehow he restrained himself as she turned to look at Dominic.

"Who knows?" she taunted. "Maybe *you'll* enjoy it, too."

Adam's lip peeled away from his teeth in a feral snarl, and he took a step toward Shae. Obviously, she was insane, because she didn't back down.

"Those are my terms," she said. "Take 'em or leave 'em."

Why would this bitch be willing to help us anyway? She was an illegal demon, after all, and Lugh wanted to make her kind as illegal in his world as they were in ours. Then again, she was a mercenary. She didn't give a damn what she was fighting for, so long as she got paid.

Adam visibly controlled his rage, then he turned to Dom and asked a question with his eyes. I was still holding Dom's hand, so I could feel how clammy it was. He didn't want to do this, though he might consent.

Looking up at his pale, scared face, I knew what I had to do. This wasn't his battle. It was mine. And for the second time in two days, I was going to have to let Adam hurt me.

"Leave Dom out of it," I said. My voice came out froggy with fear and disgust, but I soldiered on. "Whatever has to happen should happen to me, not him."

To my surprise, Dominic barked out a definitive "No!"

I blinked up at him.

Color rose to his cheeks. "I may not want to do this, but it would hurt far worse to be forced to watch Adam fuck someone else."

Now my own cheeks blazed. I hadn't really thought about what I was offering. I'd focused on the whole pain thing, had allowed myself to forget what this place was really all about.

Would I have let Adam fuck me to save Brian? And would Brian ever have forgiven me if I had? I'd never know—thank God.

"It's a deal," Dominic said, directing his words to Shae.

She smiled that unwholesome smile of hers. And I vowed to myself that if I lived through the night, I'd find a way to pay Shae back for this.

Chapter **24**

Shae left the three of us alone, slipping outside to sit on the bench and look in the window. I'd have liked to get the hell out of there, too, but that didn't appear to be among my options. Dominic looked miserable, but determined, his hands clenched into fists at his sides. When Shae beckoned the crowd of perverts over to our window, I seriously considered storming out of the room and punching that malicious little grin off her face.

Adam looked at me, then at the gathering crowd, then at Dominic. "We're not doing this."

My heart lurched, but as desperately as I longed to save Brian, I didn't have it in me to protest. That Dominic would even consider doing something this degrading for the chance to help a total stranger—and it was a chance only, for who knew if Shae would hold up her end of the bargain?—amazed and humbled me.

"Yes, we are," Dominic said. As miserable as he

looked, there was no hesitation in his voice. "I'm not leaving a helpless, unwilling victim down here."

"Dom—"

"No, Adam. I could never live with myself if I just walked away."

"I'm so sorry I dragged you into this," I said.

He waved that off. "It's ultimately my choice." His eyes locked with Adam's. "And I choose to do it."

Adam cut a look in my direction. I had a feeling this was one more sin he was going to blame me for. I had a feeling *I* would blame me for it, too.

"Stand over there in the corner," he barked at me. "Stay out of the way."

His tone would ordinarily have raised my hackles, but I sympathized too much with his anger to object to it. I meekly obeyed. Adam cupped his hands around Dom's face and looked into his lover's eyes.

"Forget about everything," he said, and the anger had disappeared from his voice as if it never existed. "Forget about everyone else. It's just me." He laid an almost chaste kiss on Dom's lips. "And if you need me to stop, say the word and I will."

Dominic swallowed hard and nodded. They both looked toward the table, and Dom heaved a heavy sigh. Then, with Adam's arm around his shoulders, he moved to stand at the table's foot. Adam stood close behind him and ran his hands over his chest, moving downward until his fingers found Dom's belt buckle. Dom leaned back against him and closed his eyes as Adam undid his pants and pulled them down.

Not surprisingly, considering how tight those pants had fit, Dom wasn't wearing any underwear. My eyes slid away, but they soon returned to the spectacle. I'm not sure if it was morbid fascination, or whether I wanted to punish myself for putting them through this by making myself as uncomfortable as I could possibly be. Whatever the motivation, I watched as Dominic bent over that table and allowed Adam to cuff his wrists and ankles to the table's legs. Adam whispered something in his ear that made him smile briefly.

From the corner of my eye, I saw movement behind the window, but I didn't allow myself to look. I didn't want to think about how many people were out there, witnessing this. Bad enough that *I* was witnessing it.

Adam left Dominic bent over that table, his ass bare for everyone to see, as he selected a paddle from among the many choices. He slapped it hard across the palm of his hand. The noise, far louder than I'd expected, made me jump. Adam frowned at the paddle and put it back, making another selection. He tried a few others, his hand getting redder and redder as he hit it. Was he punishing himself? Or was he really just testing them out? I didn't know.

He finally picked one and went back to the table. He smoothed his reddened hand over Dominic's butt, the gesture unmistakably tender.

"Ready?" he asked.

"Yeah."

Dominic's hands tightened into fists. I felt a fist-sized lump in my throat, and I pressed myself as tightly into the corner as I could, wincing in anticipation.

The table was positioned parallel to the window so that the watchers outside could see both his butt and his face. Unfortunately, my position gave me a really clear view of his butt—not that it wouldn't have been nice to look at under other circumstances! But I got to watch as the blows rained down on him and his skin glowed an angry shade of red.

Dominic was very quiet, though every once in a while a soft whimper escaped him. I don't know if it was because of the audience, or the taint of Shae's malice and blackmail, but no one watching could think he was enjoying himself. His hands stayed clenched, and he struggled feebly against the bonds, trying to avoid Adam's blows.

Adam's face was as red as Dom's ass, but it wasn't from exertion or pleasure. Fury radiated from him. If I'd been in that audience, watching for pleasure, I'd have run like hell when I caught a glimpse of that face.

Finally, Adam hurled the paddle across the room so hard it broke clean in half when it hit the wall. Even with the insulating glass, I could hear the audience outside gasp.

Then, God help me, Adam attacked his pants, getting them open and down in about five seconds flat.

I couldn't help admiring him. I just couldn't, no matter how sickening this spectacle. He had an ass a body double would kill for, lean and rounded and very, very firm. And his cock . . . Well, let's just say my earlier cucumber analogy was surprisingly apt.

He had to stroke himself awhile to get himself to full tumescence—which he did while baring his teeth in a feral snarl at the audience. I guess Shae was wrong about him enjoying this against his will, though from the look in his eyes it wasn't much consolation. He went through two condoms in his bid for safe sex, the first one tearing from too much rough handling. Then he was finally ready for action.

I looked away at first. It was just too much. But in the end, I suppose I was as much a voyeur as everyone else in the place, for my eyes were inevitably drawn back.

From my vantage point, pretty much all I could see was Adam, his body shielding Dom from view. I watched the muscles of his spectacular ass bunching and releasing, and heard the little sounds Dominic couldn't seem to help making. No matter the public humiliation, no matter his discomfort, no matter his basic unwillingness, he couldn't help enjoying what Adam was doing to him. I suspect only reluctance to give Shae any satisfaction kept him from letting loose completely.

For his part, Adam didn't make a sound. He pounded away, fucking Dom as brutally as he'd beaten him. It had to hurt, but you wouldn't have known it from Dominic's sighs and moans.

I could tell when Adam came by the stiffening of his stance and by the change of rhythm. Still he made no sound, though his breath came in ragged gasps. Looking exhausted, he leaned over Dominic's back, resting his hands on the table.

"Draw the fucking curtain," he snarled at me over his shoulder.

Outside, the audience gave an enthusiastic round of applause. I hurried to the curtain on shaky knees, wobbling on my damned high heels. I drew the curtain as fast as possible, then kept my back turned on Adam and Dom to give them a belated moment of privacy.

It occurred to me that Shae wouldn't have the same decency, so I moved to the door and pressed both hands against it. Sure enough, I felt someone trying to push it open.

"Give us a minute!" I said, not quite a shout but close to it.

Being a demon, she could have forced the door easily, but she didn't, at least not yet. I kept leaning on it anyway, putting as much of my body weight into it as I could. Behind me, I heard Adam and Dom dressing.

"All right," Dominic said a moment later. "You can let her in now."

I didn't want to, but I moved away from the door.

Shae sauntered in, looking terribly pleased with herself. She sighed with contentment.

"And you thought you couldn't put on a good show anymore!" she said.

Adam's eyes glowed. "You don't want to push me just now, Shae."

She arched an eyebrow. "Is that a threat?"

"My self-control is not boundless. Give me the keys and get the fuck out of my face." Dom put a hand on his shoulder as if to calm him, but Adam shrugged it off. "I mean it, Shae!"

She smiled. "I know you do. And I'm a woman of my word."

I had to resist the urge to snort. If she was such a woman of her word, then why was she helping us, if that's what she was doing?

Shae fished a couple of keys out of her pocket and held them up to Adam. "The big one is to the rack room. The smaller one is to the 'fire escape.'" Yes, you could hear the quotation marks around the term. "You'll wire the money to me as soon as the bank opens in the morning. Right?"

Adam nodded. "Assuming I live that long and that none of the people under my protection dies, yeah."

Her eyes narrowed. "That wasn't part of our arrangement."

"It is now."

Apparently, she wasn't entirely insane, after all. She took one look at the expression on Adam's face, then shrugged and handed over the keys.

"Fine." She looked at her watch. "It's one twenty-five. At one thirty-five, I'm going to make the call. I suggest you move your glorious ass."

For a moment, I thought we were going to have to waste precious minutes prying Adam off Shae, but he managed to control his obviously brittle temper. With one last goading smile, Shae left the room. The rest of us followed.

In the hallway, the crowd had gathered in front of another window, closer to the stairway leading out of Hell. Shae waggled her fingers at us as she climbed the stairs, but the rest of the crowd ignored us completely, enjoying whatever sick perversion was taking place behind that window.

We reached the room with the black curtain, and Adam made to slip the key into the lock. I stopped him with a hand on his arm.

"We don't even know if there are guards," I said.

He batted my hand away. "We will in a minute."

Before I could utter another protest, he turned the key and pushed the door open.

Chapter **25**

There weren't any guards. I think all three of us took that as something of a bad sign, but it wasn't like we were just going to run away. If this was a trap, then we'd already stepped into it, so what the hell.

Brian was still chained to the wall, the gag still stuffed in his mouth. Blood crusted his abdomen and soaked the front of his underwear. His head lolled, and my heart constricted to see a pair of burns, one under each armpit.

I ran to him, tears stinging my eyes. "Brian!" I cried, touching my hands to his chest, relieved to feel the beat of his heart. But he was out cold.

Dom and I held him up while Adam freed him from the shackles. His body was a dead weight.

"Oh my God, what's the matter with him?" I was reduced to a quivering mess, my whole body shaking, my brain hardly functioning.

Dom traced his finger over the crook of Brian's elbow, finding a small bruise. "They drugged him," he said. "Let's get the hell out of here. We'll figure out what they gave him later."

Adam bent and picked Brian up, slinging him over his shoulder in a fireman's carry. He moved as if the weight were nothing, heading toward the door.

I saw Brian's clothes lying in a heap in the corner, and I snatched them up. We were going to look very conspicuous carrying an unconscious, half-naked, bloody man, though I didn't suppose we had the time to get him dressed.

When we exited the room, Adam led us to the left, rather than toward the stairway leading back into the club. I supposed we were heading for the "fire escape." A couple of the perverts watching the show noticed us and made surprised noises, but no one followed.

Adam shoved the small key Shae had given him at me, and I took it. We rounded a corner and burst into another of the rooms, this one designed to look like a doctor's office, only the stirrups on the exam table came complete with restraints. I shuddered and forced my mind not to go there.

"Here!" Adam said, pointing at what looked like a locked cabinet.

I didn't question him. I rammed the key in the lock, and Dominic grabbed the edge of the cabinet and pulled.

I gave Adam a questioning look as the cabinet pulled away from the wall to reveal a doorway. He shrugged—an awkward gesture with Brian lying limply over his shoulder.

"Illegal things happen here," he explained. "Sometimes the patrons need a secret escape route."

I was definitely going to have a talk with Adam about the wisdom of letting Shae continue to operate when this was all over.

We piled into the secret hallway and pulled the door shut behind us. The screams and other unwholesome sounds cut off, though honestly, I'd been blocking them out so thoroughly it wasn't until the door closed that my mind acknowledged what it had been hearing.

We hesitated, looking at each other with identical concerned expressions, I'm sure.

"This has been too easy," I said, deciding to state the obvious.

Adam and Dominic both nodded their agreement. Then Adam took his turn stating the obvious.

"We're committed now. There's nothing we can do but move forward." He took a step down the hall, then looked over his shoulder at me. "Stay behind us."

I let them take the lead. My heart was pounding so loud I could barely hear anything else. How much time had passed? Had Shae made her phone call yet? Was that even an issue?

The questions buzzed through my head one by one, but I had no answers.

The hallway went on for what felt like a mile, but finally we reached a stairway leading up. I hoped to God it was the exit.

Adam took the lead, taking the steps two at a time despite Brian's dead weight. Dominic followed close behind, and I brought up the rear.

I hadn't even set foot on the first step yet when I heard a familiar, awful sound. A Taser shot.

Adam made a grunting noise, then Dominic yelped. I leapt backward as the two of them and Brian came tumbling down the stairs. My leap wasn't fast enough. When Dominic crashed into my legs, I went down hard, the impact on my tailbone causing me to bite my tongue.

Dominic struggled to roll off me and get to his feet.

I heard a muffled hiccup, then Dom screamed and clutched his leg as blood fountained from his thigh.

I looked up and saw a hooded, masked figure pointing a silenced pistol directly at Dominic's head. Two more masked figures descended behind him. One of those held the Taser.

Adam lay in a helpless bundle on the floor. Brian lay half on top of him, still unconscious. And Dom was in too much pain to do more than moan.

"Make any attempt to run away," the gun-wielding masked man said, and I recognized Andrew's voice, "and I'll kill both the humans." He moved his aim to Brian, and I almost screamed. But I didn't want to startle him into anything.

His eyes bored into mine, and I realized he was wearing green contact lenses for some reason. But there was no doubt in my mind that it was Andrew behind that mask, despite the difference in eye color.

"Get up slowly," he instructed me as another masked man stepped out of the stairway, making a total of four.

I wasn't entirely sure my legs would hold me, but I didn't want to know what Andrew would do if I didn't obey. I made it to my feet and stood facing my brother. Or Lugh's brother, depending on your point of view.

"Cooperate," he told me, "and no one gets hurt."

I looked pointedly from my unconscious, wounded boyfriend to Dominic, who clutched his still-bleeding leg. "What do you call *this*?" I asked. My voice was a little shaky, but I still thought I sounded rather brave.

"They'll live," Andrew said with cold calculation. "All of them. If you behave."

Why should I believe him? No reason whatsoever, except believing him was my only hope. And so I didn't fight it when Masked Villain Number Three grabbed me and slapped handcuffs on me. As soon as the cuffs were on, Andrew put away his gun.

Honestly, I wasn't stupid enough to think I could take out four men—at least one of whom was a demon—even if my hands hadn't been cuffed behind my back, but at this point, I had nothing left to lose.

I managed to stomp his instep and incite a curse from the man who'd cuffed me, but then Andrew crossed the distance between us and grabbed me. My struggles were useless as he dragged me up the stairs.

Chapter 26

The stairway exited into a parking deck. My captors pulled off their hoods before venturing out, but the deck was deserted at this hour of the morning. I considered screaming for help, but Andrew was dragging me toward a black SUV only a couple of yards away. Even if someone heard me—unlikely—we'd be in the SUV and out of here before help could arrive.

We all piled in, with me sandwiched between Andrew and another of his minions. Andrew appropriated the Taser his flunky had used on Adam, pointing it at me and smiling pleasantly.

"In case Lugh has any ideas," he said.

I tried not to think about their plans for me. And I tried not to think about what might be happening to Brian, and Adam, and Dominic. The goon squad here had let them live, but they were still in hostile territory.

A tear snaked down my cheek, and I couldn't wipe it away. I ground my teeth, willing myself to stay strong. Pain gathered behind my right eye. Apparently,

Lugh had ideas, but with Andrew's Taser, he would be as helpless as I was. That didn't stop him from trying, and I mentally cursed him. I was going to be in plenty of pain soon enough. I didn't need this.

Another tear leaked out of my eye. This time Andrew noticed.

"We'll make it as quick as possible," he assured me.

"Fuck you!" was my incisive rejoinder. I would have sounded a lot tougher if I hadn't sniffled like a baby afterward.

He continued as if he hadn't heard me. "And your friends will be fine. They can't identify us, so they're no threat. We have no reason to kill them."

Except that Adam, at least, would have recognized Andrew's voice. Andrew seemed to read that thought on my face.

"Your policeman friend might recognize my voice, but that wouldn't be enough evidence even to arrest me, let alone convict me. Not when the only thing he could see of my face was my lovely green eyes."

"And what about Shae? They've all seen *her* up close and personal."

Andrew shrugged. "She's a mercenary bitch, but she's not a killer. And, by the way, she didn't know she was driving you straight into us. She was trying to uphold her end of whatever bargain you made. It's just that you're all so predictable, it was child's play to intercept you."

I didn't dignify that with an answer. Instead, I huddled around my small hope that the boys would be okay. I reminded myself of Val's fanatical ravings about how the demons were good for mankind, etc., etc. The humans, at least, believed they were fighting for a good cause, no matter how misguided they might be. I supposed it would be harder to hold on to the illusion that they were the good guys if they went around slaughtering people who were no threat to them.

We drove first south, then west, leaving the city behind. I didn't know where they were taking me, but when we entered the Brandywine Valley, I figured we were probably nearing our destination. The Brandywine Valley is full of farms and vineyards. Quite scenic, and a great place for a peaceful Sunday drive. Unfortunately, the picturesque landscape also meant it was easy to find a place with the kind of isolation you'd need to burn someone alive without being interrupted.

We eventually arrived at what seemed to be an industrial-sized farm. We entered the farm via a gravel road. When we got to the end of the road, there was a small cluster of other parked vehicles waiting for us.

The drive had lasted long enough to slow my adrenaline rush, but now it was back full force. My heart pounded frantically, and my mouth was so dry I couldn't swallow. Lugh started pounding on the inside of my skull again, making me wince. But even if I knew how to let him take control, what could he possibly do when Andrew could Taser him into a mass of Jell-O?

My high heels and the gravel parking area didn't like each other much. The moment my feet hit the ground, I tottered, and would have fallen if Andrew hadn't held me up.

"I like your new look, by the way," he said as he steered me around a couple of the parked cars. "But you need to practice walking in high heels. You're pretty clumsy."

I tried to stab his foot with my stiletto heel, but missed. He retaliated by backhanding me. I fell on my butt on the gravel, seeing stars. I tasted blood, and gathered what moisture I could to spit at him. It was a feeble attempt, and didn't even annoy him.

He dragged me back to my feet. "I was hoping that would convince Lugh to come out and play," he said as we resumed walking.

I could see our destination now. We were heading behind a huge barn, where seven or eight people stood clustered around what I presumed was the modern version of a classic witch-burning stake—a basketball hoop set into a concrete base and surrounded by hay, kindling sticks, and fireplace logs. My footsteps faltered. Pain stabbed through my eye, and I gasped.

"You should let him in, Morgan dear," Andrew said, still dragging me where I most definitely did not want to go. "He can't save you, but he can protect you from the pain."

One of the men gathered around the stake broke off from the crowd and approached us. At first, it was so dark I couldn't see his face, but when he came closer, I got a good look.

I must have looked comically surprised, because Jeremy Wyatt—founder and head fanatic of God's Wrath—laughed at me. I shook my head, trying, but failing, to make sense of things.

Why would a man who advocated burning all demons alive have anything to do with a plot to overthrow Lugh and allow demons to take over unwilling humans at will? True, God's Wrath believed that hosts couldn't be taken over unless they were somehow unworthy, unclean people, but still . . .

"Surprised to see me, Ms. Kingsley?" he asked, still laughing at me.

His eyes seemed to glow in the darkness, and suddenly pieces of the puzzle started to fit together. "Have you been living in Jeremy Wyatt since the beginning, or are you a new arrival?" I asked. I didn't suppose it much mattered, but if I could get him talking, that would put off the whole being-burned-at-the-stake thing I wasn't looking forward to.

He smiled as if delighted with me. "Jeremy and I joined forces almost two years ago now."

Long after the fanatical bastard had started his little hate group. "I guess Jeremy is just another sinner like the rest of us," I said. Apparently, these demons were really into irony, possessing the people who would most hate to host them.

"What better way to tilt the scales in our favor?"

I didn't get that at first—fear wasn't the best catalyst for clear thinking. Then I understood. "God's Wrath isn't just targeting random demon hosts. You're targeting people who host demons who support Lugh!" Like Dominic.

"Indeed. That is, in fact, why I chose Jeremy to host me." He laughed. "His true believers would be *so* thrilled to know the cause I've been using them to fight for. But perhaps once Lugh himself is no longer agitating, these killings will become unnecessary. It breaks my heart to have to destroy my fellow demons, but it has to be done."

Apparently, Lugh really, really objected to that. The pain in my head brought me to my knees.

"Is he trying to come out?" Wyatt asked Andrew as I gritted my teeth and tried to remember how to breathe.

"I'd say so. But Morgan's too much of an idiot to let him."

I glared up at him, at the Taser he held steadily pointed at me. Maybe it would be better to let Lugh take over, to be a passenger in my own body while they burned me to death. Andrew's Taser meant Lugh couldn't save me, but like Andrew had said, he could take the pain away. I was pretty sure he'd do that for me.

But I didn't know how to let him in, even if I wanted to.

Wyatt hauled me to my feet and dragged me toward the stake. The pain in my head didn't let up. I mentally screamed at Lugh to stop it, but he didn't listen. I squeezed my eyes shut and tried to endure. Maybe it would be a relief to be burned to death, if it meant this pain in my head would just stop.

The pain was so bad I hardly felt myself being dragged into that pile of foul-smelling kindling. They didn't unlock my cuffs, just looped another length of chain through them and attached that chain to the metal base of the basketball hoop.

Lugh let up for a moment—maybe just to let me catch my breath. Wyatt stepped back from the stake, letting one of his flunkies squirt me with lighter fluid. My breath came in quick, frantic gasps. The fumes made me cough.

"You really are a fool, Morgan," Andrew told me. I looked up and snarled at him, but he didn't seem to care. "Why should you suffer, when it's Lugh's sin you're dying for?"

"Shut up, Raphael," Wyatt snapped. "What are you trying to do? Goad her into letting him in?"

Raphael laughed. "Well, yes. I don't give a shit about Morgan. My quarrel's with Lugh, and it would be more satisfying if I could hear him cursing me as I finally win our little game."

"Well he's a lot more dangerous than she is, so stop it."

"He'd be dangerous if I couldn't Taser him. As it is, he'd be as helpless as a baby. I would so enjoy his helplessness."

He flashed me an unpleasant, shark-like grin, and Lugh put everything he had into another effort. The pain was like nothing I'd ever felt before, and I thought I might pass out. My vision went fuzzy around the edges. Raphael said something, but I couldn't hear through the roaring of my blood in my ears.

I felt something inside me shift. It wasn't a physical sensation, not exactly. The best I can describe it is that it felt like a set of doors inside my head cracked open.

I seized upon that sensation, closing my eyes and using the same visualization skills I use when I'm exorcizing a demon. Only instead of visualizing a gust of wind blowing the demon away, I visualized throwing open the doors of my mind to let Lugh in.

Suddenly the pain in my head stopped completely. Not even an echo left. I raised my head and stared at Raphael, but it wasn't *me* looking through my eyes.

Raphael grinned delightedly. "Welcome, brother. What the hell took you so long?"

Lugh made a horrible growling sound I wouldn't have thought my throat could make. Raphael looked even more delighted. Lugh started to struggle against the bonds, and I expected Raphael to Taser him into submission.

But that wasn't what happened.

With what looked like a respectful nod at Lugh, Raphael turned to Wyatt. And shot him point blank with the Taser.

Chapter **27**

For a moment that seemed endless, everyone was shocked. Wyatt cried out and crumpled to the ground. Raphael put the Taser down on the ground, then plucked a gun out of the hand of the human standing closest to him. The man was just starting to protest when Raphael shot him in the head.

Lugh recovered his composure quickly and, with a burst of strength, broke free of the handcuffs. I felt the press of the metal against my skin, but it didn't hurt like it should have. I leapt out of the gas-soaked kindling, but I had no control over my own body.

Later I would panic over the sensation—like I was sleepwalking while wide awake. Now I was just happy not to be burning.

The rest of Wyatt's people converged, half of them going after Raphael, half going after Lugh. It appeared none of them were demons, because they were about as effective as yapping Chihuahuas. One of them drew a gun and shot at me. At Lugh. Whatever.

The bullet slammed into my shoulder. Painlessly. Lugh swatted the gun out of his hand, then struck him in the side of the head so hard I heard the neck snap. Out of the corner of my eye, I saw Raphael shoot two more men who were trying to grab his gun arm.

At this point, smart little minions would have run like hell, but these guys were fanatics. Even as their numbers dwindled, they wouldn't stop attacking. Lugh and Raphael picked them off, one by one, bodies piling up until the field looked like a war zone.

I suspect if Lugh hadn't been controlling me so thoroughly, I would have puked my guts out.

Finally, the last of our enemies was down. I wasn't a hundred percent sure, but I thought everyone except Wyatt was dead. I'd have felt worse about that if they hadn't been planning to burn me alive so that demons could take over the world, or whatever it was they'd hoped to accomplish.

Wyatt started to regain control of his limbs. Raphael snatched up the Taser and gave him another jolt.

Lugh crossed my arms over my chest and glared at his brother, who smiled.

"Explain," Lugh growled. Not much of a talker at a time like this, I suppose.

The smile faded from Raphael's face. A hint of some darker emotion—anger, maybe—glinted in his eye. "You're the worst kind of fool, Lugh. So bloody self-righteous and self-absorbed you're completely blind to the world."

We took a step toward him. Personally, I'd have been happy to punch the bastard's lights out. But then, I wasn't in control.

"If you'd paid attention to the world as it really is," Raphael continued, undaunted, "you'd have seen this coming. But no, you thought everyone was as honor-able as you are—that once you became king, you'd make everything right. Arrogant ass." His lips twisted in an ugly sneer.

So far, this wasn't the clearest explanation I'd ever heard.

"Raphael..." Lugh said, a warning in his tone.

Raphael shook his head. "I knew Dougal was up to something. He wasn't upset enough at the prospect of you taking the throne. He should have been rabble-rousing as hard as he could, but he wasn't. So I started dropping hints to him that you would make a lousy king. You and I get on poorly enough that he had no trouble believing I would stand against you. And so he let me in on his plan."

"The plan to force me into a mortal host and then burn me and my host alive."

Raphael rolled his eyes. "Yes, that one. And before you ask, if I'd run to you and told you all this, you wouldn't have believed me. You'd have thought I was just starting trouble. And even if you had, there was nothing you could do about it once Dougal gave your True Name to his human followers.

"The only thing I could do was try to preempt them by summoning you into a human who wasn't under their control. I'd hoped Morgan would be able to keep you hidden until I'd figured some way out of this mess."

I felt my eyebrow raise. "And how did you know I wouldn't be able to take her over? I've never heard of such a thing."

Raphael hesitated. "Block Morgan out, and I'll tell you."

Block me out? I didn't like the sound of that at all, but before I could start panicking, Lugh spoke.

"I don't have enough control to do that," he said. "Whatever you have to say, you can let her hear."

Raphael shook his head. "Then all I can tell you is that Dougal has been up to more mischief on the Mortal Plain than anyone could have guessed. I'm not sharing state secrets with Morgan, no matter what you order."

Lugh advanced another step toward his brother. "You don't get to make that decision."

Raphael's chin set stubbornly. "Yes, big brother, I do. Do you think you can torture me into talking?"

I kind of liked the sound of that. After all, Raphael might have just saved me from burning to death, but his methods sucked big-time. I remembered the burns under Brian's arms, and the blood fountaining from Dominic's leg. Unfortunately, revenge didn't seem to be Lugh's top priority. He clenched his fists in what I took for frustration, but dropped the subject.

"Once your friends knew I was in Morgan, why didn't you help her?"

"I *did* help her. I arranged for her to be arrested so she'd spend some time in jail where no one could get to her. I've also arranged for the key evidence to be 'lost' so they'll have to drop the charges. And I called her house to wake her up when Wyatt tried to burn it down around her ears.

"I couldn't prevent tonight's rendezvous without blowing my cover, but I stalled as long as I could by being a temperamental bastard when she called. I figured if you couldn't surface under these circumstances, you'd never be able to.

"And don't tell me that either one of you would have believed me if I'd come to you and told you I was on your side. Morgan doesn't trust any demon, and you've never trusted me. I was better off staying on the inside."

Lugh swept the battlefield with a contemptuous gaze. "And if I hadn't managed to surface tonight, Morgan and I would both be dead."

But Raphael shook his head. "No, brother. Only Morgan. If they'd lit the fire, I'd have had no choice but to shoot her." He looked into Lugh's eyes, and I could tell he was looking through them at me. "I'm truly sorry, Morgan. I did everything I could to goad Lugh into surfacing and goad you into letting him. But if I'd failed, I'd have had to kill you and send him back to the Demon Realm. It would have been a temporary solution at best, since they'd still have Lugh's True Name. They'd just call him into another human victim, and I'd have thoroughly blown my cover. But I couldn't have taken on everyone here by myself. I'm strong, but I'm not *that* strong."

I, of course, didn't say anything. Panic beat at me as I realized I'd probably never be able to say anything again.

"It'll be all right, Morgan," Lugh said, speaking to me with my own mouth. "I know what I did to take control, and I know how to let go."

Raphael looked shocked. "You're going to let her back into control?"

Lugh shrugged. "Even if I didn't let her, I suspect she'd figure out how to do it herself. She always managed to kick me out of her dreams when she wanted to. This will have to be a partnership, rather than a dictatorship."

"The gallant knight again, eh, brother?" There was a hint of disgust in his voice.

Lugh didn't seem to appreciate it. "You should try it sometime."

The slight tightening around his eyes suggested Lugh had actually managed to hurt Raphael's feelings. He lowered his gaze. "Do I get no credit for anything I've done? Can I never do anything right in your eyes?"

Lugh sighed. "Forgive me. I truly am grateful, even if I don't appreciate your methods."

Wyatt groaned, and the brothers both turned to look at him. He couldn't move yet, but he stared up at Lugh with a mixture of scorn and fear in his eyes.

"This is only one cell of Dougal's revolutionary army," Raphael said, his voice quiet and studiously neutral. "I tried my best to find others, but everything started to move too fast. You cannot return to the Demon Realm until we're sure Dougal's supporters can't summon you to your death. And our best hope of wiping out the conspiracy is if I stay on the inside."

Lugh was silent for a long time. I wished I knew what he was thinking, but our communication went only one way. I'm sure he "heard" me yammering questions at him, but he chose not to respond. It pissed me off, so I tried visualizing shutting the door in my mind.

Lugh winced, and I felt a fleeting spark of triumph. Yay! I knew how to make his head hurt!

Unfortunately, he had his foot firmly in that door, and I couldn't seem to shut it.

Wyatt made another pathetic groaning noise. It seemed to snap Lugh out of his moment of indecision, if that's what it was.

"He mustn't be allowed to warn anyone of your loyalties," Lugh said, looking at Wyatt. Wyatt's eyes widened in terror, and he fought to regain control of his limbs.

Raphael gave him another jolt from the Taser, then went to kneel beside him. "Trust me, my friend," he said. "You don't want to heal this."

He punched Wyatt so hard you'd have thought his head would go flying. Not hard enough to kill him, however, for I could see his chest rising and falling, though his eyes were closed and his jaw slack.

It wasn't until Raphael picked the unconscious man up and carried him toward the stake that I fully realized what they were about to do. I shoved harder on the door, though it wasn't as if I could stop Raphael my own puny human self.

Again Lugh winced, though I didn't feel like I was making any progress. But I couldn't let the two of them just burn a guy to death without trying to stop them, could I?

"Don't feel too bad for him, Morgan," Lugh said. I hated when he used my own mouth to talk to me. "Both the human and the demon are responsible for many, many deaths, most if not all of them by fire. This is a fitting end."

Yeah, I knew all that. And in a Biblical, eye-for-an-eye sense, it was hard to argue that the man didn't deserve it. But I didn't have the demon ability to shrug off necessary evils. I didn't want to be party to burning a man alive, no matter how evil that man might be—no matter how dangerous he would be to me in particular and mankind in general.

I kept shoving hopelessly on that door in my mind, knowing I didn't have enough time to figure out how to shut it before the deed was done. It had taken Lugh *weeks* to figure out how to gain control. How could I expect myself to figure it out in minutes?

Didn't stop me from trying, though.

Lugh bore the pain stoically as Raphael laid Wyatt's inert body on the pyre and squirted him with lighter fluid.

"You're going to want to step back," he told Lugh

as he tossed the can onto the pyre and pulled out a book of matches. "We put a ton of accelerant on this thing. I can't guarantee we're not about to have an explosion."

Lugh took a few steps backward. I was still trying to close the door, but my efforts were weakening. It was too late already, my sense of urgency dwindling as I realized there was no way I could cross the distance between us to stop Raphael from lighting the fire.

Raphael struck the match.

It wasn't quite an explosion, but it was close. As soon as the match hit the kindling, the whole pile blazed—a huge, wild bonfire, so hot Lugh had to take a few more steps back. Raphael ran from the blaze the moment it went up, and still he had minor burns on the hand he'd lit the fire with. The burns healed within seconds.

The brothers stood side by side, watching Jeremy Wyatt and his demon burn to death. I wanted to cry, but I couldn't, not with Lugh controlling my eyes. At least Wyatt never made a sound. I hoped that meant he never regained consciousness.

The fire roared so loudly that, at first, I didn't notice the sound of a car driving up. Neither did Lugh or Raphael, who stood gazing at the fire and, as far as I could tell, feeling no guilt over what they'd just done.

It wasn't until a car door slammed closed that we turned, ready to do battle with a late-arriving enemy.

But it wasn't an enemy who'd stepped out of the car. It was Adam.

He walked slowly toward us, looking from Lugh to Raphael, then to the bodies that lay strewn on the ground around us. I was relieved to see him alive, and I knew he deserved a hasty explanation for the carnage, but at that point, explanations weren't my first priority.

I hammered away at Lugh, trying to gain control, trying to force his mouth—*my* mouth—to form questions.

He remained in control, but asked my questions anyway. "Are Brian and Dominic all right?"

Adam's hand hovered near his sidearm. "They will be," he said, cautiously. "They've both been taken to the emergency room, but the EMS folks said their prognosis was good." He looked at the bonfire, still burning brightly, then back to Lugh and Raphael.

"Care to explain what's going on?" he asked.

Lugh did most of the talking, probably because he didn't expect Adam to trust Raphael. To be perfectly honest, *I* wasn't that sure I trusted Raphael. I mean, yeah, obviously he was on Lugh's side, but I wasn't so sure his motives were as pure as he claimed. And I don't care how bad the blood was between him and Lugh, he should have told me that he was one of the good guys. Even if he thought Lugh and I wouldn't believe him, he could have saved us both a lot of pain.

The fire was starting to burn down when Lugh finally stopped explaining. Adam looked over the collection of bodies and shook his head.

"Well," he said, in something of an understatement, "this is a bit of a mess, isn't it?"

Raphael found that funny, which made me dislike him even more. Lugh cut him a sharp look, but Raphael ignored it.

"What did you tell the police about Brian and Dominic?" Raphael asked.

"I told them my informant warned me a demon was holding an unwilling human captive in the basement of the club. The demon escaped and shot Dom to keep me from chasing him. I'll take plenty of heat for not calling in backup and for taking a civilian in with me, but I'll weather the storm eventually."

Raphael seemed satisfied with that explanation. "Then no one knows any of us has anything to do with these losers." He drew the gun with the silencer out from under his jacket. "This is the gun I shot Dominic with," he said. He handed it butt-first to Adam, who took it without a question, though the look on his face suggested he wanted to punch Raphael's lights out.

Raphael took a deep breath as if bracing himself for something. He gave me/Lugh a long, searching look, then faced Adam. "The demon who kidnapped Brian was Andrew Kingsley. He attacked you, afraid you'd be able to identify him, and you shot him."

What the fuck . . . ?

As usual, I was a little slow on the uptake. Adam's brows drew together, but even slow as I was, I knew the expression wasn't so much puzzlement as indecision.

"I'd do it myself," Raphael continued, patting the gun tucked in his belt—the gun he'd taken from the human henchman, "but I don't think any of us want the ballistics to match the gun that shot all these idiots."

My mind finally caught up with what Raphael was suggesting. For half a second, I hoped Lugh would object, but when Adam looked at him for confirmation, he nodded.

"No!" I screamed mentally, frantically shoving on the door, but it was too late.

Adam drew his gun. "I'm sorry, Morgan," he said. Then he shot Raphael . . . shot *Andrew*, my brother.

Chapter 28

The bullet slammed into Andrew's chest and knocked him backward. He fell in what seemed like slow motion, landing on his back.

With a massive burst of will, I shoved the doors of my mind shut and regained control of my body.

"Andy!" I screamed, and ran to kneel beside him where he lay. His eyes were open, his face twisted in a grimace of pain. I grabbed his hand, feeling like an enormous fist closed around my heart. So much for my thought that I'd stopped loving my brother long ago.

I couldn't form words around the lump of despair in my throat. I watched the blood spread over Andrew's chest, and knew Raphael had no intention of healing the wound.

Impotent rage freed my voice. "Heal my brother, you bastard!" Tears streaked down my cheeks. "Don't you do this!"

"Have to," he grunted. "Need to...go back home...infiltrate again." He coughed blood. "This is . . . good cover story." His eyes slid shut, but I could still hear his labored breathing.

"No! Raphael! Heal him. Please. I'll exorcize you, send you back."

But I knew he wasn't going to do it, even before he shook his head. "Too strong for you," he gasped. "Sorry."

Adam knelt beside me. I turned to him, my rage so huge I thought I might kill him with my puny human hands. He gave me a grave, regretful look.

"I had to do it, Morgan, but don't give up hope."

That made me blink. I'd expected excuses and explanations. I sucked in a sobbing breath.

"Let Lugh surface again," Adam continued. His voice was soft and gentle, like he was talking to a frightened child. At that moment, I'm not sure that was so far off. "He's a very powerful demon—perhaps the most powerful of us all. He might still be able to heal Andrew after Raphael has fled."

I blinked stupidly. "Raphael can't 'flee' unless Andrew is dead."

"Raphael can flee as soon as Andrew's heart stops beating. If I do CPR and Lugh transfers to Andrew, we might be able to get his heart beating again and heal him."

I sniffled and tried to think straight. If I let Lugh surface again, I could heal Andy *and* be rid of my unwanted guest at the same time. My life could go back to normal—assuming I didn't die or go catatonic when Lugh left me, that is. Somehow, I thought that was unlikely. If I could still function as myself even with a demon living in me, it stood to reason that I'd function without him as well.

But even if this killed me, I couldn't just let my brother die.

I took a deep breath to steady my nerves, then closed my eyes and imagined opening the doors.

Nothing happened at first. I'd been so frantic when I'd let Lugh surface the first time that I wasn't sure I knew exactly how I'd done it.

"Hurry, Morgan," Adam said. "He stopped breathing."

Adam's words injected a shot of panic into me, and the adrenaline gave me the strength I needed to open the doors. I felt Lugh fill me, felt the slight changes in my posture and facial expression that said I was no longer myself.

"Don't let go of his hand," Lugh said. "I'll try my best to save him, but if I fail, I need to be able to return to you."

Then I felt him drain away.

Adam leapt into motion, positioning his hands on Andrew's sternum and starting CPR. The pressure made more blood pour out of the wound. All I could do was pray.

It seemed to go on forever. Adam pumping away at my brother's chest, then breathing into his mouth. Despair settled over me, even as I told myself that the wound didn't seem to be bleeding as much.

Finally, Adam rocked back on his heels. Grief threatened to overwhelm me. Until I saw Andrew's chest rise and then fall.

Another rush of tears crawled down my cheeks, and I squeezed his hand convulsively.

"You did it!" I said. I wasn't sure whether I was talking to Lugh or to Adam. "Thank you."

Adam nodded, then gave me a pitying look. I didn't like it.

"What?" I asked. "Why are you looking at me like that?"

"For Raphael's cover story to stay intact, Andrew can't be hosting a demon. Raphael will have to tell Dougal's people that his host was killed. And if any of their operatives on the Mortal Plain discover he's still hosting... The fact that I managed to resuscitate him at all will put some doubt into the story, but as long as it's clear he's not hosting when it's over, Dougal's people should believe it."

I dropped Andrew's hand and scooted away. Yeah, I'd mostly transferred Lugh to save Andrew's life, but I can't pretend I hadn't also looked forward to getting rid of him.

Not that I didn't like him, you understand. His kindness and his noble cause had definitely won me over. But these last couple weeks of playing the reluctant hero had been more than enough for me! When I thought about what I'd gone through because of him—being attacked by my best friend, having my house burned to the ground, watching Adam murder my former best friend, letting Adam hurt me, almost being burned at the stake...

Let Andrew be the hero. It's what he always wanted, why he decided to be a host in the first place.

"It's too late," Adam said. "He transferred back as soon as Andrew's heart started beating."

I hadn't felt a thing. But I believed him anyway. I drew my knees up to my chest and lowered my head, hugging my knees to me and fighting despair.

"You bastards," I said, but I didn't think Adam could hear me. Lugh could. They'd let me believe that if Andrew survived, Lugh would stay with him, that I'd be free. That was as good as lying, in my book.

I really believe that if they'd explained what they were planning to do, I'd have gone along with the plan. I wouldn't have *liked* it, but if I'd thought about the consequences of Andrew showing up still hosting a demon, I probably would have agreed that I had to take Lugh back.

But there's always that hint of doubt.

Lugh can read all my thoughts and feelings. He knows me better than it's possible for any human being to know another. And he chose not to tell me he planned to move back in. Does that mean that given the opportunity to get rid of him, I would have said *To hell with the human race, just let me be free*?

I don't think that's the case. I think Lugh didn't clue me in because he couldn't take the time to explain while Andrew lay dying. That's what he tells me, though maybe he's just telling me what I want to hear.

Adam picked up Andrew's limp body and carried him to the car. He was going to have to do a lot of creative talking when he got my brother to the emergency room, but I was sure he'd manage.

And me? Yeah, I'd manage too, eventually. But I knew as long as Lugh was a part of me, my life would never be the same, would never be truly my own. And that was one hell of a depressing thought.

Brian was awake, but groggy, by the time I got to the hospital. Emotional coward that I am, I'd checked on Dominic first. Dom was doing fine—"just a flesh wound," he'd joked—and would be out of the hospital in a day or two.

My throat ached, and something I might almost have called terror tightened my chest as I walked through the door into Brian's room. I swear, if I'd seen condemnation in his eyes, I would have shattered into little pieces right there. Instead, he smiled weakly and held out his hand.

My throat was too tight for words, so I just took his hand and sat down beside him on the bed. His eyes were heavy with drugs—either the ones the bad guys had given him, or the ones the hospital had—and he didn't seem inclined to talk.

I cleared my throat to try to loosen my voice. "I'm sorry," I said. "About everything."

Another weak smile, and he squeezed my hand. His voice sounded hoarse and dreamy. "No worries. It's all over now."

I did my best not to wince, because, of course, it was far from over. But I was going to make sure that for Brian, at least, it was. I had learned a hard lesson, and I wasn't going to make the same mistake twice.

He was losing the battle against sleep, his eyes sliding shut then jerking open again as he desperately tried to stay awake. I was going to miss him more than I could possibly say.

"I love you," I told him as his eyes closed once more. This time, they didn't open again. I bent over and kissed him very gently on the lips. His eyelids fluttered, but that was all.

"I'll always love you."

When I was sure he was fast asleep, I slipped my hand out of his. I'd risked everything to save him, and I'd be damned if I let him get hurt because of me again. So I was going to be a big girl about this and do the right thing. I was going to let him go, even though he would never understand.

Even though it was going to hurt more than anything I'd ever done before in my life.

I paused in the doorway, looking back on his sleeping form. "Goodbye," I whispered. Then I forced myself to walk away.

Epilogue

Andrew survived the gunshot wound to his chest. The doctors were amazed he made it. Unfortunately, his mind didn't. It's possible he's brain-damaged from the time his heart wasn't beating. Or it could be from losing Raphael—you can't tell the difference, or at least humans don't know how yet. When he finally came to after the surgery, his stare was entirely vacant. My family is devastated. I know my mom and dad look at me and wish I'd been the one to take the bullet. Harsh, but true. If only they knew . . .

I asked Lugh whether he knew why some demon hosts, like Dominic, recovered with no ill effects, and some turned out like Andrew. He wouldn't answer me, which suggests he knows, but won't tell. Demons do love their secrets. My guess is that Raphael ran roughshod over him and broke him, but maybe I'm wrong. If Raphael returns to the Mortal Plain and I run into him, it won't be pretty. I've got a lot of axes to grind.

I visit Andrew at least once a week, timing my visit to miss any of my other family members. Those few demon hosts who've recovered from the catatonia have said they were conscious and aware the whole time, even though they couldn't control their bodies, so I talk to him and read to him. Anything to keep him entertained, to keep his mind from atrophying, assuming his mind is still there. And I tell him that I love him—something I hadn't done in far too long.

The slaughter at Jeremy Wyatt's farm wasn't discovered until days later, after a torrential downpour had washed away most of the evidence. Because many of the victims were members of God's Wrath, and because of the nature of the injuries on the ones who weren't shot to death, the authorities believe they were murdered by avenging demons. Not far from the truth. Adam assures me that no one would ever suspect Andrew or me of having been the killers. I have to admit, I see his point.

Which brings me to Brian. The drugs Wyatt's people had given him made his memory of his captivity hazy at best. He'll wear the physical scars for the rest of his life, but his mind appears to be intact. Thanks to some creative storytelling, the authorities believe it was Andrew who tortured him as a way to punish me for the bad blood between us. My parents staunchly refuse to believe Andrew's demon did such a terrible thing.

I love Brian more than ever, but I've stood firm in my resolve to break up with him for his own good. I rented an apartment in Center City and didn't give him my new address. I tried the same with my office. He found both addresses, and sends me letters at least once a week. He harbors hope that he can change my mind, can win me back. He's trying every romantic ploy in the book, from flowers, to poems, to serenades. He's one of the most stubborn people I've ever met. But then, so am I.

I don't know what's going to happen next. For the time being, Lugh is content to let me recover from the ordeals I've gone through. Eventually, I'm going to have to step back into my ill-fitting hero shoes. Because Dougal's demons are still out there, and as long as they are, I won't be safe, and neither will the human race.

The fate of humanity resting firmly on *my* shoulders? The irony is so thick you could eat it with a spoon. Lugh tells me I make a better hero than I think.

I sure hope he's right.

About the Author

JENNA BLACK is your typical writer. Which means she's an "experience junkie." She got her BA in physical anthropology and French from Duke University.

Once upon a time, she dreamed she would be the next Jane Goodall, camping in the bush making fabulous discoveries about primate behavior. Then, during her senior year at Duke, she did some actual research in the field and made this shocking discovery: primates spend something like 80% of their time doing such exciting things as sleeping and eating.

Concluding that this discovery was her life's work in the field of primatology, she then moved on to such varied pastimes as grooming dogs and writing technical documentation. Visit her on the web at www.JennaBlack.com.

If you enjoyed

The Devil Inside

be sure not to miss the next
exciting Morgan Kingsley novel:

The Devil You Know

by
Jenna Black

Coming in 2008

Here's a special excerpt. . . .

The Devil You Know

On sale in 2008

Chapter 1

There's no denying Dominic Castello is a treat to look at—the classic tall, dark, and handsome; soulful hazel eyes framed by thick lashes, warm olive skin, muscles in all the right places.... But on seeing him standing in my doorway, my first impulse was to shut the door in his face.

He must have read my expression, for he wedged his foot in the door and smiled at me. He has a sweet, disarming smile that would turn most women to jelly, but I'm not most women. Besides, his equally good-looking boyfriend was the sadomasochistic demon host who'd shot my brother. That put Dominic near the bottom of the list of people I wanted to see, with only his boyfriend, Adam, and pretty much my entire family below him.

Unfortunately, with him being well over six feet tall and at least two hundred pounds, I wasn't keeping him out of my apartment now that I'd been stupid enough to open the door in the first place.

Giving in to the inevitable, I moved away from the door, letting him come in, though I didn't actually invite him. I headed to my minuscule kitchen, where a half-full pot of coffee left over from breakfast still sat on the warmer.

"Wanna cup?" I asked without looking at him.

"Sure. Thanks."

I filled two mugs, noticing that the coffee was dark as ink and smelled stale. If it were just me, I'd make a fresh pot, but I didn't want Dominic staying that long.

"Cream and sugar?"

Dominic looked at the tar-scented swill in the cup I handed him and shook his head. "I doubt it would help much."

That almost made me smile. "So, what brings you to this part of town?" I asked, taking a sip of my coffee to prove it was drinkable and trying not to gag when I discovered it wasn't.

When Dominic didn't immediately answer, my nerves went on red alert. Apparently, this wasn't a social call, which I suppose I'd known all along.

"Maybe we should sit down for a bit," he suggested.

I really hated the sound of that—and the way he wouldn't quite meet my eyes. My stomach made an unhappy gurgle, and my fingers clenched on the coffee cup. I put it down before I took a sip by reflex.

For the last few weeks, I'd been trying my best to live under a rock. I'd had enough stress lately to last me a lifetime or three. Realistically, I knew my problems were far from over, but I'd been determined to hold them at bay for as long as possible—ideally, until I was on my deathbed.

See, here's the thing. I'm an exorcist. My calling in life, my very *raison d'être,* is to kick demon ass. Only the ones who possess unwilling hosts or who commit violent crimes, of course, but in reality I didn't like legal demons much better. So as you can imagine, my life became a little complicated when I found out I was possessed by the king of the demons, who was embroiled in a war for the throne of the Demon Realm.

For reasons neither of us understand, the demon king, Lugh, can't take control of me the way a normal demon can. Even though I'm possessed, I remain in total control of my body. For the most part, Lugh can only take command when I'm asleep, and can only communicate with me through dreams.

From the moment I found out I was possessed, my life shot straight to hell and stayed there. My best friend tried to kill me. My house was burned to the ground. I was thrown in jail for murder. My boyfriend, Brian—actually, he's my *ex*-boyfriend now, though I have yet to convince him of this fact—was kidnapped and tortured in an attempt to get to me. And, to win his aid in rescuing Brian, I let Dominic's boyfriend whip me bloody for his own amusement.

All in all, I was desperately in need of some R&R. But since I wasn't getting Dominic out of my apartment through brute force, I figured the quickest way to get rid of him was to listen to what he had to say.

I'm sure I looked pretty sulky and mulish as I led him into my living room and gestured him toward my couch. I dropped into the love seat and suffered a momentary pang of yearning for the homey, comfortable furniture that had been destroyed when my house burned down. I'd rented this apartment furnished, and nothing in it reflected my taste. This love seat, for example was hard enough to numb my ass. I hoped the sofa would have the same effect on Dominic.

"So we're sitting down," I said, folding my arms across my chest. "Why don't you tell me why you're here?"

He put his cup on the coffee table—I don't think he'd been stupid enough to take a sip, like I had—then turned so he could face me full-on. I didn't like the intensity of his expression, so instead of looking at him, I idly tugged on a loose thread on the arm of the love seat.

"Adam has found out something he thinks you should know," Dominic said.

I pulled on the thread a little harder, and the fabric started to unravel. With a grunt of disgust, I stopped fidgeting and gave Dom my best steely-eyed glare. "If Adam thinks I should know, why isn't *he* the one sitting here?"

Dominic grinned. "He thought I was more likely to get through your door."

I couldn't help a rueful chuckle. There have been times when I've said some terrible things to Dominic, but he's never deserved them. When I'd first met him, he'd been a willing demon host, and I had despised him for being the kind of weak-minded, suicidal fool who was willing to give up his entire identity to host a demon. Because the human personality was (in all cases except my own) completely buried beneath the demon's, I'd considered the human hosts as good as dead. Many people— including my entire family—considered those who sacrificed themselves to host "higher powers," as they called demons, to be great heroes. Because demons are so much stronger and so much more resilient than humans, the hosts can take on extremely dangerous tasks. But I'd always considered them sheep.

After some of the things he had done for me—and for Brian, a man he didn't even know—I now believed Dominic was a genuine hero, even without his demon. And despite my feelings about Adam, I had to admit that, most of the time, I rather liked Dom.

"Adam could have tried phoning," I said, trying to maintain my grumpy demeanor.

Dominic just laughed. "And you would have hung up on him and taken the phone off the hook."

Probably true.

"All right, you win. Tell me what he found out. I assume it's important or you wouldn't be here."

The humor faded from his face. "Yeah." He cleared

his throat, and once again his eyes slid away from mine. "This is going to be kind of awkward."

"Great."

"Adam's been doing some, er, investigation."

Along with all his other sterling qualities, Adam is also the Director of Special Forces, the branch of the Philly police department responsible for demon-related crime. The fact that he's hosting a demon himself has never seemed like a conflict of interest to the Powers that Be, though I wasn't the only citizen who questioned the wisdom of his appointment.

"What kind of investigation?" I prompted when Dominic seemed to be struggling to continue.

He huffed out a breath, and one corner of his mouth tipped up in a wry smile. "I can't think of a way to tell you this without risking bodily injury, so I'm just going to blurt it out." And honest to God, the man tensed up as if ready to defend himself. "He's been investigating you and your family."

I blinked a couple of times as I let that sink in. A low simmer started in my chest, but either I was getting more serene in my old age, or Dominic had given the statement so much buildup that nothing he said could be as bad as I expected. Knowing me, the latter is more likely.

"Investigating how? And why?"

He was still watching me warily, which meant there was more to this story he didn't think I would like. "He's been wondering why Raphael chose *you* to be Lugh's host."

Dougal—Lugh's oldest brother and second in line for the throne—had hatched an insidious plan to take over as king of the Demon Realm. He'd planned to summon Lugh into a human host and then burn that host alive, which, counter to popular wisdom, is the only way to kill a demon. Raphael, Lugh's youngest brother, had ostensibly been Dougal's accomplice, but instead of arranging for Lugh to take over the chosen host, he'd stuck Lugh in *my* body.

Turned out Raphael had always been on Lugh's side, and had summoned him into me to save his life. Somehow, Raphael had known Lugh wouldn't be able to take me over, and because of that inability, he would remain hidden from his enemies. Even when Raphael had revealed his true loyalties, he'd refused to tell Lugh how he'd known.

"I'm sure we've all been wondering that," I said cautiously. "What does my family have to do with anything?"

"You mean other than the fact that your brother was Raphael's host?"

I rolled my eyes. "You know what I mean!"

"Yes. Well. Adam figured that Raphael must have found out something interesting when he insinuated himself into your family, so Adam hoped to find out what that interesting something was."

My heart seemed to be beating louder than it should, but it was probably my imagination. "And? What did he find?"

Dominic looked even more uncomfortable. "I love Adam, but I wish he hadn't sent me to do this...."

I made a little sound of frustration. "Just tell me, already! Waiting for the other shoe to drop is killing me."

Dominic clasped his hands in his lap and regarded them with intense concentration. "He found an old, buried police report from twenty-eight years ago. About a rape." He squirmed. "The victim was your mother."

The blood drained from my face. Never had my mother even hinted that she'd been raped. Of course, my mother and I had been at each other's throats since I was about five, so I guess it isn't surprising that she hadn't shared a confidence like that with me.

Still, I didn't know how to feel. I mean ... damn! What

a horrible secret to keep for all these years. How much had that rape affected my mother's life? And her personality? Was it possible that all the things I despised about her were symptoms of that terrible trauma in her past?

Then the other shoe dropped—though I was losing count of how many shoes it had been so far.

"Twenty-eight years ago?" I asked in a hushed whisper, and Dominic met my eyes this time. His chin dipped in a barely perceptible nod, and the sympathy in his expression made my throat ache. "Then there's a chance..." I couldn't say it. My pulse was pounding in my ears, my world tipping sideways once again.

Dominic sighed. "Not just a chance, I'm afraid," he said gently. "Adam also found the record of a paternity test."

My heart clenched in my chest, and it was all I could do to hold myself together. "I guess that means my father isn't really my father, huh?" I tried for something like nonchalance, and was sure I failed.

Dominic shook his head. "I wish there were some good way to tell you this."

He looked so miserable that I was able to pull myself up by my bootstraps, at least temporarily. "You did fine," I assured him. I could only imagine how Adam would have delivered the news. He doesn't like me any more than I like him. In my more generous moments, I allow that I've given him good cause not to like me. But my generous moments are few and far between.

I guess this unpleasant truth about my origins explained a bit about my less-than-stellar relationship with my parents. I'd always assumed they favored my brother for his willingness to host a demon. My parents are members of the Spirit Society, a group that practically worships these demons. To them, there can be no greater glory than to sacrifice oneself to host a demon. The fact that they hadn't been able to brainwash me into hosting had inspired boundless animosity, but now I had an insight into what else they held against me. And it wasn't pretty.

"Not to be shitty or anything," I said, "but is there some burning reason you and Adam felt it necessary to tell me this? I mean, I've gone twenty-eight years without knowing, and I'd have been happy to go twenty-eight more."

Dominic shrugged. "Lugh can't gain control of you. There's got to be a reason, since Raphael had no trouble taking over your brother. Don't you think the fact that you and your brother have different fathers might have something to do with it?"

I leaned back into the stiff, uncomfortable cushions of my rent-a-couch and brooded a bit. I wasn't sure how I felt about this revelation. There was definitely an element of shock. I mean, how could I not be shocked? But I think I would have been more devastated if I were actually close to my dad.

Christ! Why had they done it? Why had my mother decided to keep her baby under the circumstances? Yeah, she was the pro-life type, but even if she wasn't willing to have an abortion, that didn't mean she had to keep me after I was born! Had my father known all along that I wasn't his?

The questions circled like sharks, and I didn't want to deal with them.

"Okay," I said, "let's say you're right and my biological father"—man, did that sound weird—"has something to do with why Lugh can't get a foothold. What does that gain us? We don't know who he was, do we?"

Dominic shook his head. "No. Your mother didn't even give much of a description in the police report. But the strange thing is that after she made the initial report, it appears that nothing happened."

"What do you mean?"

"I mean no one made any effort to investigate the case.

It just kind of sank out of sight, and your mother never made an inquiry. I can't help wondering why."

I had to admit, that was pretty strange. But I also had a sneaking suspicion where this was going, and I intended to nip it in the bud before it got there. "If you think I'm going to question my mom about it, you can forget it."

"Now, Morgan—"

"No!" I snapped. "I do everything I can to avoid her, even in supposedly pleasant situations. No way in hell am I asking her about a rape she never bothered to tell me about."

I was too agitated to sit still, so I stood up and paced. I wanted to pull the blanket of denial up over my head, again. After all the shit I'd been through, I needed more time, dammit! Bad enough to have to deal with royal intrigue and assassins and the fate of the human race— which, according to Lugh, could turn seriously ugly if Dougal managed to grab the throne. But to have to deal with my family issues on top of all that....

Nope, not ready for it.

Dominic's a pretty smart guy, and his instincts are good. He took one look at my face, then swallowed whatever argument he'd been about to make.

"All right," he said, standing. "I can certainly understand your position. Adam will keep poking around the old files. He'll let you know if he finds anything important."

I'm not the most polite person under the best of circumstances, which these weren't, so I couldn't manage much better than a curt nod of acceptance. Still, I did walk him to the door, which I felt was rather decent of me.

"If you ever need someone to talk to," he said before he left, "give me a call. I'm a good listener."

I couldn't help a little snort of laughter. Dom looked hurt.

"Nothing personal," I hastened to assure him. "I'm sure you're a *great* listener. But I'm a lousy talker." Which

I bet he knew already. He hadn't known me all that long, but he was far too sensitive not to have picked that up.

Dominic smiled faintly. "All right. But the offer stays open."

"Thanks," I said, and then there was nothing else to say.

After Dominic left, the apartment seemed ominously empty and quiet—just the kind of atmosphere to encourage a round of brooding melancholy and self-pity. I decided hanging around would be a bad idea, so I stuffed my Taser in my purse and headed out.

Tasers are one of the few weapons that actually work against demons. The electricity fucks up their ability to control the host body and leaves them essentially helpless. Normal weapons, like guns, might be able to kill the host, but the demon would just return to the Demon Realm. And if it ever managed to get back to the Mortal Plain, you'd be high on its shit list.

It used to be that I rarely carried my Taser when I went out. By the time I'm called in to do an exorcism, the demon has been well and truly contained and is no threat to me. Now, with Dougal's unknown minions wanting to kill me, I wouldn't go to the lobby to pick up my mail without the Taser on my person.

I didn't actually have a plan for where I wanted to go, but as I walked the streets of Philadelphia, trying not to brood or even *think*, I found myself heading toward The Healing Circle. That's the nursing home where my brother currently resides. The demon Raphael abandoned my brother's body after Adam shot him. My brother managed to survive the gunshot wound, but as is usually the case when a host loses his demon, his mind didn't survive. He's in a state of catatonia, probably permanent.

For many years, I'd despised Andrew as much as I'd despised the rest of my family. But in the horrible moment when Adam shot him, I'd realized that, despite all our troubles, I still loved him. And so even when I was otherwise trying to keep my head firmly buried in the sand, I made sure to visit Andrew on a regular basis. Usually I tried to time my visits to miss my other family members. Visiting spur of the moment like this was dangerous, but I guess after the disturbing news, I felt the need to connect to the one family member I felt comfortable with.

The fact that I could talk to Andrew without him talking back might also have been a plus.

The gods decided to have mercy on me—for once!—and Andrew had no visitors when I arrived. My parents were well-off enough to afford a private room—only the best for their favored son—so I closed the door behind me and pulled up a chair.

Naturally, Andrew had lost a lot of weight since he'd gone catatonic. He was too tall and big-boned to look frail, but he certainly didn't look like the strong and powerful big brother I'd once known.

"Hi, Andy," I said, reaching out to clasp his limp hand. My voice came out a bit raspy, and the stinging in my eyes said I was on the verge of tears. I blinked until they went away.

Andy didn't move or blink. His eyes were open, but they stared fixedly ahead. I swallowed hard. Those few demon hosts who'd recovered after being in this state said they were conscious and aware during their catatonia, even though they couldn't move or speak. Knowing that, I always tried to talk to him, keep him up to date on the news, maybe even read to him. Anything to keep his mind from atrophying inside his useless husk of a body.

But tonight, my own mind was in too much turmoil to manage banter, and I didn't want to tell him about what I'd learned from Dominic. There was always the possibility he knew, but I kind of doubted it. He would have been only three years old when the rape happened—too young to understand what was going on around him, even if he had heard whatever discussions my parents must have had as they decided to keep me.

Instead, I just sat there holding his hand. It felt strangely peaceful, and I let my eyes slide shut.

I guess I hadn't been getting all that much sleep lately. Either that or the stress of Dominic's revelation had sapped the last vestiges of my energy.

Whatever the reason, I must have drifted off, because when I next opened my eyes, I wasn't in my brother's room anymore.

When I'd first met Lugh in my dreams, his control of even my unconscious mind had been tenuous at best. I'd met him in a barren white room with no doors or windows. As his control had gotten better, the room had gotten homier.

He'd embellished it since the last time I'd been here, adding a simple geometric rug under the coffee table and a frothy potted fern on a plant stand between the sofa and love seat. I gave these details about a half-second's attention before I surrendered to the inevitable and let my gaze rest on Lugh.

Dominic is nice to look at. Lugh is every woman's sexual fantasy come to life. His skin is a beautiful burnished bronze, his hair is a silky, shiny jet black and reaches to his shoulder blades when unbound, and his eyes... They're an intense shade of dark amber, and there always seems to be a hint of light glowing behind them. And let's not even talk about his incredible body! Of course, demons are actually incorporeal, so his body was nothing but an illusion—and since Lugh has access to all my deepest thoughts and feelings, he knows exactly what buttons to push to make my mouth water. But knowing that doesn't ever seem to stop me from drooling when I see him.

He was sitting on the middle of the sofa, his long arms stretched out along the back, his ankle resting on his knee as he watched me ogle him. His sensuous lips curved into a hint of a smile. I made an unladylike grunting sound and plopped into the love seat. I didn't particularly want to talk to my own personal demon right this moment, but it would take me a while to close my mental doors to him. So...

"Long time no see," I said, fighting the urge to cross my arms over my chest in my trademark defensive gesture.

"I've been trying to give you some space," he answered.

His low, rumbling voice always seems to vibrate through my nerves. Goose bumps rose on my arms at the sound of it, and I had to fight a shiver.

"Very considerate of you." My voice sounded too breathy for the attempt at sarcasm.

"But in light of this evening's news," he continued, "I think it's time for us to do some investigation."

I suppressed a groan. "Let Adam do all the investigating he wants! That's not my area of expertise, and I'd rather spend time with my gynecologist than my mom." I tried a little harder to close my mental doors.

"There's only so long you can go on pretending none of this is happening. You know Dougal's people have been up to no good while they've walked the Mortal Plain, and you know the fate of your entire race may lie in the balance."

"Thanks for reminding me!" I snapped, allowing another wave of self-pity to break over me. "I might have forgotten all about it otherwise."

He sighed quietly. "I can apologize again for dragging you into this against your will, but my apologies don't seem to do either one of us any good. The only chance you have of returning to your 'normal' life is to help me defeat Dougal. Until then, you'll never know when one of his supporters might find out you're hosting me and try to kill you."

His words stung. "Do you really think the only reason I might help you is to save my own ass?"

"Of course not," he answered with reassuring promptness. "I just thought the reminder might hurry you up a bit."

I was working my way up to a smart-ass reply, when I finally managed to shove those mental doors closed and wake up. I entertained a few less-than-complimentary thoughts about Lugh for a moment before I remembered where I was.

My hand was still clasped in Andy's. With a start, I realized that his fingers were actually curled around mine instead of lying limply in my grip. A shot of adrenaline burst through me, and I sat up abruptly and opened my eyes.

Andy's head was turned toward me, and when our eyes met I could see the recognition and intelligence in his gaze. Without a moment's warning, I burst into tears and bowed my head over our clasped hands.